PENGUIN BOOKS
1077
MURDERING MR VELFRAGE
ROY VICKERS

£2

1st.

Murdering Mr Velfrage

ROY VICKERS

PENGUIN BOOKS
IN ASSOCIATION WITH
FABER AND FABER

Penguin Books Ltd, Harmondsworth, Middlesex

U.S.A.: Penguin Books Inc., 3300 Clipper Mill Road, Baltimore 11, Md

CANADA: Penguin Books (Canada) Ltd, 47 Green Street,
Saint Lambert, Montreal, P.Q.

AUSTRALIA: Penguin Books Pty Ltd, 762 Whitehorse Road,
Mitcham, Victoria

SOUTH AFRICA: Penguin Books (S.A.) Pty Ltd, Gibraltar House,
Regent Road, Sea Point, Cape Town

—

First published 1950
Published in Penguin Books 1955

*All the characters in this book
are purely imaginary,
and have no relation whatsoever
to any living persons*

Made and printed in Great Britain
by Hazell Watson and Viney Ltd
Aylesbury and London

I

THERE was no nonsense, Miss Parker had years ago decided, about Bruce Habershon. At twenty-seven he was nearly everything he appeared to be. Intelligent without being intellectual, confident without over-fancying himself, good looking without knowing it – the sort of man, she freely admitted, she would have chosen for herself twenty years ago. As it was, she was content to be his secretary and unofficial aunt. She had been with the firm of shipping agents all her life, and knew that Bruce was a better man of affairs than his father had been.

At four o'clock on a January afternoon she came with a special letter for immediate dispatch.

Bruce Habershon read the first few lines, re-read them without understanding. The lines showed a tendency to curve and sway.

'Mr Bruce!' Miss Parker still called him that, though his father had been dead four years. 'You had better go home to bed at once. Hot lemon and aspirins. Don't put whisky in the lemon – I think you have a temperature already. Alcohol would be definitely dangerous.'

'Afraid I'll have to take your advice. I thought I was getting a chill on Saturday, standing about after the game. D'you know, Miss Parker, I'm getting too old for football!'

'Sign the letter, please. Here's your pen.'

He rose, none too firmly.

'And don't drive yourself home. You can hire a car – or hire a man to drive you in the Chrysler. Just wait a minute while I fix it.'

'Oh no. I'm not as bad as that! Just a bit muzzy and headachy and depressed. Please, dear kind Miss Parker, don't fuss. I'll sweat it out and be back at work the day after tomorrow.'

He walked steadily enough out of the office, through Miss Parker's sanctum to the main room. The din of a dozen typewriters slackened for an instant, then returned in greater volume. Built into the room was a glass partition, providing an office for the firm's two outside men. In the waiting-room, which was empty, he sat for a moment and lit a cigarette. It tasted horrible; he put it out, hurried out of the building and turned the corner.

Near the garage was a chemist's.

'Give me a draught of quinine, will you? I have a slight temperature and want to keep it down until I get home.'

Good stuff, quinine! The medical people might swear that it didn't cure you of anything, but they couldn't deny that it brought your temperature down. He felt nearly normal as he drove out of the garage and threaded his way through the traffic. At the end of twenty minutes, with less than four of the fifteen miles to his credit, the effect of the quinine began to wear off.

'I was a sap not to buy a bottle.' He stopped at the next chemist's.

'I want a draught of quinine to get me home – have a bit of a temperature. And I'll take a bottle with me.'

The quinine steadied him and produced a slight exhilaration in which his physical senses were sharpened. The next draught carried him comfortably to the Great West Road. It was too early for the traffic peak. The arterial road was moderately clear.

'All the same, I'd better take it easy – something in what Miss Parker said. Motherly old thing! Good sort. Marvellously efficient.'

He drew out to pass a lorry. A couple of minutes later it dawned on him that he had drawn out too far and had afterwards swung in too far. In the peak hour, that might have meant a smash. He stopped, got out and stamped his feet.

'I'm all right!' He got back into the car. Before restarting he uncorked the quinine bottle, put his thumb on the first ridge and swallowed a single dose.

Perfect judgement! Exactly on the ridge. No more moony driving. The clutch was a bit fierce – he hadn't noticed it before – he would let the garage give it the once-over. Take it easy now. Dirty game risking other people's lives on the road. Decent people. Damned good sports most of 'em, if only one knew them. What was wanted was more friendliness of manner. Not so much of the friend-or-foe – anyway, you couldn't tell one from the other in the dark. He switched on the headlights.

Ahead was a car parked against the grass verge. Nobody parks on an arterial. Must be in difficulty. Chance for friendliness of manner.

The beam picked out a double registration on the parked car. A Belgian number, too. And a Daimler! Must be dear old Velfrage. A Belgian number *and* a Daimler can't be wrong.

Velfrage was a solicitor who frequently introduced valuable shipping business. Habershon meant to pull in behind the Daimler, but substantially over-shot it. He got out and walked back. It was raining lightly, had been raining for days.

'No one about. Car abandoned.'

And then an odd thing seemed to happen. The bonnet opened with a distinctly musical sound. From the interior of the engine Mr Velfrage emerged and floated lightly to the ground, looking a little feverish.

Not intellectual, but intelligent. Still intelligent enough to know that a human being cannot hide in the engine of a Daimler and that, when he appears to do so, there must be something wrong with the onlooker. Therefore, he reasoned, it must be the temperature that was getting the quinine down.

'Habershon!' exclaimed Velfrage. 'My dear boy, what a bit of luck for me!'

Velfrage was middle-aged, small and superbly tailored. A close-trimmed imperial beard masked an inconsiderable chin. In repose, he was impressive; but a fussy, apologetic manner gave him the air of being surprised at his own professional success and a little incredulous.

'The engine started missing as soon as I got into the clear, and now I can't get a spark out of her,' explained Velfrage.

'Most unfortunate! I happen to be in a very special hurry.'

Better take a tight grip, Habershon warned himself, or Velfrage might think he was drunk.

'I doubt whether I shall be much good, Mr Velfrage!' He was able to note that his own speech was clear, if a little loud. 'Fact is, I have a slight temperature. Swallowed some quinine, but it hasn't got into its stride.'

'Quinine is tricky stuff!' Mr Velfrage's thoughts were elsewhere. 'Habershon, I want to ask a favour. I'm carrying valuables and I've got to see a client. It will delay you about fifteen minutes, all told. Will you take me there? I know it's an inconvenient request —'

'Not at all! Great pleasure, Mr Velfrage! Trouble is, can I find your client? Frankly, I'm a bit muzzy! Temperature must be about a hundred – but I'm game if you are. Bring your valuables along while I start my engine.'

'It's all right – I have them on me. My luggage has gone in advance to Southampton – oh, I didn't tell you I'm off to New York for a fortnight! Must be on board by midnight. Let's see now – have I left anything in the car? Only the dispatch-case.'

He retrieved a conventional dispatch-case from the Daimler.

'Why, here's an A.A. man! They always pop up when you've decided you can do without them.'

The Automobile Association patrolman, on a push bicycle, was commissioned to have the Daimler garaged. Mr Velfrage gave his professional card and an appropriate tip, then hurried to join Bruce Habershon.

Habershon was standing by the sidelights of the Chrysler, a medicine bottle to his lips.

'I'd go easy with that quinine if I were you, old man. It's possible to take a fatal dose, I believe,' advised Mr Velfrage. 'Look here, if you're feeling rotten, why not let me drive? And I can drive you home when I've seen my client.'

'Sheer – common – sense!' exclaimed Habershon. 'Why didn't we think of that before! I was getting a bit rattled. Dirty game, risking other people's lives on the road!'

That commendable sentiment lulled Mr Velfrage's suspicions. Also, he was preoccupied with his own affairs. He failed to realize that Habershon was worse than he appeared to be.

After a few minutes of Velfrage's driving, Habershon felt the muzziness lifting. He noted that he had complete control over himself. His vision was unimpaired. He could see the ridges in the road surface; when the beam shone straight ahead he could see the individual grasses growing on the verge, stones between the grasses – some of the stones had faces and winked at him.

'My client is Mrs Rabethorpe,' Velfrage was saying in his dry little way. 'I daresay you've heard the name before?'

'No! I've heard of the Rabethorpe ruby, or emerald or something. One of those sort of Hope diamonds, isn't it, where the last owner has always jumped out of a hotel window or been bitten by a snake.'

'Oh well, one doesn't take that sort of thing seriously!' Mr Velfrage went on: 'All the same, when the Daimler stopped dead on a lonely stretch of road – and it's never stopped before, mind you! – I don't mind confessing that, for a moment, just before you turned up —'

'Did you! Damn funny! And I don't mind confessing that I thought I saw you float out from under the bonnet. I'm pretty cool now. Quinine does do its stuff, whatever the doctors say.'

'I mustn't miss the turning – it's somewhere about here,' muttered Mr Velfrage.

Habershon obligingly looked for a turning. Presently, it seemed, the problem was solved by the indirect aid of Mr Walt Disney. In the beam of the headlights a gay dwarf, with pointed cap and buckled shoes, smiled a welcome and pointed to the left.

'This is the turning, I think,' exclaimed Mr Velfrage.

Habershon felt that he ought to say something genial. He tried to remember what Mr Velfrage had said about the Hope diamond – or was it some other diamond? Anyhow, there was a diamond the size of a radiogram blotting out the whole of the back seat and blinding him with its glitter.

'Why, it's only the lights of that lorry!' He laughed aloud.

'I believe I've taken too much quinine. Soon wear off.'

'I'll see you safely into bed as soon as we're through. We shall reach my client's house in a couple of minutes.' Mr Velfrage was muttering assurances, partly to himself. 'I shan't stay a moment longer than necessary. Especially if she still has that red-headed parlourmaid. I happen to know that girl has served a prison sentence. Action for slander if I tell Mrs Rabethorpe. Very awkward!'

Presently the car turned across the side-walk, crawled between two brick pillars and up a circular drive to a modern house with a light over the door and a curtained light on a ground-floor window.

Twenty yards from the house, Velfrage checked.

'Did you see someone then? Moving away from that window?' asked Velfrage.

'Not a soul!' Habershon was convivially emphatic. 'Not a man, woman or child in the whole place!'

'It was probably an effect of shadows,' muttered Velfrage. He drove on to the front door and switched off the engine.

'I have only a trifling courtesy to perform and then I'll drive you home and phone from your place for a car to get me to Southampton. Call it three minutes, if we're lucky.'

'Three minutes!' repeated Habershon. He leant forward as Velfrage got out, put his thumb on the face of the dash-clock and watched the minute hand.

'One minute!' he exclaimed proudly. 'Better keep the thumb still. There ought to be a mark like they have on a barometer, so that you can't make a mistake.' When a man like old Velfrage said three minutes he meant three minutes, and three minutes he should have.

'Two minutes!' Quinine was good for the eyes. He could see the tiny specks of dust under the minute hand – quite distinct from the large specks of dust on the glass of the clock.

'Three minutes!' He leant over, opened the driver's door for Mr Velfrage. When Mr Velfrage did not appear, Habershon felt he must do something about it.

'Steady! May not be as clear-headed as I think I am. Margin of error for saying goodbye and good-of-you-to-callin-person. One minute would be quite good enough for that sort of thing.'

During the minute he groped for something Velfrage had said – something about a diamond. And wasn't there something else about jumping out of hotel windows?

'That's rot, of course. Quinine and temperature fighting each other. Better play for safety !'

He slipped from the car, went to the front door. Muscular co-ordination was unaffected. It was even with preternatural accuracy that he placed his finger in the dead centre of the bell-push.

2

HABERSHON'S sense of time was more than normally acute. He knew that it was seventeen minutes past five, and that the door had been opened within two seconds of his ring.

His eye was startled by the sight of a young woman so monstrously good looking that there must be a catch in it somewhere. Those gorgeous curves would probably turn into plumpness, if you gave 'em time. She was wearing a black one-piece dress, with sheer black stockings. Over the dress was a fancy apron, heart-shaped, with bib. At her hips there was neither belt nor strings – he wondered how the apron kept up. On her hair – synthetically but magnificently red – was a fancy cap, ribbony and lacy, tuning in to the apron.

'Hullo!' he said, very tentatively.

'Hullo, sir!' she answered. 'What can I do for you, sir?'

That was wrong, somehow. His febrile excitement was uneven. As clearly as if he had been in normal health, he perceived that the girl was playing a part and that she was making a poorish job of it.

'Can I come in? I want to speak to Mr Velfrage.'

'There is no one of that name here, sir.'

He stepped past her into the wide hall before she could shut the door on him.

There were persons in the room on the left of the hall, the room with the lighted windows and drawn blinds. He heard a woman's voice mutter : 'There's no damned key.'

Habershon strode towards the door. Action stimulated the conflict raging in his blood-stream – so that when things began to happen with the logic of a nightmare, he accepted it all as natural behaviour.

The sham parlourmaid shrieked and lunged at his face, meaning to scratch him. But the lunge was much too slow. He put one hand on her chin and, before she could bite, sent her spinning across the hall, to come to rest on the staircase, minus her cap.

On the other side of the door someone was making a feeble effort to prevent him from turning the handle. And someone was shouting in a whisper: "Quick – that rug!" – which seemed ridiculous!

When he had thrust himself into the room, he pressed his buttocks against the door in case the red-headed parlourmaid should try a rear attack.

He was aware of three persons – a scraggy, middle-aged woman, and two men. With a last snatch at reality he noted that they were all in evening dress, which seemed absurd before five-thirty.

The woman had run clear of the door. She stood panting, one hand on the back of an armchair, the other holding her cloak about her. From the crook of her arm dangled a small bag, blue, embroidered with the 'eye' of a peacock's feather. A dolled-up hag, he thought.

Of the two men, one seemed to be doing muscular exercise with the open door of a very large safe. On the far side of the man was that which appeared to be an artist's lay figure seated on an upright chair – for its outline was inescapably human, though the whole of it was covered with an Indian rug. Could it be Mr Velfrage? Ridiculous! Why should Mr Velfrage try to hide under a rug?

The other man was advancing, a revolver in his hand.

'Do your stuff, George!' cried the scraggy, dolled-up hag.

'Put your hands up, you fool!' snarled George, the man with the gun. Habershon observed a large, heavy jaw, prominent. It had not been shaved since morning. He could see the minute bristles.

'Put a jerk in it!' snapped George.

Someone had shouted those words at Habershon a long time ago. In a lightning flash of memory, he saw a sea of faces the other side of the ropes – saw the referee spring clear.

Wallop! He had put a jerk in it, too.

Habershon apprehended that he was involved in a brawl – a nightmare brawl, of course, where nobody brawled properly. From the other side of the now unconscious George, the other man bobbed, also holding a gun.

At that moment the red-head burst into the room. Simultaneously, the scraggy woman leaped on Habershon's back, pinioning his arms. The man, his finger on the trigger, was coming close. With the scraggy woman's weight added to his own, Habershon butted the man in the middle of his face. The woman fell off his back.

Habershon grabbed the gun – a Service weapon, of heavy calibre. The man's face was a mess, but he had risen. Better play for safety and kill him, as it was a nightmare anyway.

From behind, the red-head kicked as Habershon fired.

The bullet struck the figure in the chair, knocking it over backwards – figure and chair and rug, as if they were one.

'He's fighting drunk!' shrilled the scraggy woman. 'He's killed George. He'll kill Frank, and then he'll kill us.'

'All right, Margo!' cried the red-head.

Something heavy whizzed past his head, flung by the red-head. Habershon fired and broke the glass front of a bookcase. Then he flung the gun at the red-head and missed again. Frank was mopping blood from his eyes.

The two women rushed at Habershon simultaneously. He tried to swing the scraggy woman out of action by her cloak, but caught only her bag, because at that instant the red-head landed heavily with her nails, missing his eyes but searing his cheek.

'You little red devil! I'll kill you next.'

The girl ducked and reached the door, slamming it between them. He snatched it open, saw her running up the stairs and ran after her. Steady. Mustn't hit a girl, whatever the circumstances. Break her neck in a gentlemanly manner.

Near the top stair he grabbed her with his right hand. She did a cat-twist under his grip, then rolled forward on the landing, leaving him holding the black dress, complete with apron. He had a fleeting glimpse of muscles rippling under dazzlingly white skin – and the girl had snapped the light switch and disappeared into the upper darkness.

He was vaguely aware that he was holding something in his left hand. He thrust it in his overcoat pocket and touched a torch. With the torch he found the switch on the landing, but not the girl.

'You can't get away, Red-head!' he shouted.

He was pursuing her now with cold fury. He opened a door. A bedroom. He looked under the bed, behind the curtains, in the wardrobe, listening the while for the girl's footfall on the landing.

Four bedrooms and a sort of boudoir on the first floor. Up to the second floor. He lost consciousness of self and circumstance in his concentration of purpose.

Later he was recalled, at least to circumstance, by the conviction that he had tripped over a mat. He remembered the mat, outside a bedroom door, remembered his foot slipping – remembered curving and floating, rather enjoyably, through space – but did not remember hitting the floor. He was certainly lying on the floor.

He sat up. His eye was caught by a splash of colour – a soft Chinese red against a black which was gold-embroidered. His vision sharpened. He was gazing at a Burmese doll – a sibyl, scaled to the size of a largish baby – set on a bench upholstered in amber velvet. He laughed and rose unsteadily to his feet – in the effort, he forgot how he came to be in the house and what he had been doing.

He looked over the banisters. Lights on the two floors below. Lights on the floor above. He remembered turning on lights. Somebody else's house. Empty, he assumed, except for himself. Better turn the lights off – only polite to leave everything as you found it!

He went to the third floor – coconut matting, narrow doors, imperfectly fitted. He turned off the light on the landing; same on the second floor.

Back on the first floor he stopped, out of breath. He was on a wide landing, heavily carpeted. Against the banister rail was the upholstered bench. The Burmese doll now seemed no more than a deliberately eccentric decoration. His acute physical vision enabled him to see that on the face of the doll was a layer of dust. On the upholstery, near the doll, was the nozzle of a vacuum cleaner, but there was no cleaner in sight. A clear line on the upholstery showed where the dusting had been interrupted.

Aware that he was shivering with cold, he remembered his condition. He took another dose of quinine, waited for it to steady him before he tackled the last flight of stairs.

In the hall he paused in uncertainty. The phase of acute vision was returning and with it the fleeting sense of well-being.

"I must be pretty muzzy!" he reflected. "Velfrage jumping out of the engine! Comic-opera parlourmaids and gunmen! Must have missed Velfrage somehow!"

The front door was being opened with a latchkey.

A girl came in. Not, Habershon noted, one of the nightmare girls. A real one, who gave him some sense of proportion. A few years younger than himself. A walking suit that was exactly right. Ash-blonde and light natural colouring. Probably beautiful, but one couldn't tell. He could tell only that her face reminded him of all that was cool and restful. An attractive girl whom he could safely introduce to Miss Parker.

The thought was shattered as she caught sight of him. She gave a little gasp, then backed into the corner on the other side of the door. He was unaware that his face was streaked and had not quite stopped bleeding.

'Please don't be afraid!' he exclaimed. 'I'm not a burglar or anything like that.'

His tone to some extent reassured her. She came out of the corner.

'Is that your car outside?' she asked.

'I suppose it must be. Yes. I remember. Mr Velfrage drove for me. I came in to look for him.'

He spoke hesitatingly, reconstructing from his own confusion.

'I think not!' said the girl coldly. 'I myself telephoned Mr Velfrage's office this afternoon to tell him my aunt was not returning, and the house would be empty.'

'He couldn't have received the message.'

'I spoke to him personally.'

'Anyhow, I'm at least sure about Velfrage coming in here

16

– I came in after him, but I must have missed him. Perhaps I seem to you mad, or drunk. Try to believe that I had a temperature, and I've been taking quinine to keep it down.'

He drew out the bottle, held it for her to see, then put it back.

'I don't think you are drunk, and I do believe that you are ill. But I must insist on knowing why you are here.'

'That's the devil of it! Dunno whether I can give a clear account. A bit delirious, I think. I've been upstairs chasing one of the crooks.' He touched his cheek. 'She scratched me. Red-headed hell-cat! I have an impression of a ghastly great fight in that room.'

He turned his back on her, went into the room. It was empty. He saw it as a 'library', saw the shattered glass of the bookcase. The door of the big safe had been shut. He looked in vain for an overturned chair.

The girl was a few feet behind him.

'It wasn't all delirium!' he exclaimed. 'Look at that book-case!' He suspected that the quinine was not running true to form. 'I'm ill. I don't feel equal to explaining. There's a telephone. I'll ring the police.' He dialled Scotland Yard.

'What's the address of this place?' he asked the girl.

'The wire has been cut from the terminals,' she pointed out.

It was a few seconds before he took it in. He happened to glance in a mirror over the fireplace, saw the blood-streaks on his face.

'Good God! No wonder you're frightened of me! But it does bear me out when I say there's been a fight!'

She was not physically frightened of him – she was standing near him. Her eye travelled from his face to a glistening patch on the carpet – as if water had been spilled – then to the bookcase.

'I can see there has been a fight. I would like to know why.'

'I dunno! Can't remember. Can't concentrate. I'll go for the police in my car. Will you come with me?'

'No, thank you!'

'Because you're afraid I'll go mad and attack you. Don't

know who you are. You needn't tell me if you don't want to. I'll find out when I'm better.' His momentary clarity was passing. 'Sweat it out and be back at the office the day after tomorrow. Then I'll collect an apology from you.'

Habershon was smarting under a sense of cruel injustice. The cold air and the light rain on his face steadied him. He got into his car, took the drive with precision.

He had cleared the semi-circle of the drive, was in the straight immediately in front of the gates, when a woman stepped from the shadow and held up her hand.

He stopped with a vague idea that she wanted a lift. She hurried forward, put a foot on the running-board.

'I think you have my bag,' she said. 'Will you give it to me, please?'

'I haven't anybody's bag. I know your voice, don't I?'

He switched on the dome light.

'Why you're the one who jumped on my back!' he exclaimed, as if he were greeting an old friend. 'I say, if you aren't in a hurry, let's go back to the house and tell 'em what happened.'

'You seem to have recovered your senses.' The woman spoke severely and with some dignity. 'Give me back my bag, or I shall call the police.'

The threat banished Habershon's good temper.

'I have told you, madam, that I have not your bag. You are very rude. Please go away.'

A man's head was thrust through the opposite window.

'Hullo, Frank! Your face is a mess, old man. .... *Ah!* Not quick enough, Frankie!'

Frank had reached forward to switch off the ignition. Habershon had brought his knee up and crashed the hand painfully against the dash.

'Give me that bag, damn you, or you'll get one, this time!'

Frank had thrust a gun in at the window, but not before Habershon had meshed gear.

'All tickets please!' whooped Habershon and let go.

As he shot through the gates, the gun screeched against the windscreen and went off harmlessly. Frank was scraped off by the near-side pillar.

Habershon laughed and instantly forgot the woman, the man and the gun, as he narrowly missed one of the trees planted along the roadside. By chance he turned in the right direction for the arterial road.

He was putting on speed when the car ran into a depression in the road, now filled by the rain to a depth of some ten inches. His number plate struck the water with a thud — some few gallons landed on the bonnet and splashed against the windscreen, scaring him badly.

'Drive slowly. You're muzzier than you think you are. Drive *very* slowly.'

He was within a hundred yards of his bungalow at Stainham when he ran into a lamp-post.

3

GRADUALLY, like a slow fade-in on the screen, the confused shapes took familiar form. A blur of blue and white and pink turned into a hospital nurse – of unearthly beauty.

'Am I all in one piece?' he asked.

'Why, you haven't even had an operation! You're weak, but you'll soon be all right if you don't hurry yourself. Just sleep it off.'

He went to sleep, woke up and heard the doctor say much the same thing. He began to notice his surroundings. A small panelled room with no ceiling. A cubicle in a hospital. His lounge suit and his overcoat were hanging on the wall in front of him. The equipment of the cubicle was strictly utilitarian. Get well and get out. Good!

In time came Miss Parker with flowers and things. Dear old Parker! She was going grey and her large face was trellised with wrinkles, but she looked as if she could run the whole hospital with her left hand. No good playing the invalid with her.

'Please, dear kind Miss Parker, tell me about me. How long have I been here?'

'In a few hours you will have been here ten days. I think you're well enough now to be ashamed of yourself.'

'I'm ashamed of leaving all that work to you. I'll probably be back tomorrow or the next day. Is everything all right?'

'I don't know whether the Chrysler has been repaired yet. The estimate was thirty pounds. The insurance company may refuse payment on the ground of contributory negligence.'

'I say, Miss Parker – look here! – don't tell me I killed somebody with the Chrysler.'

'Fortunately, lamp-posts are immortal. You would have killed yourself with pneumonia if a very sensible young constable hadn't brought you here quickly. You will have to thank him when you're well. You must have got worse after you left the office.'

'Maybe! I remember stopping once or twice to take quinine. Otherwise, it's all a sort of nightmare. Don't remember crashing.'

'The less we both remember of it all the better!' pronounced Miss Parker, and Habershon was inclined to agree with her.

Three days later she delivered an ultimatum.

'The doctor approves of your leaving tomorrow, but not of your going straight to the office. A brief holiday is essential. I suggest that little place in Cornwall. You liked the Atlantis Hotel last year. I could travel down with you on Saturday and move you in.'

He protested and argued, but only as a mental exercise. Miss Parker had a moral authority which was invariably reinforced by common sense and therefore irresistible.

He saved face by demanding a report on the office. He drank in the details, which made him forget his invalidity.

'And there was our claim over that furniture from Athens – you remember? Well, I accepted a very fair offer from the solicitors – Knight and Velfrage.'

'Velfrage!' cried Habershon. 'Good! Splendid! Better than you know. He's one of the missing links. I met Velfrage on my way home. I'll ring him up.'

'You will not!' Miss Parker was unsympathetic. 'He happens to be in New York and will not be back for another fortnight. His clerk told me.'

'That tallies. I seem to remember his saying something about his luggage being at Southampton – that was while he was driving my car.'

'He was not driving your car when you hit the lamp-post.' It was Miss Parker's way of indicating disbelief. 'Anyhow, what does it matter if you did meet Mr Velfrage? You've had a miraculous escape. The crash only scratched your face, but the fever might have killed you. You'll be very unwise if you keep on nagging at your memory. The whole thing is over and in a little while you'll be none the worse, if you behave reasonably.'

Common sense again. Miss Parker never gave quarter.

The next day, waiting in his cubicle, fully dressed for departure, he thrust his hand into the side pocket of his overcoat, felt an unfamiliar object.

He drew out a small bag – a woman's bag. An evening-dress affair. Peacock blue with a peacock's 'eye' embroidered on each side. Two peacock's eyes! And fasteners at each end for a chain, broken. Somebody with a noisy taste.

The nurse – now no more beautiful than any other girl – put her head in at the door.

'Matron will be free in a minute. I've told her you want to say goodbye.'

'I say, Nurse! I've just found this!' He displayed the bag. 'It's not mine. It must have been put in my pocket here while I was unconscious.'

'That's a *gorgeous* explanation!' laughed the nurse and hurried away.

The matron did not say it was a gorgeous explanation, but she did smile as she declined guardianship of the bag. If he *really* couldn't remember, she said, it would be justifiable to look inside.

When he had bowed her out, he looked inside.

Maquillage, a latchkey, a tiny phial of aspirins, and a wisp of a handkerchief, unmarked. A small tear in the lining was obviously not wide enough for a visiting card to have slipped through. There was therefore no means, he decided indifferently, of identifying the owner.

The peacock's eye! It suggested only Kew Gardens, but he hadn't been there for years. And he had seen a peacock's eye recently, somewhere.

In the hired car that was taking him to his bungalow, he remembered that Miss Parker had told him to thank the constable on duty.

'You might stop at the local police station and wait for me,' he told the driver.

The young constable was identified as one who had just come off duty. In the presence of the superintendent, Habershon thanked him.

'When you were fishing me out of the Chrysler, constable, were there any women about?'

'Not what you'd call *women*, sir. There was a char-woman on her way home, after we'd got you into the ambulance —'

'A charwoman will not solve my difficulty.' Habershon produced the bag and laid it on the superintendent's table. He stated, in effect, that he could offer no explanation of its presence in his pocket.

'A sort of lapse of memory, I suppose, Mr Habershon?'

'Hardly that. More like a thick night. I can remember bits, but not in the right order.' He told his little tale of the temperature and the quinine.

'Well, I don't suppose you met a lady-friend on an arterial road on a wet winter's evening who asked you to take care of her bag. Must have got into your pocket on some earlier occasion.'

Habershon shook his head.

'I hadn't been to a party since Christmas. And there was no bag incident then. I can remember that kind of thing perfectly. The muzzy period only begins after I left my office.'

The superintendent gave Habershon a receipt for the bag. Later he had the trouble of looking through the lists of the last three weeks. When this yielded no result, he forwarded the bag, in accordance with routine, to the central Lost Property Office, a department of Scotland Yard.

4

Detective Inspector Kyle entered the room of the Chief Superintendent, Scotland Yard, in answer to a summons on the house telephone.

The Chief looked up from a typewritten report, indicated a chair, and went on reading for some thirty seconds, during which Kyle noticed a woman's handbag on the blotting pad, bearing the label of the lost property department.

'Well, I'm jiggered!' exclaimed the Chief good humouredly. 'Got a bit of colour for you here, Kyle. I'm not sure that it's a job for your section, but I want you to take it on. I've done most of the work for you. Look at this!'

Kyle contemplated the bag, which was passed to him. An evening-dress affair. Peacock blue with a peacock's 'eye' embroidered on each side.

'That was handed voluntarily to the Stainham police three days ago by a young man who said he found it in his pocket and didn't know how it had got there. The details are in the report which is now being typed. The report covers everything. I dictated it myself.

'Stainham sent it to L.P. as a lost bag. Whether Stainham put 'emselves to the trouble of opening the bag we don't know. Anyhow, they didn't feel round the lining. L.P. did – and found this!'

The Chief passed a little box which a layman might have mistaken for a pill box. Kyle lifted the lid and stared at a diamond, so large and with so many facets that it made one want to laugh, as if it were a practical joke.

'What is it, sir? The Koh-i-noor? The Cullinan?'

'Not quite in that class. It is somewhere among the fifty best-known diamonds in the world. There's a letter from Napoleon in the British Museum with four lines of guff about it. That kind of thing! You'll find it all in my report. Are you interested in history?'

'Well, sir —'

'Same here! We'll skip it,' smiled the Chief. 'For the last hundred years or so it's been known as the Rabethorpe diamond. Last owner, William Rabethorpe, died fifteen years ago. The diamond has been in the custody of solicitors, who have freak instructions to find the missing heir – William's long lost daughter. We can skip that too. Except for this daughter – and she must be fiftyish now, if she's alive – the family died with William.'

'How much is it worth?' asked Kyle.

'The experts wouldn't commit themselves. As a diamond, it seems that it's worth around fifty thousand pounds. Then there's the collector-value – the history and the legend and the whatnot – which might double the price.'

Kyle returned the diamond but retained the embroidered bag.

'A firm of solicitors!' ejaculated Kyle. 'They didn't think the diamond would be quite safe at the bank, so they asked a lady-friend to keep it in her best bag?'

'Wait for the laugh! That bag, with diamond in the lining, had been in that man's pocket while he was lying in Stainham hospital for a fortnight. And no one has reported the loss of the diamond. That's why I think it might turn out to be a job for your section after all.'

The Chief may have flattered himself a little, but it was certainly a good report, Kyle admitted, when he had read it. He wasted no time in reflection. It was a sound rule never to try to be ingenious until you have exhausted the obvious. So he called on Messrs Knight & Velfrage, solicitors, custodians of the Rabethorpe diamond – and asked for Mr Knight.

'Mr Knight,' he was told by an elderly clerk, 'has been dead this many a year. Mr Velfrage is in the United States. Mr Clawson is acting for the firm in Mr Velfrage's absence.'

It was a large suite of offices in Chancery Lane, where rents are high. The elderly clerk took him along a corridor, in which he passed a door labelled 'Mr George Clawson, LL.B.', to Mr Velfrage's room, where Clawson was temporarily enthroned.

'Mr Velfrage is in New York, Inspector. I'm his managing clerk. Glad to do anything I can for you.'

'Thank you.' Kyle observed a man in the middle or late thirties; intelligent eyes, rather prominent jaw; employed a good tailor. 'Has Mr Velfrage been away long?'

'He sailed on the night of January the fifteenth.'

'And you expect him back – soon?'

'He did not give a date. He said he would stay in New York for a fortnight or three weeks. He may cable us when he has decided to return – he may not. My chief,' added Clawson with a smile, 'makes rather a point of never giving unnecessary information, even to his colleagues.'

'But you have heard from him since he left?'

'No. Our last exchange was in this room, about lunchtime, on the day he sailed. I can see that you think that extraordinary. You would not think so if you knew Mr Velfrage.'

'Can I have his New York address, please?'

'Certainly!' Clawson wrote the name of a world-famous hotel and a world-famous ship, and passed the slip to Kyle. 'I confess I'm getting a little anxious, Inspector. Have you any reason to believe that something may have happened to Velfrage?'

'A query has reached us indirectly, in a roundabout sort of way, concerning the Rabethorpe estate,' evaded Kyle. 'I believe this firm is the trustee?'

'Correct!' said Clawson.

'We've been given to understand that the estate is worth upwards of a quarter of a million pounds. And on top o' that, there's the famous Rabethorpe diamond?'

'Correct again,' said Clawson. 'Though I'd better admit that I'm speaking on hearsay. I've never seen the diamond, and Mr Velfrage has never mentioned it to me. Of course, the diamond, with its ill-luck legend, and the rest of it, is pretty well known.'

'I'd chance the ill luck – if the firm ever wants to give it away,' said Kyle with ponderous good humour. 'Thank you, Mr Clawson.'

The shipping company confirmed that a passage had been booked by Mr Velfrage. Further enquiry elicited that the booking had not been taken up. The ship had sailed without Mr Velfrage.

The central index of air-passenger traffic contained no mention of Velfrage.

Finally, a return cable from the New York police made it abundantly clear that Mr Velfrage had not arrived in New York since 15th January.

He caught Clawson just as the latter was about to leave for home.

'Mr Velfrage booked his passage for the fifteenth but he did not sail. If he is in New York, he has slipped past the authorities with a false name,' said Kyle, and left Clawson to go on from there.

Clawson registered distress – in strong-silent form.

'Before I get excited,' he said, 'I want to try someone who may help us.'

As he spoke he turned the pages of the telephone book. Presently he was giving the name of the firm.

'Clawson speaking, Miss Velfrage. Would you mind telling me whether you've heard from your brother in the last week or so? As you probably know, he sailed for New York on the fifteenth – at least, I understood him to say that was where he was going – and he has forgotten to cable his address. . . . You've heard nothing at all? . . . Oh no, please don't worry. I expect we shall hear in a day or so.'

Clawson replaced the receiver and gazed gloomily at Kyle.

'I don't, of course, expect we shall hear from him. I expect he is dead!' His expression became almost fierce. 'If it's in your mind, Inspector, that Velfrage has absconded, I invite you to forget it. I can tell you that the affairs of the firm are in good order. I've watched Velfrage pretty closely. If he isn't exactly rich, he's very well covered. He lives alone in a flat in Kensington, with small-scale personal expenses. I was speaking to his sister who is his only relative as far as I know.'

'Let's see how it adds up.' Kyle's tone was conciliatory. 'He walks out of this office at lunch-time on the fifteenth and as far as you're concerned walks off the earth.'

'Not quite! I know where he was at about five in the afternoon of that day. Just a minute!' Clawson opened a drawer and took out a receipted bill from a garage at Kew Bridge pinned to a notification from the Automobile Association.

'Velfrage told me in here that he was driving himself in the Daimler to Southampton and would call on a client – unspecified – on the way. On the seventeenth, I received this bill for towing his Daimler a couple of miles along the Great West Road and making a repair. It can't have been an accident or the A.A. man would have reported.'

That was all Clawson had to say. Kyle went to the A.A. central office, where he was shown the patrolman's report. After giving the patrolman his instructions, Mr Velfrage was driven off in a Chrysler (number noted) by a man with whom Mr Velfrage was talking when the patrolman arrived on the scene.

When he was back at the Yard, he sent the number of the Chrysler to Register.

In a few minutes the owner's name was returned as Bruce Habershon, with an address in Stainham.

Kyle stroked his chin. To make sure that memory was not tricking him, he turned to the Chief's report. He was not mistaken. The bag with the peacock's eye – the bag in which the Rabethorpe diamond had been found under the lining – had been handed to the Stainham police by Bruce Habershon, with an address in Stainham.

By eight o'clock he was hearing from the superintendent at Stainham the detailed story of Habershon's surrender of the bag.

'We have no record of Habershon,' said Kyle. 'Have you anything on him locally, for small stuff?'

'Anything on Bruce Habershon? Meaning convictions?' The superintendent laughed loudly, then apologized. 'Why, his father used to be chief magistrate here. And if you'd happened to be interested in amateur boxing, Mr Kyle, you'd know Mr Bruce well enough. When he was up at Oxford he beat the Cambridge man two years running. Heavyweight, yes! And his last fight – well, he lost that on points

28

to the champion of the Army, but he had bad luck. That sergeant – he must have got a freak jaw —'

'D'you reckon I shall find Habershon at home?'

'Not at his bungalow, you won't. He's on holiday – convalescent. I don't know where he's gone, though I did hear it was down in Cornwall. You'd have to ask at his office. Shipping agents. It was his father's firm and it's his now. They'll tell you, Mr Kyle. I'll guarantee you won't get any hanky-panky from them.'

On the way back Kyle surveyed progress.

Mr Velfrage, prosperous solicitor and custodian of the Rabethorpe diamond, disappears for more than a fortnight and no one seems to notice. Ditto the Rabethorpe diamond.

Velfrage is last heard of as entering a Chrysler car in company with its owner, Bruce Habershon. A significant juxtaposition, suggesting that Habershon has murdered Velfrage and stolen the diamond.

But it is the same Bruce Habershon who hands to the police the vanity bag containing the diamond.

Not knowing that the bag contained the diamond.

Which suggests – in spite of that superintendent's guarantee – that there must be some hanky-panky somewhere.

No good worrying about that yet awhile. Exhaust the obvious by interviewing Habershon.

5

FOR Bruce Habershon, the first three days of his enforced holiday were the worst. A short ride on an elderly cob in the morning, a short walk in the afternoon, dinner, and bed at ten, made up his day. The Atlantis kept one wing open during the winter for a clientele of prosperous old maids and retired military men. As there were fewer than fifty guests there was a general tendency to sociability.

On his third evening Habershon was buttonholed in the lounge by a general's wife whose husband neglected her.

'Oh, Mr Habershon! I wonder if you're superstitious! Look at this.'

She fluttered an illustrated weekly and compelled his attention to the photograph of an American industrial magnate.

'*Mr Sundius K. Gallerton,*' he read, '*who is reported to have offered £100,000 for the Rabethorpe diamond. The diamond which, like the Hope diamond, is believed to bring violent death or crushing misfortune to its owner —*'

There were several lines of it, which Habershon thought it unnecessary to read.

'I suppose if you begin by believing that sort of thing you may increase your liability to accident!' he said with mechanical amiability. He escaped as soon as he could and forgot the incident until he was getting into bed.

The Rabethorpe diamond!

It was as if someone had spoken it aloud.

'Somebody else was talking to me recently about the Rabethorpe diamond – oh yes, old Velfrage!'

Having thus settled the matter, he went to sleep. From the start he had decided that, as he was going to the expense and trouble of an unwanted holiday, he would not spoil it by nagging his memory about the events of that night. Now and again at odd moments he broke the resolution. Confused pictures and disconnected phrases would loom up – a swinging right at a man with a gun, a red-headed girl whose clothes he had torn off her back, a grinning Disney dwarf, a fantastically enormous diamond, old Velfrage floating out of a carburettor and telling him he ought to be in bed! Addled, nightmare nonsense that must be forgotten as soon as possible.

On the fourth night, at dinner, he was pleased to note a new arrival whose appearance promised a more lively companionship. He saw an erect, well-preserved man in early middle-age who had probably got his slight limp from a bullet – which was true, though Habershon would have been surprised to learn that the bullet had come from a crook; for there was nothing about Detective Inspector Kyle to label him a member of Scotland Yard. His bony, intelligent face, with wide blue eyes and benevolent expression, suggested a lawyer with a good practice and a large family. The poor chap, thought Habershon, had probably come down to convalesce, and would be bored stiff in a day or two.

Kyle was able to observe Habershon at leisure. Looked a good type, popular too! Few of the guests passed his table without stopping. Not of much use to a policeman, by the look of him.

In the lounge after dinner Habershon heard the faint whispering sound behind him made by Kyle's shuffle. He turned and grinned amiably.

'I expect you've come for a cure of some sort, sir, as I have?'

'I've come to see you, Mr Habershon.' Kyle's tone was as friendly as the other's. He produced his card.

'Good Lord!' Habershon looked guilty of almost every crime a man can commit. 'Have I – have I put my foot through the law somewhere?'

'Not as far as I know!' chuckled Kyle. 'What about a spot of coffee?' There was no difficulty in finding a quiet corner in the half-empty lounge. 'It's about that bag.'

'Bag?' echoed Habershon. 'Oh, I remember! Peacock's eye! I swung it on the local police before I came here.'

'That's the one that's causing the trouble, Mr Habershon —'

31

'Can you tell me where I picked it up?'

After the long journey from London, Kyle found the question somewhat discouraging.

'You see, if you could start me off I might be able to go on,' added Habershon.

The waiter brought coffee. A retired colonel stopped to invite Habershon to join him in an expedition for conger eel.

'It might help us very considerably, Mr Habershon, if you could piece together what happened before you had your crash.'

'Not a hope! The doctor told me that quinine, if you mess about with it, as I did, will produce a kind of drunkenness. It ranks in my mind as a frightfully thick night, in which one remembers some things that did happen and some that couldn't have happened. For instance, I have a clear picture of meeting a man I know and giving a lift after his car had broken down. But Miss Parker, my secretary, seems to think I couldn't have. Anyway, he's in the States.'

Kyle's interest quickened at the last words.

'If you remember that he was a friend, you probably remember his name?'

'Oh yes, that's perfectly clear. I even remember some patter about New York and Southampton and luggage in advance – which links on to the States. He was a solicitor I do lots of business with – a man called Velfrage.'

The right answer! The long journey from London had not been wasted.

'Please go on, Mr Habershon. That makes sense.'

'Only because it's the sort of thing that *could* have happened. Just as vivid in my mind are things that could *not* have happened. When I met him – if I did – the delirium and the quinine-drunk, or both, had started. The muzziness would come and go. I remember his driving my car, because he said I was too ill to drive – which probably didn't happen, because if he thought I was as ill as that, he wouldn't have left me. There's no memory of parting from him, either. Of course, there must have been longish lucid intervals, though I don't remember them. I didn't crash until I was practically home.'

'Aren't you unintentionally exaggerating the delirious element?' Kyle was treading very carefully. 'For instance, we know that Velfrage stopped on the Great West Road about that time with engine trouble, that an A.A. patrolman took over the car, and that Velfrage went off in a friend's car. There can surely be no doubt that the friend was yourself.'

'Splendid! I wish I could piece it together – I'd quite given up trying. It's irritating not knowing what sort of a goat I may have made of myself.'

Habershon's face clouded. Kyle was able to reassure him.

'Don't worry about that, Mr Habershon. What did your doctor tell you? – that misuse of quinine can produce a kind of drunkenness. I have had this kind of conversation we're having now a great many times – with alcoholics and dope fiends. You won't mind my lumping you in with them for the moment. I can tell you that before you and I have finished we shall have linked up the bits you do remember – and they'll remind you of the rest.'

'That's a relief, anyhow!' There was an element of doubt in Habershon's voice. 'In the meantime, my account of anything is no good until it's confirmed. We can prove I met Velfrage. But if we go on, I shall tell you things no one can prove, because they couldn't have happened.'

'You'll tell me things that *seem* as if they couldn't have happened,' corrected Kyle. 'That'll be because you're remembering bits in the wrong order, making nonsense. Push on a little, and the things that seem absurd begin to slip into proportion. Perhaps this will help you – we know that Velfrage did get into your car.'

'Did he? I can't be sure. Listen! My version is that Velfrage was going to call on a client, then drive me home and hire a car to Southampton. Well, he couldn't find the turning. So up jumped a Walt Disney dwarf, all smiles, pointing out the turning!'

'Yet you're clear-headed about it – able to remember it as an absurdity,' Kyle pointed out.

'That's true!' To Habershon it was a welcome discovery.

He went on: 'The little I have remembered is mixed up with odd bits of conversation about almost everything. For instance, there's an interlude with the Hope diamond, or one of those diamonds that kill people. The Rabethorpe diamond – that's the one!'

Kyle took up his empty coffee cup and pretended to drink. Velfrage! The Rabethorpe diamond! Both had clicked into place in a few minutes. It looked as if the whole case would be handed to him on a plate.

The Stainham superintendent was right. There was certainly no hanky-panky about this young man. With careful prompting, he would soon be able to remember how he got hold of the bag – and what he had done with Velfrage.

6

HABERSHON was emphasizing the fantastic element in his recollection.

'Whether Velfrage said so or not, I got it into my head that he was taking the Rabethorpe diamond to his client. In a few minutes, there's the diamond behind me on the back seat, the size of a radiogram and glittering like mad.'

'Probably you were startled by a flash of light, or something,' said Kyle. 'Leave that sort of thing to sort itself out. Skip the fantastic and concentrate on the real.' Kyle had already noted that those of Habershon's statements that were credible in themselves dovetailed with the facts he had obtained in London.

'I believe we're in for some more conger eel,' said Habershon, who had spotted the colonel returning. 'If you want to go on with this, what about coming up to my room?'

Five minutes later Kyle turned up in Habershon's room, carrying a concertina dispatch-case. From it he took the evening-dress bag with the peacock's eye.

'Have a good look at it, Mr Habershon. Handle it. Maybe it'll remind you.'

Habershon took the bag, turned it over, opened it.

'I don't remember this cut in the lining – quite a big one,' he remarked.

'Our fellows probably did that,' Kyle hastily assured him. 'Anyhow, you remember the bag?'

'I remember puzzling over it in hospital and taking it to the local police – nothing else.'

Kyle returned the bag to the dispatch-case. Perhaps it would help later when they had found something definite to work on. For half an hour he put questions without result.

'We seem to stick, Inspector, don't we?' lamented Habershon, lolling back on the pillows. 'That Disney dwarf – as real to me as Velfrage's Daimler – is the first incident in a delirious nightmare. We turn into a drive. Velfrage seems to drop out of the picture then. A comic-opera parlourmaid lets me into the house. Soon I'm fighting a lot of men and women. The men are armed, but I knock them down – like those absurd sloshing scenes on the films – I grab their guns and fire at people in general.'

'You *can* slosh, Mr Habershon! Oxford gave you a half blue for – er – sloshing.'

'But you can't get realism into what I did that night. There's a point where I'm chasing a girl up the stairs. I tear her clothes off.' He hesitated. 'I'm not trying to get fresh with her. I'm trying – good Lord! – *to kill her*!'

With a sudden movement his hand went to his cheek. He sprang from the bed, stared at himself in the mirror.

'She scratched my face – a hell of a scratch! I believe – I believe I can see the marks.' Impulsively he turned to the detective. 'Can you see any marks – this side?'

'Excuse me.' Kyle tilted the other's chin so that the light should fall at an angle. 'Yes, I think I can see three, possibly four, streaks, beginning about an inch below your eye.'

Habershon looked long at the detective. When he spoke his voice was thin and high pitched.

'Inspector! Suppose I *did* kill that girl!'

'Now, young man, pull yourself together!' said Kyle. 'Suppose you did kill her, eh? In the state you were in, you couldn't have concealed the body. It's over a fortnight ago. Someone would have to do something about that – which means call the local police.'

'*Phew!*' Habershon mopped his face with a handkerchief. 'Thanks a lot, Inspector! I never thought of that.'

It was a large single bedroom with one armchair and a small writing-table. Habershon turned away from the dressing-table and resumed his seat on the edge of the bed. The silence lasted while Kyle filled and lit his pipe.

Suddenly Habershon laughed.

'That girl with her clothing torn off and her nails on my face! I may have thrown myself about in delirium at the hospital and a nurse may have scratched me by accident. Perhaps the hospital has a record?'

'I wouldn't worry 'em!' said Kyle. 'We're getting along fine. No need to rush things.'

A note of irritation crept in as Habershon asked :

'I say, Inspector, is all this soul-searching pinned on to a bag that's worth about three quid at the outside?'

'Not the bag itself, of course!' hedged Kyle.

Habershon waited. Kyle saw that he had no choice, if he wished to keep the other's willing co-operation.

'Mr Velfrage has been reported missing. There's the bare possibility – hardly more – that this bag may be a clue to his whereabouts. That's why I want you to remember all you can about it.'

'Missing!' repeated Habershon. 'Half a minute! Remember what I said about luggage and Southampton? And, now I think of it, my secretary told me he was in New York.'

'He is not in New York.'

'Oh, I say, Inspector! You don't know Miss Parker! She's practically never wrong about anything.'

'His firm believed him to be in New York. You may take it from me that he did not leave this country for the United States.'

That, coming from a Yard inspector, was final.

'Well, I'm skew-wiffed!' Habershon's thoughts were wholly on Velfrage's disappearance. 'He isn't the kind who would slope off with a girl. And you can rule out the possibility of his bolting with his clients' cash. Poor old blighter – something must have happened to him. He's a good chap, in a dry sort of way.'

He followed thought of Velfrage for some seconds and continued :

'I saw a reference to that Rabethorpe diamond in a paper last night. That's how I remembered it.'

Kyle waited. As nothing was added, he took from the dispatch-case a copy of the same illustrated weekly.

'That's it!' said Habershon. 'I didn't read the patter —'

'Better read it now. It may remind you of something Velfrage said.'

' " . . . is believed to bring violent death or misfortune to

37

its owner." Yes, I read that bit.' Habershon resumed : ' *"For fifteen years the diamond has been in the custody of trustees of the considerable estate of the late William Rabethorpe, whose will strikingly revived the legend of evil. Under the terms of the trust* 'the trustees, their heirs or assigns' *are to hold the estate — including the Rabethorpe diamond or the proceeds of its sale —* 'until such time as my daughter Elsie Amelia shall have been found alive and of sound mind.' *Mr Gallerton, himself a distant connexion of the Rabethorpe family —"* '

Habershon returned the paper absent-mindedly.

'It's brought something back to you, Mr Habershon?'

'Yes — something Velfrage said. *"My client is Mrs Rabethorpe. I daresay you've heard the name before."* '

'Good!'

'But unhelpful!' protested Habershon. 'How can she be William-Diamond-Rabethorpe's daughter if she's called "Mrs" Rabethorpe?'

'Ah! That's the sort of question we'll have to keep until you've remembered something about that bag.'

Habershon was trying to link Velfrage on to the bag with the peacock's eye. But that bag could not be made to fit into a picture of 'old' Velfrage. The diamond was a different matter.

'I say, Inspector, is that Rabethorpe diamond missing too?'

Kyle reflected that the admission might defeat his purpose. He decided on evasion.

'We have reason to believe, but no proof, that Velfrage was carrying it when you met him — perhaps intending to take it to New York and sell it to Mr Gallerton. We are not looking for the diamond as such. My assignment is to find Velfrage. If the diamond is going to help, I am interested in the diamond.'

'You can count me in, Inspector.'

'In what way, Mr Habershon?'

'I can't see the sense of catching conger eels!' exploded Habershon. 'I mean, if you'll promise not to tell my secretary, I'll slope back to Town tomorrow.

'And you and I,' he went on excitedly, 'will drive along the Great West Road and see if we can find that house.'

'What house?' asked Kyle blankly.

'The house of Velfrage's client. If it exists. And if I can find it – though we can't expect Disney to help us this time! You see, if there was a house, I might have entered it. And although the sloshing business and the girl on the stairs take a bit of swallowing – well, there may have been a real girl there with a bag. With a peacock's eye! Cut the bit about my tearing her clothes off. Isn't all this what you meant when you said the bag might be a clue?'

'Y-yes, that's what I meant, I suppose – more or less,' asserted Kyle.

'It would be grand to help you find poor old Velfrage. Pretty obvious that something has happened to him. I mean – well, he may have been murdered, mayn't he?'

7

BRUCE HABERSHON, as Miss Parker had observed, was everything he appeared to be. When he told Detective Inspector Kyle that he was anxious to help, he meant it. That the reconstruction might prove dangerous to himself did not occur to him. His attitude to the police, like that of most of his type, was one of benevolent indifference. One took the police force for granted, like the other public services. Kyle he accepted as a mature and reasonable man with whom one could be perfectly frank.

Shortly after four-thirty on the following afternoon they were sitting together in a police car at the beginning of the Great West Road.

'The light is about the same!' exclaimed Habershon. 'That gives me every chance.'

Perhaps his very eagerness let him down; for Kyle drove some five miles through the growing dusk without eliciting any response.

'No good, Inspector! It couldn't have been as far out as this.'

'Funny!' ejaculated Kyle. 'You know this road pretty well, don't you?'

'Been over it regularly for years without taking any notice of it.'

The Great West Road is much like any other arterial road to look at, with ribbon-development of factories and houses, behind which are flat square miles of market gardens.

Kyle drove back, nearly to the London extremity.

'We'll try once more, if you feel up to it, Mr Habershon!'

It was close upon five. Kyle turned on the headlights. There was a silence of several minutes, during which Habershon's spirits sank. He had the impression that the detective was beginning to doubt his whole story.

'See if this will help the memory! I can tell you that this

spot is within a hundred yards or so of where you saw the Daimler.'

'Fine! Now let me get out, talk to an imaginary Velfrage and get in again.'

Kyle was ready to humour him in anything. He intended to give the mental blackout theory every chance to establish itself. In the meantime he waited patiently while Habershon slipped out of the car and then got in again. The trick seemed to be effective. When they restarted, Habershon rapped out :

'Slower! Keep her down to about twenty-five. Velfrage was driving gingerly and keeping well in. I remember noticing the grass.' When Kyle complied : 'I say, Inspector, have you got a lot more facts up your sleeve?'

'One or two. But it's no use prompting you until you're stuck. What's-er-matter?'

Habershon had clutched his arm.

'Do you see what I see?' cried Habershon. *Walt Disney's dwarf!*'

'Jee-rusalem! You're right! That's Grumpy or Happy or something. Seen it in the kids' books!'

In the beam of the headlights, some fifteen yards from the roadway, stood the dwarf with pointed cap, bowing, smiling, and pointing to the left. Kyle had slowed. Beside the dwarf was a notice board : *The Snow-White Chalet. Fully Licensed Car Park. Teas.'*

'That ticks off number one of the nightmare!' said Kyle. 'Turns out to be something perfectly reasonable.'

'Beginner's luck!' laughed Habershon. 'Hold the line – more coming through. The house we're looking for has a drive. It's not the next turning – the one after – yes, second on the left.' He added : 'A "T" turn, not a cross-roads.'

Suddenly Habershon's spirits sank below zero.

'I don't like that dwarf!' he said uneasily. 'We thought it was something that couldn't have happened, and it's turned out to be real. I mean – some of the beat-up and shoot-up stuff may turn out to be as real as the dwarf.' He paused. 'The girl with the red hair, for instance.'

This was serious. Kyle stopped the car and lit a cigarette

partly to gain time. He was convinced that Habershon was no crook. But he was hefty and spirited. There was no guessing where a man like this would stop – given that the quinine had fuddled his sense of proportion.

'You're getting a bit nervy about this job,' said Kyle. 'Why? Because you've started wondering what the hell you're going to remember next.'

'Quite right, Inspector! I have a feeling that if I don't do my stuff neatly and remember all the right things, you'll begin to wonder what sort of game I'm playing.'

'I know you're not playing a game with us, Mr Habershon,' he said, with complete conviction. 'I'm as sure as I've ever been of anything that you are honestly doing your best to help us find Velfrage. Now let's concentrate on spotting this house with a drive.'

They found a 'T' turn and a house with a drive. They found, in fact, three such turns and a hundred or so houses with drives, for they had run into a prosperous little dormitory area – an oasis in the vast area of market gardens.

They drove up one tree-lined avenue, down the next, and back again.

'I'm stuck!' grunted Habershon. 'Shake that sleeve of yours, Inspector.'

'Huh! Means we'll have to call on every one of those houses and see if we can find another bit o' your nightmare lying about. That's a job for the staff, and we'll get the local police to help. Maybe you're tired and we've done enough for tonight?'

Ahead of them, a car suddenly sprouted a silver halo which spread outwards, fountain-wise, from its wings.

'Stop!' cried Habershon. 'I ran into that water.'

Kyle stopped, and said nothing. In Habershon, the silence bore fruit.

'Push on to that watersplash, please. . . . Now turn, getting your back wheels touching the water. When you start, give plenty of gas on the gears. When you're in top, give her just long enough to start picking up, then brake her down. We ought to stop near where one of those trees has only a few inches clearance of the drive.'

'I reckon that will be about a couple of hundred yards!' muttered Kyle.

'I can dimly remember being attacked on my way out,' contributed Habershon. 'A man and a woman. Yelling for a bag. Good lord! – it may have been *the* bag! Then someone fired a gun. Can't fix the details yet.'

The rule of thumb proved sufficient for their purpose. By some thirty yards, they overshot a property where the tree was within a few inches of the fairway of the drive.

'Is this it?' asked Kyle.

'Looks like it – but so do the others. Let's take a chance. If we fall down, I'll leave it to you to bow us out.'

Kyle turned into the drive, noting that the name of the house, picked out on a brick gate-post, was Woodville.

'Okay?'

'The drive is the right shape. The shemozzle – if there *was* one – took place in that room with the lights on – to the left of the front door.'

They got out of the car. Habershon, in his preoccupation, took charge.

'I press the bell-push.' His finger touched dead centre. 'The door should be opened by a young, tallish parlour-maid, red-haired, somewhat luscious – on consideration, definitely somewhat luscious!'

For the next twenty seconds he was hoping rather desperately that a red-headed girl would appear.

8

THE door was answered by a corpulent woman in a grubby apron, who looked more like a temporary cook than a parlourmaid.

'Who is the owner – or tenant – of this house?' asked Kyle.

'Mrs Rabethorpe,' answered the woman aggressively. 'Why shouldn't she be?'

'Please tell Mrs Rabethorpe I would like to see her.'

'What's the good! She's got company. She won't leave 'em.'

'I think she will.' Kyle produced his official card.

'All right, then!' The woman grudgingly admitted them. 'You'd better wait in the morning-room.'

It was a wide hall, certainly the kind of hall which Habershon remembered. The staircase, up which he had – or had not – chased the girl, was in the right place. The hall he remembered was like any other of its kind; but this one, he now noticed, had a certain individuality. A table, bench or chair of old oak had unmistakable quality. But the parquet was uneven and cracked. One of the three large rugs was very good, the other two nearly shoddy.

They were taken across the hall to a small room, part living-, part dining-room. The ill-favoured woman slammed the door on them.

'Definitely not luscious!' grinned Kyle.

'But the name of the owner is right!' Habershon spoke in an excited whisper.

'That doesn't mean much! When she shows up, touch your tie with your right hand if you've seen her before. If you haven't seen her, move your head as if your collar were too tight.'

Habershon had barely finished repeating his instructions when the door was opened – impulsively, as if by an eager child.

'Good evening! I've never met anybody from Scotland Yard before.'

The putative Mrs Rabethorpe was a tall woman, fiftyish, dressed floppily in an elaborate semi-evening dress that defied current fashion, her large hands jewelled but tobacco stained. A woman, one could tell at once, who had savoured life to the full and meant to enjoy the dregs. A woman who had been petted and spoilt, yet a woman who could never have had any physical beauty. She was not plain – she was magnificently ugly. A small, disharmonious nose, very large mouth and lips, large eyes with laughter wrinkles, large ears and large ear-rings – altogether, she looked like an eighteenth-century portrait in oils of one of those ungainly, brainless women who inexplicably ensnared a succession of princes. Her voice alone was soft and feminine.

She surveyed the two men with ripe appreciation. The elder was the kind one would choose for a husband if one wanted to settle down. The younger, with his crisp hair, regular features, and his general air of having jumped out of the sea, would have thrown her off her balance thirty years ago.

'It really is very kind of the police to take all this trouble over a trifle – it makes one feel so well protected!'

Habershon was trying not to show his bewilderment at her conception of what was trifling. For Kyle's information, he moved his head as if his collar were too tight.

'Not at all!' Kyle was well trained in conducting conversation in the dark, the cardinal principle being to let the other side turn on the light. 'We like to leave no stone unturned. I gather you were expecting me, Mrs Rabethorpe?'

'Frankly, no!' admitted Mrs Rabethorpe. 'I have a few guests who are taking me on to the theatre after dinner. But do sit down and tell me exactly what you want me to do.'

'It would be most helpful if you would give me your own account of what happened in this house on the evening of January the fifteenth.'

'Well, you realize it won't be my account because I wasn't here – it will be my niece's account – she should arrive at any minute – I had to send her to Town for some shopping today. And of course I believe every word she says, as she's a very truthful girl. But young girls who have no experience of life do sometimes tell the most incredible stories about young men. Why, for instance, should there be blood on the young man's face?'

Habershon tried in vain to catch Kyle's eye.

'I haven't heard that part,' said Kyle.

'Celia says she let herself in with a latchkey and found a young man standing by himself in the hall, looking idiotic. She says he had a nice voice and was probably very handsome if it hadn't been for the blood on his face – that's why I suspect she invented the blood, unconsciously of course! There's some absurd tale about fighting with a woman who had scratched him and smashed the glass in the library bookcase. He said she had red hair – which is almost uncanny, because I had a red-haired housemaid. She was good at her work but such a thief that I let her go when I shut up the house for my trip to Belgium. I don't see how the young man could have known that – and anyhow she wasn't here that night. Nobody was here —'

'But apparently the glass in the library was smashed!' Kyle reminded her.

'Oh yes! Celia's man must have done it. And to prove he wasn't a burglar, which I don't suppose he was, he offered to call the police. I know it sounds fantastic, but that's what Celia will tell you when she comes in! The young man was very drunk.'

'And did he call the police?'

'No. The telephone wire had been cut. But we've had it repaired. And we've had a new glass put in the bookcase. The whole thing cost less than a couple of pounds. So I don't feel I'm justified in worrying the police any further. But I do appreciate —'

'Excuse me, Mrs Rabethorpe, why didn't – Miss Celia – call the police herself?'

'Fenton, her name is. She did call the police, in person. After the young man had gone. Because she thought she heard a revolver go off in the drive – probably a tyre burst.

And the police said it must have been an attempted burglary, and it was lucky I hadn't lost anything.'

Habershon sighed with relief. The local police had found nothing significant – certainly not the corpse of a red-headed girl in an upstairs room.

Habershon, ignoring Kyle's instructions, thrust in a question :

'Did Miss Fenton say he was drunk, Mrs Rabethorpe?'

'No. She said the poor fellow was ill. He told her he had taken a lot of quinine.' Mrs Rabethorpe chuckled wickedly. 'I never heard that excuse before! As I said, she is very inexperienced.

'The whole thing,' continued Mrs Rabethorpe, 'arose through my having to dine with a client in London immediately on my return from Belgium. I do a certain amount of dealing in *objets d'art* – a dear friend left me his business some years ago. Mr Velfrage, my solicitor, was to have met me here to – to show me something before going to New York. But I had to put him off – because of the client —'

'To *show* you something, Mrs Rabethorpe?' interrupted Kyle.

'It sounds mysterious, doesn't it? – and so it is, when you come to think of it !' As Kyle was unresponsive, she added : 'Have you ever heard of the Rabethorpe diamond?'

Habershon contrived to kick the heel of Kyle's shoe, but the latter was watching Mrs Rabethorpe.

'I can't wear diamonds – I never could ! Pearls, rubies, almost anything, but never diamonds!' Mrs Rabethorpe sighed. 'And I would certainly never wear that one. I'm superstitious, you know. So when Mr Velfrage said he had a buyer at a special price – Americans are wonderful for special prices, don't you think? – I was enthusiastic. But I thought I would like to see it before it went to America for good.'

'Is it *your* diamond, Mrs Rabethorpe?' asked Kyle.

'We don't know yet. There's a large fortune – about a quarter of a million, I think Mr Velfrage said – as well as the diamond, of course. Left by the man who seems to have been my father. Awaiting a claimant, you know. And we're all quite certain that I am the right Rabethorpe – only, a judge has to agree before Mr Velfrage can do anything. As he seems to have run off on his own, Mr Clawson will do it all. He says it will be all over in a day or two, but I'm not letting myself think too much about it.'

'But you are *Mrs* Rabethorpe?' put in Kyle.

'Oh well!' Mrs Rabethorpe gurgled girlishly. 'It's so troublesome to start a new name every time one has a new friend. So we generally used mine. So much simpler for forwarding letters. Oh, here is my niece, letting herself in!'

She got up and opened the door.

'Celia – in here, darling!'

The men had risen. Kyle saw a good-looking young woman, becomingly dressed, possessing a certain natural dignity that was free from assertiveness. Habershon saw a girl unlike any girl he had met, except in day-dreams. The ash-blonde halo was a beacon, pointing the way back to an orderly life, in which crooks and detectives were as remote as the Himalayas.

'Celia, this is Detective Inspector Kyle, who wants to hear about your mad burglar. And this is – er – his colleague.'

Celia Fenton gave Habershon a momentary glance, in acknowledgement of the introduction. About to speak to her aunt, she froze into immobility. Then, very slowly, she turned and looked full at Habershon, who returned her gaze.

'I have come to collect that apology, Miss Fenton,' said Habershon.

'The handsome burglar – why, of *course*!' Mrs Rabethorpe shrieked with delight. 'I knew he couldn't be a policeman!'

'I don't owe you an apology.' The girl ignored Mrs Rabethorpe. 'You pretended I thought you were a burglar. Nothing of the kind. I thought you were irresponsible.'

'Because your doctor gave you too much quinine!' whooped Mrs Rabethorpe. 'Now, you two go and fight it out over a cocktail, while the Inspector and I have a brandy and soda. I'll just see that the others have all they want. Dinner isn't for another twenty minutes, thank heavens! That cook has a vile temper.'

Habershon had detached the girl. To an onlooker it would have appeared that each had been looking for something and had found it, to their joint contentment.

'I'm talking rot. I'm the one to apologize for frightening you.'

'I was *frightened*, after you spoke. A bit startled and up-side-downish. One doesn't often meet a strange man in the house who explains that he can't explain why he's there but wishes he could.' As their laughter mingled, she added : 'What was it all about, really?'

'I don't know.' His elation vanished. 'I wish to heaven I did ! It's quite true about the quinine. The result is I'm still frightfully muddled as to what did happen that night.'

'I understand. Tough luck !' Instead of the shrinking he had expected, she showed a warm readiness to share his problem. 'My brother took whisky in the belief that it would cure influenza, and I helped him through a blackout very like yours. So I've had some experience. Will you let me try and help you ?'

'Will I let you !' he echoed.

'Then come into the hall and do what we did that night. Perhaps everything will come back with a flash – it did with my brother.' As he hesitated, she added : 'You don't have to be awf'ly solemn and earnest. Make a sort of charade of it.'

Kyle had been listening with both ears.

'That's an extremely good suggestion, Miss Fenton,' he said. Mrs Rabethorpe had returned, carrying decanter and glasses on a brass tray : mechanically he took it from her and set it down. 'I'd like to see it tried out – if Mrs Rabethorpe will allow us.'

'I'm enjoying every minute of it, Inspector. I told the others not to make a noise.' She sighed. 'Everybody laughs so loudly nowadays.'

As Celia and Habershon passed into the hall, Mrs Rabethorpe added : 'Don't they make a fine couple ! I suppose he's in a good position ? He looks as if he were.'

'I expect so.' Kyle was not interested in match-making.

49

He stood with Mrs Rabethorpe by the staircase, while Celia Fenton took charge.

It was unlucky, thought Kyle, that they had happened on a party. In spite of Mrs Rabethorpe's warning, a gust of laughter sounded through the door of the library. But the noise seemed to have no disturbing effect upon Habershon, who was giving his whole attention to Celia Fenton.

'You were standing about here – a little farther back. Let me push you. That's right – hold it while I go out and let myself in. Remember, we don't have to behave like actors – just remind each other of what happened. You're looking solemn again. Take it as a game.'

When Habershon heard her key being inserted in the front door, he found himself visualizing her. His memory of their original meeting became vivid.

The door was opened. The girl came in, shut it, then looked at Habershon.

'The left side of your face is covered with blood which has run to your collar. I back away into this corner. Now you carry on from there !'

'I come a bit nearer, but stop – about here – because I see you're frightened. I tell you I'm not a burglar and won't hurt you.'

'And I say I'm not frightened but want to know what you are doing in the house.'

'Yes – and that stumps me. I don't know why I'm in the house.'

'All the same, you give me an explanation,' said Celia. 'What was the explanation?'

From the staircase, Kyle was listening acutely. If Habershon could not answer, the girl obviously could, and he would ask her afterwards, if necessary.

Habershon was still sticking.

'I'll give you a clue. As I said, you give me an explanation, but I tell you politely you're a liar. . . .'

She waited a full minute.

'Can you go on? No? More clue, then ! I tell you I know it isn't true, because I did something with a telephone —'

'Why, I was coming in here to join Mr Velfrage !' cried

Habershon. 'I can rip along now. You told me you'd tele-phoned his office, saying your aunt couldn't turn up, and I said he couldn't have got the message, because he did come here. And you said he did get the message, because he him-self answered you on the phone. Then I told you I'd been fighting with that red-headed girl and I saw you didn't be-lieve me. And I said, "Come into this room" – or something like that. I turned my back on you and went into the room.'

Habershon turned his back on her and moved towards the door of the library – presumably, thought Kyle, to burst in upon the party. Damn the party, anyway!

Near the door Habershon stopped short. Without effort on his part, the memory focus changed. Instead of the mo-ment in the hall with Celia, he was visualizing that earlier moment when he had first entered the house in search of Mr Velfrage.

'The red-headed parlourmaid objects and attacks me.' The words were coming fast, and his voice had dropped to an excited half whisper. Kyle and Mrs Rabethorpe crept forward. 'I put my hand on her chin and send her spinning across the hall, and she flops on the staircase.'

He turned his gaze from the staircase to the door of the library, pointed at it, as if accusingly.

'Someone inside that room tries to prevent me from turn-ing the handle. All the same, I turn it and fling the door open.'

His eyes were fixed, almost glassy, so that he seemed to be staring through the door.

'In front of me, with one hand on the back of a chair, is a scraggy woman. She's out of breath. The other hand is across her chest, holding her cloak. Looped at her elbow on a chain is a bag – a blue bag – with a peacock's eye!'

With the last words he gripped the handle, flung the door open and thrust himself into the room.

The next instant he felt exactly what he had felt when the sergeant had landed the pivotal blow that won the fight for the Army.

Opposite him, sitting at ease in the chair against which

she had been leaning at his first sight of her, was the scraggy woman.

Astride the hearth, a cocktail glass in his hand, was George, the heavy-jowled man he had knocked senseless.

On the other side of George – standing, as before, by the safe – was Frank, the man he had butted, now snapping a lighter.

George, Frank, the scraggy woman! One of the gang missing. No doubt because he had killed her upstairs?

He turned sharply. She was standing almost behind him. The red-headed girl, magnificent now in a long-skirted evening dress of black.

The party was regarding him with polite surprise. From behind, someone took him by the arm and urged him forward.

'Here you are, everybody! Meet Celia's burglar!' whooped Mrs Rabethorpe. 'Isn't he the nicest burglar in the world!'

9

Sight of the scraggy woman, the red-head, George and Frank left Habershon dazed, but triumphant. The dread that he might have killed the red-head was removed. For a minute he could think of nothing else.

To the outward eye he seemed no more than a man who had horned in on a party and was ready to be apologetic about it.

Mrs Rabethorpe was making introductions.

'Margaret, dear' – this was the scraggy woman, the very same dolled-up hag – 'meet Mr Habershon – Mrs Wellard, who has that lovely house next to this – oh, and Detective Inspector Kyle, who solved the mystery for us.'

In Habershon's mind the haze was clearing. Mrs Wellard had bestowed a meagre nod on each man, as might a hostess of some standing who intends to reserve judgement. Nevertheless, it was Mrs Wellard who had carried the bag with the peacock's eye – it was Mrs Wellard who had jumped on his back.

The red-head sidled up. Seen at close quarters, the black gown was an overdress which threw a green aura, enhancing her rich natural colouring. Not that anything about her needed enhancement.

'This is Prinny Loftus – you've heard of her, of course – she's on the stage.'

'Every Monday morning, for an audition,' smiled Prinny, giving her hand – the hand that had scratched his face. Poise, gracefulness, style – not a trace of the shrill virago who had twisted out of her clothes and fled into the darkness.

'Mr Keller' – this was Frank, whom he had butted in the face – 'and Mr Clawson. George, dear, look after the drinks.'

'I know your voice on the telephone,' said George. 'I'm with Knight & Velfrage. Gin and orange?'

Velfrage's managing clerk! Mrs Rabethorpe's voice penetrated to Habershon.

'And then Celia and Mr Habershon acted it all in the hall, and he remembered absolutely everything except the other people he met in the house. And as there weren't any, of course, that part doesn't matter.'

'How could he meet people who were not there?' demanded Mrs Wellard, who affected to be a bit of a bully.

'I expect he's psychic – I am myself, you know, and I can sense it in others.'

Prinny's smile invited Habershon to laugh at Mrs Rabethorpe's extravagances.

'I'm afraid you're going to be one of her best stories. In time, you'll wonder what really did happen to you.'

I tore your clothes off your back, you luscious little hellcat. Aloud, Habershon told her about the quinine.

'Awful for you – you must hate talking about it!' said Prinny, and presently was telling him a light-hearted anecdote about an encounter with a customs official. The anecdote was banal, but she told it as if he alone could be trusted to appreciate it. This girl could make you listen to her and wonder about her when you didn't really want to.

Mrs Wellard was sunk in her own thoughts. Mrs Rabethorpe and Kyle were drinking brandy and soda, Keller was cutting in, making himself agreeable to Kyle, who was laughing.

Habershon was struggling against the suspicion that – without fever or drug – he was again witnessing something which could not happen. Mrs Wellard owned the lovely house next door! George was an associate of Velfrage. Keller was amusing the Inspector. Prinny, the fake parlourmaid hell-cat, was making a very good job of being charming. It was as fantastic as Walt Disney's dwarf coming to life on the Great West Road.

The sour-visaged cook-person announced that dinner was ready. Kyle was asking something of Mrs Rabethorpe.

'Oh, of course! As long as you like. Do make yourselves at home and ring for anything you want. Not that anyone will answer the bell, I'm afraid. Trained servants seem to be extinct nowadays. My niece is not coming to the theatre and she will look after you.'

Automatically, Habershon helped them chatter themselves out of the room.

Kyle himself was chattering now, though they were alone.

'Quite a nice party in the end! Your path seems to be littered with red-heads, old man. Hm! Ah well, I've found you often save time in the end by investing a bit in making yourself agreeable.' He set down his empty glass. 'D'you get any reaction from this room?'

10

WITH an effort Habershon succeeded in giving attention.

'I don't know.' Habershon looked about him, noting details for the first time.

It was the kind of room, found in most prosperous suburban houses, generally called a library or a study, but rarely used as such. Bow windows giving on to the front garden; smaller windows facing the door; leather armchairs; a writing-table; a glass-fronted bookcase; one or two upright chairs. The safe struck the only unusual note, for it was of the kind one would expect to see only in an office, being some five feet high and proportionately deep.

By the fireplace was an Indian rug of fine workmanship. His eye lingered on the rug – turned from the rug to the safe. He wished he could stop staring at that safe.

He became aware that Kyle was waiting for him to speak.

'That bag with the peacock's eye! That chair over there is the one – the scraggy woman – was leaning against – with the bag dangling from her arm.'

'Good work!' said Kyle. 'Keep going.'

Habershon made no response. What was the use? The reality of the plaster cast of the dwarf had given substance to one of his fantastic assertions. That sort of luck wouldn't happen twice. If he were to blurt out that he had found the gang, Kyle might not believe him, without supporting evidence.

'The bag with the peacock's eye!' repeated Kyle. 'Wait a minute!'

He went to the armchair near the safe where he had left his dispatch-case. He took out the bag, held it against the chair where the scraggy woman had sat.

Habershon was unresponsive.

'I can produce a bit out of the sleeve for you, if you're stuck,' tried Kyle. 'Listen! I know the owner did not hand you this bag. I know you must have taken it from her by force.' Kyle was speaking slowly and insistently, as if trying to penetrate the other's sub-conscious. 'Try to remember why you took this bag with the peacock's eye – from the scraggy woman – by force.'

'I've gone cold for the moment!' Habershon had decided to go on the defensive. 'And anyway, why do you emphasize force?'

'You remembered that this bag was dangling from her elbow. It was a fancy chain. Microscopic examination bears that out – it showed that the bag had been wrenched from the fasteners here.'

'I don't go through life yanking women's bags off their arms!' He spoke with nervous irritability. He was hardly thinking about the bag – his eyes were again on the safe. 'We have to be careful with this business of what I remember, Inspector. Pass it through a sieve of common sense.'

'Isn't that what we're doing?' suggested Kyle patiently. 'The woman didn't put it in your pocket. If someone else grabbed it, he didn't put it in your pocket either.'

'But why should I grab it? There was nothing in it I wanted. I looked inside before I took it to the local police.'

'Take it easy!' Kyle returned the bag to the dispatch-case. 'We know you didn't intend to steal it.'

That sounded comforting, but to Habershon there was a catch in it.

' "Intend"!' he echoed. 'But you do claim to know that I did – *in fact* – steal it, however innocent I might be held *in law*.'

'Well – yes, if you like to put it that way,' Kyle would not shirk the issue. 'If you hadn't brought it to the police – if we had found it on you – I'm not prepared to say how far the quinine, and the rest of it, would have saved you.'

Again Habershon's eye raked the room, again coming to rest on the Indian rug, but still without association.

'We don't know what happened here, but we do know that I am in it up to the eyelids. This is getting rather grim for me, Inspector. True that I couldn't have killed the red-head. But there's no memory at all of meeting Velfrage in

57

here, though I am quite certain that I entered this house in order to collect him.'

'Then what have you to worry about?'

'If I can't remember Velfrage, there may be others I can't remember. Suppose I killed one of the crooks and the others carried his body away?' he challenged. 'If they don't hang me, they'll send me to a criminal lunatic asylum. And I've got to help you put me there.'

Showdown, thought Kyle. He made a quick decision, based on the belief that Habershon was the kind of man he appeared to be.

'That's true!' said Kyle. 'If there is a murder in the background – as there may be – I may have to use the facts you and I have found while working together in a pally sort of way. Perhaps you'd rather stop?'

'Back out now – and give you the moral certainty that I've remembered something dangerous to me!'

'That's true, too! You're in a tight spot, Habershon. But I reckon you're not the kind to sit down and cry about it. You're more likely to take a bet on your own innocence and damn the consequences – including me!'

'I don't feel as heroic about it as that.' Habershon smiled wanly. 'But if this investigation were to come to a dead end, I'd spend the rest of my life waiting for the police to tumble on to something and drag me off to jug.' He added : 'I've no real choice, so we'll pretend I like it. Go ahead, Inspector.'

'That's what I thought you'd say, and I'm glad you said it. You spoke of the crooks. How many were there?'

As Habershon hesitated, Kyle decided to rush him.

'We'll try Miss Fenton's method. If you mean to play ball, get back against that door.'

This, thought Habershon, was a safe line. It would help Kyle to work his own way to the truth about Mrs Rabethorpe's party – that the scraggy woman who had leapt on his back was Mrs Wellard, who owned the lovely house —

'You've just forced your way in. You're looking at the scraggy woman with the bag,' said Kyle. 'Got the picture? Anybody else in the room?'

58

'Plenty. Over where you are. A man – they call him George – comes at me with a gun. "Hands up" and that kind of thing.'

'And what do you do?'

'Slosh!' grinned Habershon. 'He falls down – there – and stays put. I capture his gun.' Habershon frowned. 'But there was no gun in my pocket at the hospital.'

'N'em mind! Any of his friends ask for a return match?'

The treatment was not working as well as it had worked with Celia Fenton. Memory was returning, but in patches.

'There's another man over there – the other side of the safe. He's called Frank. The safe door is open. But there's something between me and the man.'

A long pause. A car was heard in the drive – then the chatter of the party getting into it, to be driven to the West End.

Kyle went to the big safe and gripped the handle. The safe was locked. He slipped silently from the room, to return a few minutes later carrying a screen.

'I can't open the safe door for you because, Miss Fenton tells me, the keys were kept by Mr Velfrage while Mrs Rabethorpe was in Belgium.' He set the screen to represent the open door of the safe. 'Does that help you?'

Habershon did not answer. Kyle gave him a reminder.

'There's that other man with a gun – Frank, you said. Standing about here, I suppose? And you said there was something between you and Frank?'

Habershon came to life.

'Something that can't hit me or shoot at me. It isn't the women.' He looked helplessly round. 'Might have been a chair.'

Kyle placed an upright chair near the safe.

'A bit nearer the safe – now forward a little.' Again Habershon went cold for a minute or more.

'That rug!' he exploded.

He snatched it up, draped it over the back of the upright chair.

'No! Got it wrong somehow.' He raised the rug, hesitated.

'Let me hold it,' offered Kyle. He held the rug at various

angles to the chair – then sat on the chair, holding it up in front of him.

'Over your head!' cried Habershon. 'That's it! The angle is about right, though you're much too big. But we've fixed it, Inspector! There's something on that chair – let's call it an artist's lay figure – with that rug covering the top part. But that doesn't make sense.'

'Keep going,' urged Kyle. 'We'll work it over afterwards.'

'Frank is coming at me with a gun. He daren't shoot where he stands – the women are behind me. He must get in close first. I'm just going to run in myself, when a woman – Margo – the scraggy woman – leaps on my back. Frank is sailing in for a close-up with gun – I butt him in the face – he goes down, but not out – comes up bleeding and unsteady. I grab the gun. I fire at Frank, but miss. I hit the lay figure.'

Habershon paused. Presently Kyle asked :

'D'you mean the bullet hit the – the lay figure?'

'Yes. Knocked it clean over, chair and all!'

Kyle avoided the other's eye as he asked :

'What did the lay figure look like?'

'Dunno. The rug went, too – probably driven in a bit by the bullet. Is there a bullet hole in that rug?'

'Half a minute – yes, there is a hole that might have been made by a bullet. Keep going, Mr Habershon.'

'I can't. Red-head had joined the party by this time. There's a mix-up, with the two women attacking me at once. Oh yes! – I fire again and break the glass of that bookcase. A bit muddled here! I throw the gun at Red-head. She has scratched my face and I'm angry. I want to kill her. I run upstairs after her. Catch her by the dress – it rips, and she wriggles out of it and runs on into the darkness. I run after her —'

Habershon broke off and stared at Kyle with an air of discovery.

'D'you realize, Inspector, that I've remembered everything – up to that point. There's a straight sequence of events from my meeting Velfrage on the Great West Road to my running after that girl with her dress in my hand. Then comes the gap.'

'Should be easy to bridge it,' said Kyle. 'A girl playing hide-and-seek in her underclothes makes a sharp mental picture. Did you catch her?'

'I don't know. I do remember prowling from room to room. Meaning to kill her, Inspector. No mental picture of underclothes or anything else until —' He hesitated. 'There *is* a mental picture of a gorgeous red petticoat – or something – surrounded with black and gold.

'I know! I'm lying on the floor – then picking myself up and staring at a large Burmese doll. It's the doll's dress I'm blithering about. On the first-floor landing.'

'Sounds a bit loopy to me!' commented Kyle.

'Come and check up!' He grabbed Kyle by the arm and hurried him up the stairs.

'There you are, Inspector! You thought I had dreamt it. I don't believe I've dreamt anything. It's all real.'

On the upholstered bench sat the doll, large as a baby, resplendent in Chinese red and gold embroidered black.

Celia Fenton watched them from the hall, observed that they needed no help. Without seeing her, they returned to the study.

'I found myself gazing at that doll,' resumed Habershon. 'Whether I was lying on that floor for seconds or minutes, or more, I've no idea. Then I turned off the lights, went downstairs, reaching the hall a few seconds before Miss Fenton turned up. Then there was the attack on me in the drive. Then my crash into the lamp-post. If I was lying on that floor for a few seconds only, there may be no gap to bridge. On the other hand —'

'Leave the gap for the moment,' advised Kyle. 'Come back to Miss Fenton —'

'Good Lord, Inspector!'

'What on earth's the matter *now*?' Kyle himself was showing nerviness.

'The sequence with Miss Fenton is fairly clear. She comes into this room with me. But there's no George on the floor down there. They must have carried George away – I don't suppose he could walk far after what he'd taken on the jaw. *And* another thing —'

Habershon was groping in memory. Kyle was feeling the strain.

'What other thing?' he growled.

'Where is Velfrage?' demanded Habershon.

Kyle had been hoping that question would not be asked. It would have to be stalled. Habershon was talking on :

'I'm quite confident about all I've said, so far. But there must be a slip-up somewhere. Don't you see, Inspector? Velfrage doesn't figure in my little tale at all. Yet he *did* come into this house and I *did* come in to fish him out. It's time my memory found him.'

'Let's stick to the system,' urged Kyle hastily. 'Take things bit by bit. After it's all over, you come into this room with Miss Fenton. The telephone is cut – the glass of the book-case is broken. What else?'

'The place was in a bit of a mess, of course.'

'Did you notice anything else in the room?'

'Can't think of anything special.'

Kyle had been holding back his key question.

'What about that lay figure?' he asked. 'Was it still lying on the floor? Over there by the safe?'

'N-no. Didn't notice it, anyhow, though I remember noticing that the safe door had been shut. We needn't rack our brains about that lay figure. We can check with Miss Fenton.'

Before Kyle could stop him, Habershon had rushed from the room. The dining-room door was open. Celia had heard and came into the hall.

'I say! Did you ever have an artist's lay figure in the house? I mean, was there one in that room when you came in with me?'

'No – I'm quite sure there wasn't. Did you think there was?'

'I did, but I see there couldn't have been. Part of the nightmare element!' He went on : 'We're getting the main lines straight, thanks to your starting me off. There's still a gap. And a wall!'

A wall over which Kyle must be induced to climb to the truth about Mrs Rabethorpe's party.

'It'll come right if you don't hurry it,' said Celia. Again he felt reassured by her serenity, by the conviction that she would be right when everyone else was wrong.

'We're being a frightful curse to you,' he apologized. 'But I believe the Inspector has nearly finished.'

'Take as long as you like. Let me know how you've got on before you go.'

He hurried back to the library. Kyle had been making notes and was reading them over.

'We can forget that lay figure,' announced Habershon. 'Probably the rug was on the floor and wiggled when my bullet landed – and I've got the whole thing criss-crossed with some other incident.'

'I should think that's about right!' agreed Kyle – the first time he had definitely misled Habershon. He had guessed the truth about the supposed lay figure – knew that Habershon must guess it too, as soon as he sat down to weigh up his own story. In the meantime, so much the better if his attention shifted away from it.

'Have you picked anything out of my ravings, Inspector?'

'Quite a bit! It's clear that when both those women attacked you, you must have grabbed that bag without knowing it – probably stuffed it into your pocket while you waited for the next bit of rough-house.'

'Good! That's the common-sense compromise!' exclaimed Habershon. 'Unless it's because you've suggested it – I can almost remember it. I think it was just before Red-head scratched me. Yes, by Jove! – and it was the scraggy woman and Frank who attacked me in the drive, asking for the bag which I thought I hadn't got.'

He moved to the middle of the room.

'I found the bag in the left pocket of my overcoat. That works out. I was standing at an angle – like this. Coming at me on my right was Red-head —'

'Let's see – what was Red-head's name?'

'I don't remember – probably they didn't happen to call her by name. Let's get back to the bag, and link up with the car incident! Much nearer to me was – Margo, the scraggy —'

He had hovered over the name, had been on the verge of saying 'Mrs Wellard'.

'Margo, the scraggy!' exclaimed Kyle. There was a long pause before he went on : 'Margo equals Margaret. Margaret – Wellard! Frank – Keller! George – Clawson! Add the red-head, whose name wasn't mentioned in the brawl. Why didn't you tell me at once, Habershon?'

'Because I thought you wouldn't believe it until you'd worked it out for yourself. And now that you have worked it out – damned if you haven't set me wondering whether I'm raving!'

'You're not raving. I have a line of my own in support. I don't say in proof – but definitely in support.' He was thinking of George Clawson. That Velfrage's managing clerk should be in that house at all was highly significant – in view of what Clawson had said in the office about Velfrage's movements.

Habershon had dropped on to the settee and was looking profoundly depressed.

'What's biting you, Habershon?'

'I don't quite know. I suppose I'm afraid I'm pulling my own leg. This evening I came into the room remembering that I had seen inside it a scraggy woman and two men and, later, a red-headed girl. When I opened the door, the first thing I saw was a scraggy woman. Mrs Wellard *is* scraggy. Two men, as well. And a red-head – how many thousands are there in London, I wonder!' He added : 'I may have made myself recognize them, because they were in my mind —'

'Then you have a pretty fat coincidence in three names and a hair colour being right?' suggested Kyle. 'Four coincidences in one!'

'Y-yes. All the same, it seems somehow as if —'

'As if it couldn't be true!' interrupted Kyle. 'Any more than it could be true that a Disney dwarf popped up from nowhere to show you the way!'

'Aren't we overworking that poor dwarf?'

'No, we're not!' snapped Kyle. 'You're going to meet that dwarf again and again, in different forms. When you find somebody doing something you would never do – something that seems absurd – you don't have to accuse yourself of being crackers. Think of that dwarf incident – and wait for the reasonable explanation.

'And while we're on the subject,' continued Kyle, 'don't put too much down to that quinine. So far, the quinine has not invented anything.'

'It seems to have invented that lay figure in a chair with a rug over it,' Habershon pointed out.

'Admittedly, it can't have been a lay figure,' conceded Kyle. 'But there was *something* there – something which you failed to observe accurately. I'm not denying that you were sort of drunk – even if you didn't have a drink.'

'All right!' Habershon was apologetic. 'In future I'll take everything as it comes. Agreed that there was something in a chair and that it had a rug over it.'

Abruptly, Kyle turned away – went to the telephone with its little table and chair by the window. Habershon took no notice. His thoughts had left the problem of the gang – had fixed on something that drove out everything else. He knew now why he had been fascinated by that safe.

When Kyle had finished telephoning he found Habershon standing over him, his lips tightly drawn.

'Inspector – that "lay figure" may have been Velfrage!'

'It may have been anything!'

'I fired at it. The bullet went through that rug and knocked the whole thing over.'

'Maybe you did, maybe you didn't!'

'Let's stick to what we know. We know that Velfrage drove me here. We know – through Miss Fenton – that he did not leave with me. When did he leave the house? *How* did he leave the house?'

He turned from Kyle as if he were being drawn against his will – turned to the safe.

'Velfrage was a small man.' Habershon's voice was little above a whisper. 'That safe is big enough. Inspector, for God's sake, have it opened!'

'Didn't you hear me phoning? The team will be here within an hour.'

Instantly Habershon's self doubt and hesitation vanished. If that safe were found to contain the body of Velfrage, he himself might be under suspicion, might even be arrested while investigations were made. That meant that he must act quickly.

Kyle was explaining that Miss Fenton had given permission on behalf of her aunt, thereby rendering a warrant unnecessary.

'It may be a three-hour job getting that safe open. There's no need for you to wait, Mr Habershon. You've given us plenty to work on – and you've had a tough day for a convalescent.'

A polite way of kicking him out. Friendly enough, but it only meant that Kyle knew he wouldn't be such a fool as to bolt.

He rang the all-night garage at Stainham, learnt that his car had been repaired and was ready for the road.

Kyle had left the room. Through the open door Habershon could hear him talking to Celia Fenton.

Kyle's dispatch-case was where he had left it, in the armchair by the safe.

Habershon tiptoed to the armchair. Celia was explaining something. Kyle would probably not come back for at least twenty seconds.

Habershon opened the dispatch-case, took out the bag with the peacock's eye – and closed the case.

11

STAINHAM was but four miles distant. The car was at the door in ten minutes.

In that time Habershon had elicited from Celia that the party had gone to St George's Theatre and would have supper afterwards at Manotti's.

'Mrs Rabethorpe will have a bit of a shock when she comes home and finds the police busy with her safe,' he suggested.

'Nobody ever knows how she will take anything,' said Celia. 'I tried to get a message to her at the theatre, but they couldn't identify as I didn't know the ticket numbers.'

'I'll warn her for you – I'll catch the party as they're leaving,' he offered. Before she could accept or refuse he added with a grin and a stage whisper, 'Scotland Yard thinks the poor brain is overtired and needs sleep. But I have to go up to the West End anyway, as I left my things at the club.'

He had the impression that she knew he was making an excuse, but that she didn't mind. She was preoccupied – apparently with the same preoccupation as his own.

'Are you absolutely certain,' she asked, 'that Mr Velfrage drove you here?'

'Absolutely! There's independent proof that he was in my car with me. Also, I remember it clearly. Another thing – that safe was open when I was in the library. Mrs Rabethorpe said Velfrage had the key. Velfrage must have opened it.'

'There might be another key in existence,' she demurred. Her eyes were anxious. 'And wouldn't it be rather unusual for a solicitor to open a client's safe when she is not present?'

'Very unusual!' he agreed. He remembered Kyle's warning about actions that seemed unreasonable because the reason was unknown.

'And the red-headed maid brawling with you – that was

unusual too!' she said quickly. 'Before you opened the library door this evening – that's what you said.'

'And you think that was nightmare pure and simple?'

'No, I don't! It partly adds up. I daresay my aunt mentioned that she did employ a girl who had red hair. An unpleasant person – she used to read one's letters and eavesdrop. She was paid off before we left for Belgium.'

'Then she couldn't have been the girl!' said Habershon.

'I'm not so sure. She didn't want to be sacked – seemed to like being here, though we weren't very cordial. She could easily have found out that we expected to be back here that evening. She may have turned up on her own and started cleaning – knowing that would be the way to persuade my aunt to let her stay on.'

'My red-head was not your ex-maid.' He would have told her that the girl was Prinny Loftus, but for his need to leave the house as soon as his car turned up. 'I'll tell you my theory later.' He added : 'For one thing, if it had been your girl, you'd have found her after I had gone – probably hiding under the kitchen table. Or she'd have turned up next day.'

He could see she wanted to say something more. While she was hesitating, wheels sounded in the drive.

'There's your car!' She touched his arm to detain him. 'I was going to say – wouldn't it be wiser to grope through the blackout with me rather than with the police, if there is any blackout left?'

As he hurried away, he saw in her words only a desire to help him. He knew he must get clear of the house before Kyle opened his dispatch-case and discovered the loss of the bag.

It was twenty to ten when he reached the bungalow. By ten he had cleaned up and was adjusting his dress tie. By a quarter to eleven he was in the foyer of the theatre, with some five minutes in hand before the curtain fell.

As the minutes dragged, he felt something approaching stage-fright. It would not be enough to detach Mrs Rabethorpe – he must also detach at least one member of the gang. He would have to be jocular and slangy.

Clarity had come when Kyle had told him that the safe was to be opened. In that moment he had seen the immense significance of the bag. It was probably his one and only chance of making the gang show their hand – a chance which Kyle's official position would prevent him from taking.

Scotland Yard had come into the case on that bag. He himself had snatched the bag from the scraggy woman – Mrs Wellard.

Mrs Rabethorpe had confirmed that Velfrage had intended to come to the house to show her the Rabethorpe diamond before it was sold in America.

Habershon was able to add that Mrs Wellard, supported by Frank with a gun, had stopped him in the drive and demanded that bag – which made it a reasonable guess that the bag contained the Rabethorpe diamond hidden in the lining or a secret compartment.

If he was right, the gang might believe that the Rabethorpe diamond was still concealed in the bag. And if they believed that, they would try to get it back.

The St George's Theatre, built in the eighteen-eighties, had the advantages, as well as the drawbacks, of an old-fashioned theatre. The foyer, which yielded no revenue, was wastefully large.

At the first thin trickle of those who do not wait for curtain-fall, Habershon took up his position. The trickle became a flood, and the Rabethorpe party was in the middle of it.

'Mrs Rabethorpe. Don't be alarmed. Can I speak to you – urgent!'

He said it loudly enough for Mrs Wellard to hear. Presently he had succeeded in drawing his quarry out of the main stream into one of the wasteful bulges of the foyer. The party, which had acquired another man to make even numbers, followed Mrs Rabethorpe.

'The police are breaking open the safe in your library —'

'I'm so glad!' exclaimed Mrs Rabethorpe. 'I hate safes, with all that bother about not losing the key. And I want those miniatures. How nice of you to come and tell me!'

'Miss Fenton tried to ring you here. As she couldn't, she

gave the police permission. Matter of form. They could easily have obtained a warrant.'

'What's this about a warrant?' demanded Mrs Wellard, who was next to Mrs Rabethorpe. George and Frank were behind Habershon. Prinny was waiting on the fringe with the extra man. It was going to be easy after all. He ignored Mrs Wellard's question.

'Miss Fenton feared it might be a shock to you —'

'What's this about a warrant?' repeated Mrs Wellard.

'I don't know. They're being fearfully hush-hush – they even served a warrant on me for something or other. Might as well read it and see what it's about.' He was playing the cheerful young ass with complete success, at least as far as Mrs Rabethorpe was concerned. 'Can't think where I put it!'

He started his little pantomime. He thrust his hand into one breast pocket of his dress overcoat, pulled out the brochure of an hotel, put it back, went through the motions of delving into the other breast pocket. This time, he pulled out the bag with the peacock's eye, half turning so that George and Frank should see it. Then he slapped the bag back in his pocket, as if he had made a gaffe in revealing it. He could not tell whether it were fact or fancy that he had heard the men gasp.

But it was Habershon himself who received a shock.

'Where did you get that bag, Mr Habershon?' demanded Mrs Wellard. 'It's mine.'

The very last thing Habershon had expected was this open avowal.

'I – really, I don't think it can be, Mrs Wellard —'

'It is – I'd know that peacock's eye design anywhere. Will you have the goodness at least to let me look at it?'

'I'm awfully sorry, Mrs Wellard. I was going to explain that it's part of the stage props of what we call that nightmare of mine —'

Mrs Rabethorpe cackled. George was trying to butt in.

'I am not concerned with your nightmares, Mr Habershon.' Mrs Wellard was at her most formidable. 'I am asking you for my bag.'

'I must say, Habershon,' cut in George, 'that I can't see what objection you can have —'

'Then I'll tell you,' snapped Habershon. 'I am required to give this to Inspector Kyle without allowing anyone to handle it. I am sorry to appear discourteous to Mrs Wellard, but I have no choice.' He turned to Mrs Rabethorpe. 'I'm afraid I've disturbed the party for nothing. Please try to forgive me.'

It was impossible for Mrs Rabethorpe to be angry with a handsome young man. She beamed on him and he escaped to the Chrysler.

He had made the tactical error of parking near the theatre. He was delayed for some minutes by the sudden crowd of cars as the theatre emptied. When he got clear he had bad luck with the traffic lights. By the time he reached the Great West Road he knew for certain that he was being followed. The follower was a large car. For all he knew, it might be carrying one of the gang or the whole party. As he touched the wide arterial road he trod on the gas.

The big car had greater acceleration but a lower maximum speed. At sixty it nearly caught him – at eighty-five he was well ahead. At that speed he would reach the turning in less than a minute.

In ten seconds he had realized that their purpose was not merely to stop him and argue about the bag – and leave him alive to tell the police of their interest. They meant to shoot him, or wreck the car and take the bag while he was unconscious – or dead.

A laugh broke from him. To smash a small car with a big car, both at speed, was a matter of timing.

The same truth applied to smashing a big car with a small car.

He eased down to seventy. It was tricky work, judging the distance by the pursuer's headlights on his mirror, but it had to be done. The big car had to be very close. Fortune had given him a fairly greasy road surface. To make use of the gift there must be only about twenty feet between them. That would tempt the big car to follow his skid.

Already Walt Disney's dwarf, marking the turning,

glowed dimly in the extremity of the beam. The needle showed sixty-five miles an hour.

Now!

The timing ran to small fractions of a second, whereas the movements of hand and foot had to be started something like a whole second in advance. If the skid were too wide, the penalty would be exacted by the kerb on the opposite side.

Clutch out and in again at full throttle as he brought the steering over – sharp snap with the handbrake, quick as a boxer's tap, and he had made the turn – very nearly a clean, right-angled turn.

Even as he straightened he heard the crash of the big car as its rear wheels hit the opposite kerb. The driver had held the handbrake a twentieth of a second too long.

He hoped that Mrs Rabethorpe was not on board – whether she was one of the gang or not, he rather liked her. The fate of the others slithered out of his thoughts. The next job was already demanding his attention – for the next job was Inspector Kyle.

12

As Habershon turned into the drive of Woodville, he observed that the front door was open. A couple of men were sitting smoking in one of the police cars. He went in, found Kyle on a bench in the hall, his dispatch-case by his side. The door of the library was ajar.

'I hoped you had gone home to bed!' Kyle's tone was by no means welcoming. 'It may be another hour yet before they've finished in there.' Without change of tone he continued: 'If you're looking for my dispatch-case, it's right here where I'm sitting.'

Habershon produced the bag with the peacock's eye.

'I'm sorry I had to play a lousy trick like that – but I'm glad I got hold of the bag! I flashed it at the theatre party, but wouldn't let anyone touch it. Mrs Wellard claimed it as hers. Where do we go from there, Inspector?'

He paused, hoping that Kyle would be impressed. With maddening slowness the detective opened his dispatch-case and replaced the bag. Habershon had the impression that his trick had cost him the detective's confidence.

'Are you sure she said it was hers?' Kyle's tone was wintry, even sceptical.

'I have taken no quinine tonight,' said Habershon stiffly.

'Then she has only to ask me to let her have her property.' Kyle was ponderously sarcastic.

'Whatever they planned to do about the bag,' said Habershon, 'they'll have to change tactics. They counted on smashing me up before I could get here. I was followed from the theatre by a big car that obviously meant to ram me.'

'Who was in the big car?' asked Kyle.

'I don't know. The whole gang may have been on board.'

'Did you actually see any one member of – the gang, as you call them?'

'No, I didn't let 'em get close enough. Coming off the

73

main road, I skidded the corner at about sixty – with that dwarf grinning at me! The other car tried to do the same and came unstuck. A skid at speed takes a bit of doing in a big car. I heard it crash.'

'So you heard it crash, eh! Did it by any chance burst into flames too?'

When Habershon did not answer, Kyle got up from the bench, switched the telephone extension to the hall and spoke to the local police, giving particulars of himself.

'I'm speaking on information received,' he concluded. 'If there *has* been a smash, please ring me here as soon as you can.'

Kyle resumed his seat without comment. Habershon took the oak chair on the other side of the hall table. The silence was disturbed only by the voices of the safe-breaking team in the library. Within ten minutes the telephone rang.

Habershon grinned as Kyle answered it. The grin widened as he heard Kyle say:

'Ah! Will you give me the registration number? . . . The other man wasn't injured then? . . . Many thanks!'

Kyle immediately rang Scotland Yard, quoting the registration number of the car. He waited, the receiver to his ear, for something over a minute, then replaced it with a muttered acknowledgement.

'One of the non-existent gangsters hurt in the imaginary car smash, Inspector?'

'Getting sore with me when I'm doing my job is a sign that you need a night's rest,' returned Kyle. 'It's Mrs Wellard's Rolls. There were two men in it. One was unhurt. He had telephoned for ordinary car hire and took the other man off to a private house in Kew.'

'Am I forgiven for burgling your dispatch-case?'

'You've got away with it, anyhow! Though, mind you, they'll have a tale ready. And as to the car, you've no evidence that they tried to ram you.'

A man of the foreman type stood in the doorway of the library.

'We oughter be through in about ten minutes,' he announced, and gave technical details.

'Right! Lock the door on the inside, will you? Knock on the door when you've finished.'

Wheels sounded in the drive. A taxi deposited Mrs Rabethorpe, Mrs Wellard, and Prinny Loftus. The extra man of the party had been shed.

'Oh, there's Inspector Kyle!' exclaimed Mrs Rabethorpe. 'I'm glad you've opened the safe for me. Can I go and get those miniatures?'

Kyle explained, but was interrupted by Mrs Wellard asking for Frank Keller and George Clawson.

'They're not here,' said Kyle. 'I understand that they had a road accident on the way back. But it appears that neither is seriously hurt.'

'Well, I'm glad they're not hurt, but it's most aggravating,' said Mrs Wellard. She glared at Habershon. 'After your remarkable behaviour in the matter of the bag, Mr Habershon, Mr Clawson thought I had better be legally represented when you handed it to the police. He and Mr Keller tried to overtake you. You may come to the conclusion that the accident was the result of your conduct.'

'I'm afraid it must have been!' Habershon was impatient to turn her over to Kyle. 'But no doubt the Inspector will allow you to see your bag.'

'No doubt!' echoed Mrs Wellard meaningly.

Kyle went to his dispatch-case.

'Is this your bag, Mrs Wellard?'

'Yes.' The answer was definite, uncompromising.

Mrs Wellard took the bag to examine it.

'It's damaged,' she grumbled. 'It had a chain.'

She opened the bag, stared into the interior, then clutched the hall table, steadied herself into the oak chair.

Her hand was groping inside the bag.

'Someone has cut the lining!' she exclaimed.

Kyle waited while she recovered her breath. Mrs Rabethorpe called to Celia Fenton, who answered from upstairs. Prinny Loftus was trying to catch Habershon's attention and failing. Celia joined the party in the hall.

'When was that bag last in your possession, Mrs Wellard?'

'About two months ago – the day before Mrs Rabethorpe shut up the house and went to Belgium.'

She turned to Mrs Rabethorpe.

'Elsie!' She made the name sound like an accusation. 'Do you know who stole my bag?'

'No, but do let me guess!' chirruped Mrs Rabethorpe. 'Why, of course! It must have been that charming little Austrian who told you he was a count?'

'It was not!' snapped Mrs Wellard. 'It was that red-headed slut you employed as a housemaid.'

Habershon glanced at Kyle, wondering whether he would see that this was a mere elaboration of the tale that began with George Clawson rushing back to 'represent' Mrs Wellard.

'The day before you left, you sent her with a note, returning my opera glasses,' Mrs Wellard was saying. 'The girl came to the front door, and my housemaid, Bessie, let her wait in the hall. I cross-examined Bessie and became quite certain in my own mind that the red-headed creature had stolen the bag while Bessie was bringing the note to me and waiting for an answer. As I now have the bag, we need not discuss it further.'

'Quite so!' agreed Kyle. 'But we must ask you to let us keep it for the present.' Kyle was returning the bag to his dispatch-case when there came a loud knocking on the inner side of the library door – the agreed signal that the safe had been opened.

Kyle knocked back and was admitted. He relocked the door.

'We needn't stand about while they're making their little notes and things!' said Mrs Rabethorpe. 'Come along, everybody! The dining-room would be best – the drinks are in there. Celia, you and Mr Habershon take charge. Prinny, darling, you look cold!'

While Habershon followed the others to the dining-room he imagined the scene in the next room – the safe with the door open, the mechanics standing around. He dragged his thoughts from useless speculation, forced his attention to his surroundings. Through the chatter of Mrs Rabethorpe he observed a fine refectory table, so dark with age that it was almost black; but the effect was spoilt by Regency chairs, good in themselves, but out of harmony.

He followed Celia to a massive Victorian sideboard, rare enough now to have acquired an oddity value. She opened two of its six cabinets. By the earnestness with which she directed his efforts to help, he sensed that she, too, was feeling the strain.

Celia mixed the drinks and Habershon handed them on a huge silver tray with a castellated surround. Mrs Wellard first. She thanked him coldly without an upward glance – a dowager whom he had offended. He tried in vain to visualize her shrieking and leaping on his back in the course of a gun-fight.

Prinny Loftus, who had been looking bored, brightened when he turned to her.

'The police are in an efficiency mood,' she said. 'D'you think they've put a guard on the door?'

'Probably. Why not open it and see?'

'They might let me out and then I'd miss the fun.'

Mrs Rabethorpe next. She promptly ignored Mrs Wellard, who was explaining something.

'Oh, thank you, Mr Habershon!' The old-time gush suited her personality, as did her fashion-blind clothes. 'Isn't it wonderful that you knew it was Mrs Wellard's bag! Don't pretend to me that you're not psychic, young man. You must come to tea and talk about your experiences, and I'll tell you mine.'

'I shall love to hear yours,' returned Habershon. This sort of patter at least kept his thoughts from the gnawing problem of the opened safe. Mrs Wellard cut in and Habershon escaped to Celia at the sideboard.

'Prinny is all by herself – go and talk to her,' said Celia in an undertone.

'My case is more desperate than hers. I want to hear about your brother.'

'Need you make small talk to me?'

'It was a thoughtless remark. I apologize.' He was

77

ashamed of himself. 'I want to hear about your brother but not, of course, now.'

She nodded in full understanding.

'Whatever they have found – in there – must not make any difference to us,' she said. 'We won't accept any theory until you've remembered everything. Will we?'

'We will not, Celia. But I may remember – well – something horrible.'

'You may!' she agreed calmly. It was her calm that rebuilt his courage. Refusing to give optimistic assurances, she conceded the point as logically valid, while she herself remained a living vote of confidence. He gazed at her with open gratitude, seeing her as physically slender and almost fragile, yet strong as civilization. For the first time he understood that men can lean on women's strength. With an intuitive flash he wondered whether he had for years lent on Miss Parker's strength.

Prinny came over and joined them – Prinny, the highly decorative hell-cat. He did not contrast the two girls, because their personalities could not meet. Celia recalled him to his normal self – Prinny was a luscious will-o'-the-wisp.

The threesome was ill assorted. The chatter faltered. He was about to mix Prinny another drink when Detective Inspector Kyle entered the room.

'I want Miss Fenton and Mr Habershon, please. And I would be glad if everybody else would remain in here for a few minutes.'

The dining-room was next to the library. Kyle took them across the hall to the little morning-room.

'You and Mr Habershon have more information than any of the others,' said Kyle. To Habershon it sounded strained, as if Kyle meant more than he said. 'I want your help by yourself first, Miss Fenton. Will you come with me while Mr Habershon waits here for us?'

Alone in the morning-room, Habershon definitely disbelieved Kyle's excuse for taking Celia off by herself, but would not let himself speculate. He must concentrate on unmasking this gang of genteel, middle-class crooks.

Minutes passed before Kyle came in – alone.

'Ready for you now!' he said with false breeziness. 'Listen! Better take a firm hold on your nerve —'

'Thanks – but I've seen a corpse before now. If Velfrage was killed by a single bullet, it was I who fired it.'

'It isn't Velfrage – that's why I warned you.'

'Then who the hell —?'

'That's what I want you to tell me. If you're ready!'

In the library the door of the big wall safe was fully open, but the screen had been placed, hiding the interior.

At a word from Kyle, one of the men folded back the screen.

Huddled inside the safe was the corpse of a red-headed woman dressed only in a petticoat slip and stockings. The slip had a wide tear on one side.

His eyes returned to the dead face and lingered there, while he asked himself whether he recognized it. In a second of clock time he seemed to ask the same question a dozen times without finding an answer.

MECHANICALLY, Habershon followed Kyle back to the little morning-room, feeling as if he were walking the deck of a ship at sea. He had whipped himself into certainty that the body of Velfrage would be found in that safe.

'Well?' demanded Kyle. As he spoke he locked the door.

'I'm as foxed as you are, Inspector!' Habershon was slow to recognize his personal position. 'I haven't the least idea who that girl is.'

As if he suspected evasion, Kyle asked :

'Ever seen her before?'

'The devil of it is, I don't know for certain!' Habershon tried to pace the little room, gave up the attempt and sat down. 'At the first glance – no. But when I looked a second time at the face, I wasn't so sure.'

'You noticed that her clothes had been torn off her back. Is she the girl you chased up the stairs?'

'I repeat that the girl I chased up the stairs was Miss Loftus – or her identical twin – if she has one.'

Kyle looked blank. Habershon went on :

'Don't ask whether I've made a mistake. I haven't. That dead girl – whether I've seen her before or not – is not a bit like her. She's obviously much smaller, and her hair is more ginger than red.'

Habershon had the feeling that he was beating the air.

'I say, Inspector, it looks as if this is going to be damned awkward for me, if you don't believe me!'

'It's a good deal more damned awkward than you know! That body was identified by Miss Fenton as that of the girl they used to employ here.'

'That about puts the tin hat on!' Habershon sank into a chair, rested his head in his hands. 'I've just begun to see it from your point of view. I tell you I chased a girl, tore her clothes off, that I believe that, in my muzziness, I meant to kill her. I was more than half afraid I had killed her – until

I saw Miss Loftus tonight. If she had had an identical twin – and that twin were in the safe –I would believe now that I had killed her. As it is —'

Habershon broke off, clapped clenched fists to his cheek-bones.

'Good Lord! I've thought of something!'

'Going to share it?' asked Kyle.

'That thing I thought was an artist's lay figure – covered with that rug! We know it was not a lay figure. Suppose it was that girl? I told you I fired that Service revolver – knocked the whole layout over.'

'Stop working yourself up like that!' snapped Kyle. 'The doctor had a good look for a bullet wound – and then I asked him to look again. There's no bullet wound. That girl was strangled.'

'Huh! That settles that!' Habershon stretched and relaxed. 'I know I didn't strangle *that* girl!' He added : 'But, of course, *you* don't know I didn't.'

'Quite right – I don't!' Kyle was uncompromising. Habershon hurried on.

'I coupled up Mrs Wellard with that bag. That would seem to support my statement about the gang. But Mrs Wellard said the girl stole the bag – which passes the bag to the girl and makes everything worse for me.'

'It does!' agreed Kyle.

'Worse than you think, Inspector!' The mental habit of regarding the police as friendly protectors was too ingrained to be cast off in a moment. 'You told me just now you've identified the body. Well, Miss Fenton told me tonight that she thought the red-headed kitchenmaid probably did sneak back here. Miss Fenton took it for granted that she was the girl I scrapped with. Unless I can scotch Mrs Wellard's lie, everyone will say that I snatched the bag from that girl and killed her.'

'You've told me what I was going to tell you,' growled Kyle. 'And I advise you not to tell it to anybody else.' He hesitated. 'If you were a married man, I'd say don't tell your wife – even if you were on your honeymoon!'

Habershon nodded.

'Inspector, admit that you can't bring yourself to believe that those respectable-looking people can possibly be a criminal gang!'

'I don't have to believe things – I only have to prove 'em. I don't have to believe you killed that red-head – I only have to prove it. Or prove somebody else did. I'm counting on you to go on giving me all the help you can.'

There was more coming and Habershon waited for it.

'What you've told us about the gang, as you call it, will have to be backed up with proof. If they are a gang, they'll try to make sure whether you recognize them or not. They may try roundabout ways. If they do, you can report to us —'

He broke off at a heavy knock on the door.

'Mrs Rabethorpe says she's ready now, sir.'

'Right! I'm coming.' As he unlocked the door, Kyle told Habershon in an undertone : 'We have to get her to confirm the identification – she'll probably make a scene. Excitable woman!'

Kyle did not reverse the key and lock Habershon in. Nevertheless, Habershon perceived that Kyle would have to arrest him, even though he believed him innocent of deliberate crime. Kyle didn't have to believe things – only prove 'em. The friendly manner was just manner.

Behind him, the door opened noiselessly. Celia looked up at him with eyes that seemed to trust him, to remind him that there had sprung up between them an understanding which rendered formality absurd.

He knew she was waiting for him to speak. This was going to be awkward. How could he talk about his memory without telling her almost everything! He took both her hands.

'This is pretty ghastly for you, Celia!' he said.

'Do they suspect you?'

'They're keeping an open mind.'

Her hands told him that this was not what she wanted to hear. Whatever he told her, he must stop short of his identification of the gang. Moreover, questions about the dead girl might lead him into difficulties.

The question promptly came.

'Was she the girl who brawled with you?'

Kyle's words were fresh in his memory; ' . . . *even if you were on your honeymoon.*' Irrelevantly, the words made him certain that he wanted to marry Celia and live serenely ever afterwards.

'The police take it for granted that she was. And, of course, I can't contradict them.'

'You didn't recognize her —'

He was deliberately slow in his denial, hating himself for using a device. He feared, too, that it would fail – as his devices failed with Miss Parker.

'For all I can tell, I have never set eyes on her.'

'For all you can tell!' she echoed. 'Then you're not positive it was not Bradburn who scratched your face – that was the girl's name!' She sounded desperately miserable. 'I was hoping – d'you know, I had the queer impression this evening when you were speaking to Prinny Loftus, that you thought it was she!'

What an exasperating coincidence, he thought, that she should make that particular remark!

'I expect that was a spot of telepathy.' He smiled to discount his own words. 'I've run across some half a dozen red-headed girls since it happened. Each time I've sized them up, wondering whether I'd found the crook girl. Lucky for me that Prinny isn't telepathic too!'

She seemed satisfied with his answer. It was a bit thick having to treat her as a possible antagonist – as a possible member of the gang. There was something about her that made him feel tremendously alive, able to tackle anything, in the certainty that he would put up a good show.

'Don't strain the memory – give it a chance to pick up on its own. If it doesn't, we'll try again together – if you like.'

He was about to answer when Mrs Rabethorpe's voice screeched in the hall.

'Celia, where are you? Oh dear, I've never *seen* so many policemen! *Ce*-lia!'

Habershon waited a couple of minutes after Celia had left the morning-room. This round was going badly. Everything now depended on his ability to procure evidence against those soft-boiled gangsters.

Obviously, he couldn't collect evidence if he were 'detained pending inquiries'. He gazed thoughtfully at the window.

Useless to make any furtive movements in a house full of policemen. He lit a cigarette and strolled into the hall.

Ambulance men were removing the body. An officious young policeman motioned him to stand back. He nodded and ignored the injunction – followed in the wake of the ambulance men and made his way to the Chrysler. He revved up, in order to make a din. The constable at the front door took no notice. Habershon let in the clutch.

As he was approaching the gates, a taxi turned in. His own lights revealed the passenger as George Clawson. No bandages were visible : he was sitting well forward, apparently none the worse for the smash.

On the drive home Habershon was thinking mainly of Celia. It was not at all surprising that there should be some kind of telepathic sympathy between them. It often happened, he had heard, when people were exceptionally well suited to each other. It was a pity that the one thought she had picked up from him was that one about Prinny. Fortunately, no harm had been done. If he had told her the whole truth about the gang she would have been unable to keep the secret, however hard she tried. A girl like that would be incapable of bluffing and stalling and deceiving, even in a good cause.

His brick-built bungalow, with a large garage and a small garden, combined the advantages of house and flat for a bachelor who did not spend much time at home.

He discovered that he was hungry, foraged among the iron rations and produced himself a cold supper, with biscuits in place of bread.

While he was eating he decided that he must confine his luggage to a couple of suitcases. His first step must be to procure lodgings in London where he could lie doggo while making a flank attack on the gang.

He was packing when the bell rang – a needlessly long

ring, given that the caller had seen lights in the bungalow. He guessed Kyle – come to explain in a friendly, elder-brother manner, that he must arrest him on suspicion of murder!

He opened the front door. It was not Kyle, but George Clawson, Velfrage's managing clerk – the genteel gangster who had threatened him with a gun and taken a crack on the jaw for his pains.

Round number three, thought Habershon. If there was to be another gun, there would be another crack.

'May I come in, Habershon?'

'Certainly!' Leave the initiative with the opponent until he shows his hand. 'I admit I was just going to bed, but – have a drink!'

'Thanks!'

Habershon's sitting-room had a certain heartiness. There were college groups on the walls – an almost studied shabbiness in the two large comfortable armchairs. The whisky was kept in a Victorian tantalus.

'Dessay you heard – we had a hell of a smash tonight. Keller is cut about a bit and suffering from shock. S'matter of fact, we were trying to overtake you.'

'Why?'

Clawson grinned. Habershon put a siphon beside him.

'Thanks.' Clawson added soda, waited for Habershon to do likewise.

'We want that diamond back, old man. Don't say "what diamond?" The Rabethorpe diamond!'

'And what in hell makes you think I have it?'

'Meaning you haven't got it?' asked Clawson.

'Of course that's what I mean!'

'How d'you *know* you haven't got it, Habershon? You don't remember what happened that night. Or do you?'

14

THIS was better than Habershon had dared to hope. Instead of his having to chase the gang, they were positively chasing him. And they seemed to think he was suffering from a total blackout.

'Theoretically, I don't know that I didn't burgle the Tower of London and pinch the Crown jewels. Practically, I'm certain that I stole nothing. You can't call that bag a theft.'

Clawson gazed thoughtfully at his glass.

'The best whisky I've tasted for years!' He put down his glass on the wide flat arm of the chair. 'It's a delicate situation, Habershon. I'd better tell you how we stand – how I stand – how you stand, because you obviously don't know. Do you remember picking up Velfrage on the Great West Road?'

These questions about memory would be tricky. He must be careful not to whittle down the supposed black-out. Above all, he must make Clawson believe that he had no memory of the gang that could identify any of them.

'I remembered when the police told me the precise circumstances.'

'They got 'em from me – I paid a bill for towing in Velfrage's Daimler. Now, I happened to know unofficially that Velfrage had withdrawn the diamond from the bank. He didn't tell me so – he always played the oyster with his own staff.

'The next thing that happens is Mrs Rabethorpe's nonsense about Celia's comic burglar. Who turns out to be you. In the course of reconstructing your memory, with Celia's help, you say in Mrs Rabethorpe's hearing that you had a scrap with a red-headed housemaid. Add the Wellard's bag, possession of which you cannot explain; add that Bradburn, the housemaid, stole the bag – that she is known to have

been a crook, snooping for a chance of grabbing the diamond —'

'And we conclude that I killed the housemaid, stuffed her
in the safe, and as an afterthought pinched the diamond?'

'I think she pinched the diamond and you took it from
her. There was something about your having fought with a
gang. If you did, it was her gang.'

'Then I'd have found the diamond when I regained consciousness in hospital. In the bag, by your hypothesis.'

'Unless you had passed it to Celia. Or unless Celia took it
from you when you were in an irresponsible condition.'

'That's a damnable suggestion, Clawson —'

'It's not a suggestion at all. I am telling you what your
position will be, as seen by a coroner's jury and as seen in
the police reports. Kyle may believe in your – call it non-
criminality – as sincerely as I do. And Celia's. But these in-
spectors have to write reports. And their seniors decide
what's to be done.'

In a sense, Habershon was shocked by the calm reason-
ableness of the man. There was nothing defensive in his
talk. He was making a marvellous job of building his own
background of broad-minded respectability.

'My one suggestion,' continued Clawson, 'is that you have
concealed the stone – in complete innocence, of course. I
propose that we put our heads together, work out where it
is – and then I can "find" it in the wrong deed-box at the
office. That would dispose of a very probable murder charge
against you.' He added : 'You can't prove that you were irresponsible that night. Celia's statement that you talked a bit
wildly would mean nothing.'

Habershon sensed that the moment had come for him to
'collapse'. He could build the collapse on Clawson's belief
in a total blackout.

'You've been stating the police view, Clawson. But you're
making a very convincing case that all this may actually
have happened.' Habershon paced the room, his chin on his
chest. 'And I can't produce a penn'orth of evidence that
convinces even myself.'

He held up his hand to prevent Clawson from interrupting.

'Wait, please! I want to ask you something, Clawson.'
Habershon paused, to register inner conflict. 'Clawson! Did
I – *did* I – kill that red-headed housemaid?'

'*Huh!*' There could be no doubt that Clawson was startled.
'I – I don't want to make you feel worse about it than you
do, old man. Don't you remember *anything* about her?'

'Yes. That's the devil of it. Too much or too little. I have
a blurred recollection of a brawl in that study. Of a red-
headed housemaid who scratched my face. Of chasing her
up the stairs, intending to break her neck. Of catching her
at the top of the stairs and tearing her clothes off – meaning to break her neck, Clawson!'

'That's pretty near the facts – I understand that the dress
had been torn off.' It was Clawson now who thought he was
having all the luck. 'Go on.'

'I can't. There's a total blackout as her dress comes off in
my hand.'

'What's the next memory in point of time?'

'Of myself standing upstairs somewhere – alone and quite
calm – staring at a Burmese doll in a window-seat.'

Clawson kept a poker face, but his voice was not free from
elation as he asked:

'Then you don't deny that you killed the girl?'

'I don't deny that I *may* have killed the girl. I simply
don't know. You will say that I cannot be any more certain
about the diamond. Only, I do remember wanting to kill the
girl and I don't remember anything at all about a diamond.'

'Good enough for me! I believe you've got the diamond –
unknowingly. I'm going to put up a proposition. Half a minute. I'd better pay off that taxi.'

While Clawson was away, Habershon reflected that he
had put over his tale. His virtual admission of murder would
act as a guarantee for all his statements about his memory.

'Can I take another whisky?' As Clawson helped himself,
he continued: 'You may have heard that Mrs Rabethorpe
is claiming the Rabethorpe estate – through the firm, which
means me.' He added as an afterthought: 'Unless, of course,

Velfrage shows up. The application will be heard in a day or two. The estate includes the diamond or its value. I want to recover that diamond for her. It isn't insured.'

Habershon shrugged his shoulders.

'You're certain to be arrested fairly soon – after the inquest, at the latest,' said Clawson. 'I'll tell you what I can do for you. If you will co-operate in reconstructing your own memory of what you did with the diamond, I'll keep you out of the way of the police.'

'Suppose we find the diamond?'

'I'll do my best to produce it publicly, as I said, in such a way that it will do you good.' He added, as extra inducement : 'And, mind you, it's possible we may tumble on proof that you did not kill the girl. What about searching this place first?'

'You can, if you like. But it's no good. I never reached home that night. Had a smash and was taken to hospital.'

There was the problem of his accounting for having the bag on his person at the theatre. He would have to risk a plumb lie.

'Somehow, I drifted to the club – remembered tonight that the bag was among some things I left there.'

'All right ! We'll get away first and I'll come back and search here afterwards.'

'Before I accept your help, Clawson, understand that at this moment I've no reason to believe that I ever touched that diamond.'

'I'll take the risk. We can use your car and dump it in the West End. You go and pack some clothes. The sooner we get you where Kyle can't find you the better.'

As Habershon took the wheel of the Chrysler, some of his physical fatigue slipped away, while he revelled in his luck. The fact that the gang was ready to adopt him settled so many anxious problems. The riddle of Velfrage's whereabouts must be left to Kyle – unless it tumbled from the lips of the gang. He was almost able to believe that the job would be easy.

In the West End he ran the car into an all-night garage, on Clawson's advice, giving his own name. While the man was making out the ticket, Clawson went to a telephone booth in the garage, carelessly leaving the door unfastened. Habershon could hear what he said.

'If your spare room is empty, I want you to put up a friend for me. . . . You'll see – we'll be along in half an hour or so.'

Leaving the garage they walked along Oxford Street until they met a cruising taxi. George Clawson gave the address of another all-night garage in Hampstead.

'The driver won't notice us particularly,' said George. 'Lots of provincials leave their cars there to avoid driving in Central London.'

In fifteen minutes they arrived at the garage and paid off the taxi.

'Feel like a stroll on the Heath? I thought not, but it's good for our health, old man – with special reference to the local bobbies. About one per cent of the population of Hampstead still consists of artists and poets who actually do walk on the Heath in the small hours.'

In bright moonlight they skirted the fringe of the Heath, then turned back into Old Hampstead and presently into a side street which abruptly took on the semblance of a country lane. Presently, Clawson led him through an archway, wide enough to give passage to a stage-coach. They were walking on cobbles, overgrown with weeds.

The carriageway gave on to a tiny courtyard, one wall of which towered out of sight, being the rear of a block of modern flats. They turned left as they emerged from the archway. The moonlight revealed a low wall and beyond it an orchard : against the building, of which the arch was part, was an external flight of old stone steps with a very new handrail.

Clawson mounted the steps, Habershon following. The door was opened as they reached the narrow platform at the top.

'So *you* are the mysterious friend ! I'm so glad !' exclaimed Prinny Loftus. 'Why didn't you say so, George? I was afraid you were going to plant a girl on me.'

'Tell you in a minute, m'dear. Don't let's make a noise on the doorstep. The fact is,' he chuckled, 'we're dodging the police.'

15

THEY were standing in what had once been a harness room, but was now artistically disguised as a hall. There was a door on the left of the front door and another in the opposite wall. Prinny led the way down a narrow corridor decorated to look like the corridor of a railway train. The little procession ended in a sitting-room over the archway. Here the railway note was sustained by two high-backed settees looking like sections of a dining-car, a luggage rack running the length of one wall, square windows operated by a strap, and two large, impressionistic pictures of a locomotive engine.

Prinny caught Habershon gaping at a radiator which tailed off into surrealism.

'A dear artist friend did the whole thing for me out of scrap, charging minus nothing when you think what furnishing costs nowadays,' she explained. 'If you can't be rich, you have to be freakish. What were you going to say?'

'I was trying to work out some sort of apology for upsetting you at this time o' night.'

'Upsetting me! That, kind sir, has been impossible this many a year. Oh no – that's a line from a play I've just lost a part in! Sit down and look jolly. George, pour him a drink.'

She was wearing a sleeveless green dressing-gown over green pyjamas, so that the whole seemed to be a single garment of vaguely Eastern design. She had removed her make-up so that her face was as white as her arms, which were very white.

'The point is,' she went on, 'there's no one else in this place. You aren't married or anything, are you?'

'I'm all right that way,' he assured her. 'But what about you?'

'It'll help. I'm all out to get a bad reputation without working for it. It's expected of one in my position. George dear, you pig, you've taken the last of the gin!'

'I was pouring it for you. Habershon and I will rub along

on the whisky. Prinny! Loll back somewhere, darling, and listen. Hands folded and no interruption! You know what a jam I'm in over that damned diamond and Velfrage and one thing and another. The long and the short of it is that Habershon thinks he might be able to help us find the diamond.'

'That's fine! I do hope —'

'Shut up, darling – that's only the opening! After the inquest on that girl, it's ten to one the police will have to arrest Habershon, even if they don't think he killed her any more than we do. So it's all pull together, if you see what I mean – that is, if you will let Habershon stay here until we all know which way the cat jumps.'

'Very lucid, George! No wonder your clients adore you! Of course he can stay here as long as he likes!'

'Thanks, Prinny,' said Habershon.

'Don't mention it, Mr Habershon, I beg.'

'Bruce to you!' he returned. This pally, no-nonsense girl was very easy to get along with – this luscious little hell-cat who was helping to plant a murder on him. That white face under the shimmering bronze of her hair looked strangely pure – if you kept your eye off the pyjamas.

'We'll go into the details tomorrow,' said Clawson. 'He's dropping with sleep now, and so am I, and you ought to be.'

'I'll take you to your room,' said Prinny.

'Habershon doesn't need the honoured guest routine!' snapped Clawson. 'Comrades in misfortune – that's what we are! I'll help him up with his traps and ask him if he's sure he's got everything he wants.'

'Yes, George dear. Good night, Bruce.'

'Good night, Prinny. You must be the most good-natured girl in the world!'

'*Sh!* Keep all that for when we're alone. George is so jealous.'

The by-play, thought Habershon as they left Prinny, was rather disturbingly natural. Strange that Prinny should find any difficulty in getting on the stage – if she had ever tried.

In the hall Clawson picked up one suitcase. With the other Habershon followed him up a ladder-like staircase at the end of the corridor. On the floor above was another corridor like the one below except that it was distempered instead of decorated.

The spare room was furnished adequately but inexpensively and followed no definite scheme. It was presumably over the sitting-room, but it was a good deal smaller. In the opposite wall was a communicating door. It was a little stuffy. Habershon opened the window.

'Prinny likes to put herself over as a hard-boiled baby!' said Clawson. 'I daresay you've spotted that she's little more than a country girl talking big.'

'I've no complaint. She's been very nice about all this.'

'She'll look after you. As a matter of fact, she thinks I've been useful to her. She had some bother over the tiny property her father left her. She knows I'm in trouble over this diamond and she'll pull her weight.'

As soon as Clawson left the room, Habershon tried the communicating door, to find it locked. As he was turning the handle in the opposite direction he heard the unmistakable sound of a soda siphon, then of a cigarette lighter.

The sound was coming upwards through the floor, which was of polished boards, bare except for a couple of rugs near the bed.

Prinny was filling up her glass with soda and lighting a cigarette! A moment later he heard George's voice. Luck again, and in a big way.

'I'll just have a final and then buzz off. You needn't worry about Habershon's comfort. He's pretty well all in.'

'Poor boy! He's rather desperately attractive. You know that, don't you?'

'I know he's the typical open-air hearty. Drinks milk and goes to bed at ten. Don't you be a fool, m'dear!'

'That's just what I'm not being. I'm sensible enough to know that he throws my judgement out of gear. George – is he a crook?'

'Crook. Good Lord, no!'

'I'm glad to hear you say it. But I do wish I could be sure.'

There was a short silence, presumably while Clawson addressed himself to his whisky. So far, Habershon had heard every word distinctly. He keyed himself to pick up vital information.

'If you mean, did he kill that girl? – I don't know.'

'But you told me —'

It was Prinny who had interrupted herself. There was a distinct pause before Clawson spoke.

'I thought he did, but now I'm not so sure. I asked him outright.'

'And he said he didn't?'

'No! If he had, I might not have believed him. He said he simply didn't know. Admitted that he might have. You couldn't get better proof that the chap is playing straight with that quinine story.'

Habershon, crouching by the communicating door, tried to work it out. How could the gang be in doubt as to who had killed the girl?

'And doesn't he know whether he has stolen the diamond, either?'

'He does not. At least, he says he's pretty sure he never saw any diamond. But he admits that if he can't be sure about the murder, he can't be sure about the diamond. Let him have a rest here. Then he'll do his best to remember. If he forces himself to remember about the murder, he may remember what he did with the stone.'

Habershon observed that Clawson was giving Prinny a truthful account of their conversation at the bungalow. Why bother? Prinny, as one of the gang present at the time, must know the underlying facts about the diamond and the murder. And about Velfrage. Prinny herself had tried by force to prevent him from entering the library to look for Velfrage.

'I was just wondering,' continued Prinny, 'whether the whole thing might be a bluff. I mean, suppose he and Velfrage set out to steal the stone together —'

'That's a silly suggestion! Velfrage didn't know the Daimler was going to break down and that Habershon would be there to give him a lift.'

'N-no. I see now he couldn't have! Try it the other way

round. Suppose the police think you did something funny with the diamond at the office —'

'The police only guess it's missing because Velfrage is missing.'

'All the same, they might think you had murdered Velfrage. And suppose Habershon is a police spy?'

'Why the devil should he be? He'd have no interest. He's a well-to-do business man.'

'Then what about this? The police found the diamond on Habershon — who stole it without knowing what he was doing —'

'The police have not found the diamond – or they would have had to notify me as Velfrage's representative. Besides, you're forgetting that bag! Habershon must have taken that bag from the dead girl. Time and place prove it. It's a million pounds to a biscuit that the girl had already pinched the diamond and put it in that bag – obviously hiding it in the lining – you could see the gash. Remember that Habershon himself was in possession of the bag *tonight* – at the theatre. That's why we went after him – in the hope of stopping him before he could reach the police. Why can't you believe that Habershon is the decent sort of chap he appears to be?'

'Because I want to believe it so much that I don't trust myself. But I'm going to believe it now. I don't care tuppence if he did murder the girl, as long as he can get away with it. But suppose he murdered Velfrage too? A beautiful young man with two murders tied to him is a bit much for a poor girl to cope with.'

'Who says he murdered Velfrage? Who says Velfrage has been murdered by anybody? The servant girl must have worked with a gang. My own guess – and I admit it's a guess – is that if Velfrage *was* murdered, the girl's gang murdered him, and that Habershon was trying to save the old man and somehow managed to scupper the girl and walk off with the bag. In a lucid interval Habershon found the diamond – at least, I hope he did – put it on one side – probably meaning to take it to the police as soon as he felt better – and then forgot where he put it. Habershon doesn't remember anything about Velfrage after he entered Elsie's house to look for him.'

'All right!' There came a ripple of laughter from Prinny. 'I believe Habershon is as good as he looks. *Now* are you satisfied?'

There was a short silence during which Habershon tried to face the stark fact that the conversation he had overheard was utterly inconsistent with his identification of Clawson, Prinny and the others as the gang.

'No more whisky! Plenty to do tomorrow. Good night, m'dear.'

'Good night, George. And if I do fall for Habershon, it'll be your fault. Go out quietly – he may be asleep.'

There was the sound of the sitting-room door being opened and shut, without noticeable quietness – then of Prinny putting the glasses on a tray – of Prinny yawning deeply.

Habershon straightened up from his crouching position. Prinny was the red-headed girl whose clothes he had torn off. George Clawson was the man he had knocked out. On that point it was not possible he could be wrong. The conversation he had overheard indicated that it was not possible he could be right.

His breathing became troublesome, producing a wave of faintness. He stood by the open window facing the block of flats. He changed his position so that he looked obliquely over the low wall at the orchard. The moon was waning. For ten minutes or more he stood thus, steadying his nerve.

There came a sound immediately under the window. He leant out. A dozen feet below, Clawson was descending the stone staircase.

Clawson was half-way down the steps when, behind him, the front door was shut on the latch.

'I thought he went home more than ten minutes ago,' reflected Habershon. 'And I thought he left Prinny in the sitting-room.'

Anyway, what did it matter! He was tired beyond the capacity to worry. His last thought as he fell asleep was a restful memory of Celia Fenton. But he dreamed that she pointed at him scornfully, telling him that he was wrong about Prinny Loftus being a crook. Then Kyle floated into the dream, shouting that the whole gang had been killed in an imaginary car smash.

By half-past nine Habershon was descending the ladder-like staircase, fully dressed. From the kitchenette – a cubby-hole in the corridor, Prinny called to him.

'Breakfast in the sitting-room in five minutes.'

'Let me help.'

'No. Keep walking, or I shall scream. I've forgotten my housecoat.'

It was not easy to tell when Prinny was fooling. He felt sheepish as he remembered her remarks about his own at-tractiveness, eavesdropped through the floor-boards.

In the bath he had come to terms with himself. It would be futile to chase his own tail, proving and disproving in-compatible theories. Let it slide. Concentrate on a single tar-get – to discover what he had done in the interval between pursuing the partly-clothed red-head – Prinny or Bradburn or neither – and staring at that Burmese doll. The guilt or in-nocence of himself and Prinny and of everybody else would then take care of itself.

In the meantime, take Prinny as he found her, accept her help in dodging the police, without feeling squeamish about it.

When she appeared, he turned to help her with the tray.

'Don't be a perfect gentleman, there's a dear! Just swing that little table round and we can have the tray between us. All meals here are tray-meals.'

There is an art of tray-mealing, which Prinny understood. The breakfast was a little masterpiece of makeshift. Prinny, he noted, took the trouble to be efficient in small things. Prinny – he was annoyed to find himself thinking about her as a woman.

'George telephoned half an hour ago,' she told him. 'Mes-sage for you. He has searched your bungalow – as agreed, he said – and found nothing. He thinks the police have not yet made any inquiries about you.'

'They're certain to call me this morning. It may not dawn on them until this afternoon that I've bolted. That gives me a few hours to put my affairs in order.'

'Take my car any time,' she offered. 'I keep it in the Eagle Garage. I'll tell them my brother may come for it. They won't believe you're my brother, but they'll let you take it.'

He thanked her, and added : 'Then I must start work. I've undertaken to remember how I stole the diamond. And how I killed a girl —'

'Or how you only tore her dress off her and left her – unmolested?'

Uncertain what to make of that remark, he went on :

'Damned funny that I don't know, isn't it? I say – don't you feel a bit squiggly about it? Alone in here with a chap who may be a girl-killer?'

'I'd be terrified – only, I don't believe it.'

Habershon blinked. The gang – if they were a gang – would surely encourage him to believe that he was the killer.

'The girl-killer, as you call it,' she continued, 'is always a morbid type. You can tell they're morbid, even if you can't tell they're girl-killers.'

'That only applies to the maniac murderers.'

'It would have been a maniac murder if you had done it. You didn't know you were stealing a diamond – if you did steal it. So there was no motive.'

'Yes, there was – she made me savage. She attacked me – scratched my face —'

'Oh no, Bruce ! I've seen that girl, spoken to her a good many times. She was the cringing, sneak-thief type.'

'Very well !' For an instant only he hesitated. 'In that case it was not the dead girl who scratched my face, but some other girl. I still bear the marks of her nails. You can see them if you look closely.'

'*Really?*' Prinny sprang up, slithered round the tray to his side. 'Do let me see !'

She tilted his chin to the light, as Kyle had tilted it.

'Yes – there are marks !'

She touched his cheek. Caressingly, her cool finger-tips

travelled the length of the dimly discernible scars, while Habershon's memory turned somersaults. Her nails had made the scars which her finger-tips were now soothing. It was her dress that had been torn off her back – oh, let it slide!

'But I still don't believe you killed her.'

'I wish you could convince me, Prinny.'

Her eyes seemed innocent as a child's.

'I'll try. Where were you both when you tore her dress?'

'At the top of the staircase. She left the dress in my hand and bolted along the landing. Then we're back in the black-out. I may have caught her somewhere in the upper part of the house.'

'And killed her? Being too muzzy to know what you were doing?'

'I suppose so.'

'Be your age, Bruce!' The sudden sharpness of her voice flabbergasted him. 'You weren't too muzzy to understand your own danger. You were smart enough to carry her downstairs and hide her in that safe!'

Habershon relaxed. This was the line he had expected 'the gang' to take.

'You've stated the police case very ably,' he said.

The grey-green eyes were gazing at him steadily, pos-sessively. Colour was creeping into her white cheeks. She put a hand on his wrist.

'Please!' she ejaculated. 'Please, Bruce, do what I ask. Will you?'

He nodded indifferently, had the impression that she was putting on an act.

'In the corridor, between the kitchen and the hall, you'll see a door, flush with the wall. It's a cupboard. Open it. Look inside. Then argue with me as much as you like.'

Her manner had a genuine urgency. Without a word he got up, found the door of the cupboard and opened it.

'Well, I'm damned!' he exclaimed aloud.

Sitting on a shelf in a lifelike pose was a Burmese doll, the size of a baby.

Prinny had come up behind him.

'Have you seen that doll before, Bruce?'

'Yes. I saw it – or one like it – on a bench on the first-floor landing when I was on my way down – just before Celia came in.'

'When you saw that doll on that bench – had you got a corpse in your arms?'

'No. Absolutely, definitely no!'

'Oh God, that's a relief!' cried Prinny. 'At least, you know now that you did not put the body in the safe!' There were tears in her eyes. 'I had to stage-manage it, Bruce, so that I could spring it suddenly on your memory – so that you needn't go on worrying.'

'Prinny, you're a darling!' Impulsively, he put an arm round her, meant to peck her cheek out of gratitude. Instead, her mouth found his.

It was not a kiss of congratulation – it was not a pally, Bohemian kiss – it was a kiss to which no qualifying label could be attached. It stood magnificently as a kiss in its own right. Habershon guessed that, before it ended, it would turn her into his friend or his enemy.

He could have shouted with relief when interruption came with a thud on the front door, then a couple of flapping blows, as if someone were knocking with the flat of his gloved hand.

Prinny motioned him to silence, dragged him by the hand into the hall, thrust his coat and hat over his arm and pushed him into her bedroom. It was he who frustrated her attempt to shut the door.

He heard her open the front door.

'Frank!' There came a ripple of laughter. 'You look like the advertisements for Somebody's Bandages.'

'Never mind that! George said he'd probably be here.'

'He isn't. He —'

'We must get him at once. Listen! I've got proof that Habershon's loss of memory is a stunt. That funny business with Margo's bag last night was a trick to draw our fire, and I shouldn't be surprised if —'

'Good *morning*, Keller!' Habershon emerged with a grin. 'I say, you have been unlucky! Never skid a big car at speed until you know where the kerb is. You look as if you ought to be in the surgical ward.'

With the last words Keller recovered from his surprise at seeing Habershon.

'That's where I've been. In the surgical ward – of the Stainham hospital. When they had winkled a bit of Rolls-Royce out of my arm, the matron gave me tea in her room. We small-talked about car accidents, Habershon. She told me about a young man who was brought in with concussion – before I left I found out the exact time. This young man showed her a woman's bag with a peacock's eye design, saying he couldn't remember how he got hold of it. Can you go on from there, Habershon?'

16

'My dear fellow, you're ill!' said Habershon. One arm was in a sling, both hands were bandaged, and another bandage was visible under the turned-up collar of his overcoat. The thin, bony face was uninjured, but his eyes showed strain bordering on panic.

'You haven't answered my question.'

'You've impugned my good faith to Prinny, and you'll answer my questions first. Did I show that matron the diamond?'

'It wasn't there by that time. You had passed it to the woman who came to see you. I've found out that a woman did come to see you. P'r'aps you'll tell us who the woman was.'

Poor Miss Parker, thought Habershon.

'I'll tell Prinny after you've gone, if she wants to know.'

'There's another thing – who brought the police to Elsie's house last night if you didn't?'

'There are lots of "other things", old man. Granted that I took the diamond from the lining of the bag, what did I do with it? Prinny and George and I are working on that. And how did the body get into the safe?'

Keller's jaw dropped. He swayed, propped himself against the wall.

'The body!' he gasped. 'Velfrage's body in the safe! It *can't* be!'

'Frank darling, you're nowhere near it!' cut in Prinny. 'Velfrage's body indeed! Bruce is right – you're ill. Come and sit down and I'll get you some hot rum and lemon. Don't try to talk about things.'

'The doorkeeper said Habershon was brought in with concussion at six-fifteen —'

'That doesn't help unless you can tell us what time I left Woodville,' Habershon said quickly. 'And as you weren't there, you don't know.' He added, to Prinny : 'I'll be back about seven, if convenient.'

'Righto, if you're sure you don't want the car I'll use it after lunch.'

'Don't let him go,' blustered Keller. 'He's evaded every one of my questions.'

'That's quite right, old man. You explain to Prinny why I'm telling her all these lies. See you later. Take care of yourself.'

Twenty minutes later Habershon was speaking from a call-box to Miss Parker at the office.

'Good morning, Miss Parker.' His tone was placatory. 'I'm in Town, and I —'

'It's a great pity you didn't stay in Cornwall, as you promised.'

'You'll be nice about it when you know why. Listen. In a few minutes a messenger will bring you a cheque on my private account. I want you to cash it and bring it in currency to the Casserole Café in Theobald's Road. I'll be there in an hour from now. Repeat that, please.'

'There's no need – my hearing is perfect. And you will turn up at the office this afternoon !'

Habershon scowled as Miss Parker cut off. It was, he thought, rather cheek – saying 'you will' turn up at the office. Her tyranny was tacitly understood to be confined to personal matters. In business she was a subordinate. It might even be necessary to remind her of that fact.

She arrived at the teashop a few yards ahead of him.

'Morning coffee for two,' he ordered and waited for her to speak. In spite of the grim business ahead, he was personally nervous of her.

'Morning coffee !' She snorted. 'And that absurd conversation on the telephone ! Where do you suppose this sort of hole-and-corner behaviour will lead us ?'

'It wasn't absurd. You've got the cash, haven't you ?'

'Much against my better judgement !' She handed him a large wallet. 'You might just as well have drawn it yourself. The bank clerk will tell the police.'

She had not lowered her voice. The waitress bringing the

coffee and biscuits would have heard if she had been listening.

'Funny you should mention the police, because —'

'It's not funny at all. Detective Inspector Kyle was in the office when you telephoned.'

'Oh-h! I see why you put in that bit about my coming to the office – what did he want?'

'Information about you.'

'Good Lord! What did you tell him?'

'Everything I knew about you that could possibly interest a policeman. I neither flattered nor spared you. On the whole, the interview was satisfactory. On his side he gave me the cardinal facts. He asked me to impress upon you that it is absolutely necessary for you to keep in close touch with him. And I quite agree.'

Miss Parker approved of Scotland Yard, so Scotland Yard was all right. Indeed, if she were sitting in the House of Commons instead of a teashop there would have seemed nothing outrageous in the reflection. In Habershon's eyes she was a woman of commanding presence, well dressed, too, in a style that stood aloof from fashion.

Presently he drew from her the gist of Kyle's statement, which was sufficient for his immediate purpose.

'You have reached,' said Miss Parker, 'the years of discretion. I do not need to remind you that the first essential is absolute frankness with the police.'

'I've tried that. I have been utterly frank. And it has got me in this mess. I know as well as you do that Kyle does not believe I'm a criminal – at least, he believes that I never had any criminal intent. But he doesn't know whether I did or did not kill that girl, and steal the diamond. I have to prove my own innocence.'

'You don't prove your innocence by running away – which is what that money is for, I suppose?'

'Kyle will have to arrest me – or somebody else will – after the inquest. I can't prove anything when I'm locked up. As long as I'm at large there's the bare chance I shall be able to prove something – one way or the other.'

'One way – *or the other*?' demanded Miss Parker.

He hung his head, like a small boy before an inquisitorial governess. The gesture expressed his actual feeling.

'I myself don't know for absolutely certain that I did not kill her.'

'What nonsense!' ejaculated Miss Parker. 'Fancy talking to me like that!'

'I'm afraid it isn't nonsense.' He had as suddenly become a mature man. 'Listen! I identified – to Kyle – four persons. I was positive I had seen those four persons in that house when the crime was being committed. Kyle himself convinced me that I was not deceiving myself. My own version of what took place – my own belief that I did such-and-such – is based on that recognition of those four persons. Four persons, Miss Parker!'

'Don't keep saying "four persons". What about them?'

'Since my conversation with Kyle, I have – I have some reason to doubt my own identification. I've overheard two of the four persons talking about the affair – when they didn't know I was listening. What I heard was not – well, it was not consistent with my previous belief.'

For the first time in his life he observed that Miss Parker was impressed by something he had said. When she spoke, her voice held a new note.

'Do you mean, Bruce, that you half suspect that you may have killed a woman?'

'That's about the size of it!'

'Oh, my dear boy! You must certainly do all you can to remove the doubt from your own mind. I refuse to accept it as anything but a doubt. I can tell you – though you won't believe me – that you could never kill a woman, quinine or alcohol or anything else notwithstanding!'

Good old Miss Parker – she believed in him a hundred per cent. But her assurance was valueless. He vividly remembered his determination to kill the red-head. *A* red-head anyhow.

'What do you want me to do?' asked Miss Parker.

'Go to a good private detective agency. Have these four persons shadowed. I've written them down. Let 'em start with the girl – Miss Prinny Loftus. She's taking her car out of the garage after lunch.'

After discussing plans for communicating, Habershon was about to go when Miss Parker detained him.

'In part of my conversation with Inspector Kyle,' she said, 'there was a curious cross-purpose. I thought he suspected you – since we are talking about these dreadful things – I thought he suspected you of killing Mr Velfrage!'

Habershon nodded reflectively.

'And you weren't so positive that I could never possibly kill a man?' he asked.

'That is an unnecessary question!' reproved Miss Parker. 'Of course, I know that when they aren't quite themselves men do sometimes attack each other. But – as I understand it – there is no proof that Mr Velfrage is dead, is there?'

'None!' snapped Habershon, his nerves on edge. 'That's one of the horrors I may find under one of the stones I'm trying to turn.'

'Anyhow, we needn't meet our troubles half-way!'

That little platitude settled on Habershon's courage like a wet blanket. The very tone in which she had uttered the words betrayed her fear that he might have murdered Velfrage – made it seem credible that he had murdered Velfrage.

His talk with Miss Parker had cleared his own thoughts on one point. To her he had spoken aloud a truth which he had partly concealed from himself. He was no longer certain that he had not killed that girl.

There was that maddening blackout between the moment when he had torn the dress and the moment when he was looking at the Burmese doll.

'But I hadn't got a corpse in my arms when I noticed the doll. Good old Prinny!'

Reasons for, reasons against! Dog chasing tail! He turned into a telephone booth and rang Celia Fenton.

'I want to accept your offer, if it's still open. Can you cope with me this afternoon?'

'Easily!' she answered. 'Aunt Elsie will be with her cor-setière in Town. That means the whole afternoon. And the staff – meaning that awful cook – has left in a huff. We shall have the place to ourselves. Come as early as you like.'

'Three o'clock, then. I say, I want to keep out of the way of the police.'

'I don't think they're likely to come again. If they do, you needn't show yourself. Come in by the garden door – it's in the road that runs parallel. I'll be on the watch for you.'

It would be safe to use the Chrysler until after the inquest. At three o'clock exactly he entered the garden. Over the hedge, he viewed the back of Mrs Wellard's 'lovely house next door'. The loveliness escaped him. He observed that the windows needed cleaning.

Celia was coming to meet him. At sight of her, memory of Prinny's kiss intruded, but vanished when Celia spoke.

'You don't *look* like a fugitive from justice.'

'I don't feel like one, now.' Her presence was rapidly restoring his self-confidence. Thank heavens she wasn't luscious!

'I'd like to have a go at that staircase,' he told her. 'I simply must find out what I did in the upper part of the house.'

17

In the hall, Celia opened the oak chest.

'Put your hat and coat in here, or I shall look foolish if the police call and I tell them there's no one at home.'

Even that sort of thing seemed rather fun. He became aware of her slenderness in a skirt and jumper of the same silvery grey. Her dress was as unstudied as her movements, but both awoke in him a sense of fitness. She was stimulating but unprovocative – he could absorb himself in her without losing his own sense of proportion.

It was she who directed his eyes to the staircase.

'The girl was on the landing – I had one foot on the top stair when I grabbed her,' he explained. 'I got a good grip on her clothes. I think she did as much of the tearing as I did. She slithered to the floor, then up and away – leaving me holding most of her outfit. Thin black silk and a fancy apron – I can remember the feel of the stuff.'

Celia looked doubtful.

'What is it?' he asked.

'I'm trying to see it in my mind's eye.' She smiled. 'It comes out rather like those bedroom-farce films. Someone clutches a dress – there's a terrific sound of tearing – the girl pirouettes prettily, and the dress comes away without any bother with the sleeves – and there she is in her ravishing underwear!'

'H'm! I don't suppose I noticed the dress details. But there's a clear impression that she was more or less dressless and that I had most of it in my hand.'

Celia moved to the staircase.

'Come along!' she urged. She stopped at the landing.

'No reaction!' he moaned. 'I have a feeling that nothing is going to happen.'

'Because you've worked yourself up into a lather! Why, your hands are shaking! I can feel them.'

She had taken him by both hands. Abruptly she dropped

her grip. She was staring intently at something, it seemed, in the space over his shoulder. He turned round, saw nothing but the underside of the staircase to the next floor. He had sensed a change of mood in her.

'What is it?' he asked.

'Nothing!' Her tone was strangely curt. There was a short silence. 'We're beginning in the wrong way. Come downstairs again.'

He was piqued by what he regarded as her lack of frankness. He wanted to draw her attention back to himself. Some evil genius prompted him to ask the same grimly humorous, self-mocking question he had asked Prinny.

'Aren't you afraid to be alone in the house with a man who may turn out to be a girl-killer?'

She caught her breath and faced him.

'Yes – just a little. Or I would be, if I let myself think about it like that.' She laughed self-consciously. 'One fear cancels out another. I'm more afraid of running away from the job.'

'Well, I'm damned!' he muttered. Such self-assurance as remained to him had received a violent shock.

Celia went to a cupboard under the stairs and produced a black overall. While she was putting it over her dress, their eyes met.

'When we were working on my brother's blackout,' she said, 'the only really difficult part concerned an incident of which he was ashamed. He did not want to remember – and so he genuinely could not remember.'

He was startled again – to him her words seemed to be not far removed from accusation.

'D'you think that applies to me, Celia?'

'I can't tell. But don't let's cheat ourselves. We may find that you did nothing in particular – upstairs. But we may find —'

She did not go on. It was unnecessary.

'Nevertheless, I want to get to the bottom of it,' he said. 'Police or no police.'

'Good – that's settled!' she exclaimed. 'Now, I'll run up the stairs and you run after me. I'll fall down. Then you give me time to run away and hide. Remember what I told you, don't act it – only imitate what happened. Ready?'

'Ready!'

He gave her about as long a start as the other girl had had, then ran after her. Her doubt of him doubled his determination, doubled his power to concentrate. He ran up the stairs as if he were again running after the red-head.

He caught Celia's overall and ripped it off. As he did so, it was as if he had started an engine that drove his memory.

With the tearing of the garment came savage anger – echo of the anger he had felt against Red-head. He was in no sense in a trance. His state was that of a person sitting in a theatre, feeling intensely the emotion depicted on the stage, yet aware that he is a member of the audience.

He no longer needed to remember – he had only to observe.

He observed that he was wrapping the torn garment round his right wrist.

The landing was well lit with daylight from the bow window. As if unaware of this he switched on the light, strode forward and opened the first door.

As before, he noticed no detail of the room. But he looked under the bed, in the wardrobe, behind the curtains.

Along the landing into the next room – and the next. At the end of the landing he turned back and made for the staircase. He was neither walking nor running. He was moving in a swift, padding glide. Already he had forgotten the existence of Celia Fenton. He was looking for a red-head whom he was going to strangle.

On the second floor he repeated his search, which took on a certain rhythm – pushing the door open to its extremity, turning on the light, swiftly and economically probing each possible hiding place.

On to the top floor. To the first room. To the second. To the third – the room that had been Bradburn's.

Unlike the other rooms, this room was in darkness. He did not notice the difference. The room had been in darkness when he had visited it before.

He snapped on the light. It was a ceiling light, badly

placed. It threw a beam on a curtained corner, which served as a wardrobe. As on that memory-fogged night, he again saw the tips of a girl's shoes, showing beneath the hem of the curtain.

He backed to the door, his eyes watching a spot near the centre of the room : he shut and locked the door, removed the key and dropped it in his pocket. With slow, deliberate movements he unwrapped the overall from his right wrist, rolled it up and tossed it under the bed.

Then he strode to the curtain and flung it back.

The next instant he drew back with a startled cry, which broke his concentration.

This time, too, there was a girl. Only the girl was Celia Fenton. Pressed against the middle of her, Celia was holding a revolver levelled at him.

'What have you remembered?'

His world tilted sideways. He saw her as an enemy, more subtle than Prinny, more formidable than Kyle. It was as if Miss Parker had revealed herself as a dance hostess.

He remembered Kyle's advice. When something inconceivable seems to be happening before your eyes, wait until events provide a reasonable explanation.

18

'WHAT have you remembered?' repeated Celia.

'Everything up to the moment when I pulled the curtain. When it turned out to be you – well, it was a bit of a shock!'

'What a pity!' She came from the recess, laid the revolver on the whitewood dressing-table and pulled up the blind, letting in the daylight. 'I've overdone it and broken your train of thought. I was "acting on information received", as the police say.'

The impression lingered that she had had it in mind to shoot him. He drove it out by forcing himself back to the matter in hand.

'Could you see what I did when I came into this room?'

'You rolled up my overall – what's left of it – and flung it under the bed.'

'That's important!' He nodded as he ticked off each point. 'I searched every other room for Red-head. I didn't search in here. Because she was here!'

Celia walked past him, sat on the edge of the bed.

'Let's keep our heads!' she said. 'Do you definitely remember seeing her in here?'

'N – no. I blacked out when I saw you – with that gun.'

'Then you only infer that she was here?'

He did not answer. She left him in silence to arrange his thoughts.

'In those other rooms I felt as if I were actually looking for Red-head. And watching myself looking for her.'

'And there was some change when you came into this room?'

'Yes. I was no longer looking for anything. I had finished looking. That can mean only one thing.'

'Oh, nonsense!' she said impatiently. 'It's impossible to be as definite as that. We needn't get the creeps about it. Let's go on with it.'

'How?' he demanded blankly.

'Let's do this bit over again. You come into the room again, repeat your actions – and this time I won't interrupt.'

He agreed without enthusiasm, moved towards the door.

'Wait a minute, Bruce. Let's have our stage props. You must do your act with my overall.'

He remained near the door while she stooped to recover the overall. When she pulled it from under the bed, she was startled to find that she was pulling another garment with it.

'Bruce! *Look!*'

In one hand Celia held the black overall – in the other a torn black dress of washable silk and a fancy apron. She spread them out for him.

'Those are the things Prinny was wearing!' he cried spontaneously. 'And I flung them there, under the —'

'*Prinny?*'

He realized his slip, knew that he must cover it.

'A super-imposed image!' he said with elaborate indifference. 'You twitted me about it last night, if you remember.'

'I felt sure that Prinny was in your mind!'

He let her remark hang in the air. He began to pace the little room, stopped opposite the mirror, noticed that his collar was rumpled and his tie disarranged. While he was making the adjustment the pale wintry sun illumined a line of burnished copper on the shoulder of his coat.

A hair from Prinny's head! That disastrous kiss! When Celia and he had been standing at the top of the stairs, she had been looking, not over his shoulder, but at it.

'I've been to Prinny's flat,' he said. 'She showed me a Burmese doll.'

'She bought it from Aunt Elsie. There's one exactly like it on the landing downstairs.'

'That was the point of showing it to me. I told her where I had seen the doll's twin. She sprang a question on me. When I saw the doll on your landing, was I carrying a corpse in my arms? Well, I knew that I wasn't. That little trick of hers gave me hope.'

'Hope?' repeated Celia.

'Don't you see! If I killed that girl in this room' – excitement came into his voice – 'how did I get her body to the safe?'

'That seems to me pretty good proof that you did not kill her.'

He did not answer – sunk in his own thought.

'I say, Celia! Suppose I *did* find a girl in this room – and it wasn't the girl I was chasing?'

'Making two girls?' she asked. 'And one of them Prinny?'

'As a starting point – yes!'

'Then Prinny would be the one whose dress you tore?' As he assented, she went on : 'The dress itself can settle whether it was Prinny.

'Prinny,' she continued, 'is three inches taller than I am and a good deal fuller. And I am a good deal taller and fuller than Bradburn.'

As she spoke, Celia removed her belt and slipped out of the grey skirt and jumper.

'It's important that you should see for yourself. With a couple of pins – here we are ! – I can make it hold together enough for our purpose. . . . Now look !'

It could hardly be said that Celia was wearing the black dress. But she had certainly put it on. The fancy apron seemed to have slipped upwards.

The hem of the skirt hung above her knees.

'If Prinny had worn this dress, it would have looked like a tunic. Not that she could have squeezed into it. I couldn't have, but for the huge tear – you can see miles of bare back, can't you?'

Habershon accepted the conclusion – that the red-head could not have been Prinny.

'But there's a catch in it somewhere,' he exclaimed. 'Why – good heavens! – a girl thinks I'm going to strangle her. She bolts into this room – hears me opening the other doors – coming up the stairs. She would have locked the door. She could have put in a spot of screaming while I was battering the door down.'

'Splendid!' There was no surprise in her voice, only approval. 'So now you needn't suspect yourself of murdering

the girl. But you did come into this room, Bruce. You abandoned pursuit of the girl all of a sudden – probably forgot
her.' She paused and added : 'Because you saw someone
else in this room?'

'Sounds reasonable!' With sudden determination he
snatched Celia's overall, then pulled down the blind.

'Give me half a minute!' she asked. Perceiving his inten-
tion, she took up the revolver, went into the recess and drew
the curtain.

He went over to the door, stood leaning against it while
he concentrated his thoughts. In a few seconds he was
ready.

As before, he unwrapped the overall from his right wrist
and tossed it under the bed. As before, the tips of the shoes
were visible below the hem of the curtain. As before, he
strode to the curtain and flung it back.

This time, he avoided looking into her face. He waited,
swaying a little, his eye on the revolver.

'Got it!' he exclaimed. 'She said she would shoot me if
I didn't leave the room. . . . Wait! I remember. It came out
in a shrill, whining cockney. *I ain't seen nothink. Lea' me
alone! can't yer, or I'll blow yer guts out.*'

'And I said – can't remember the exact words – something like : *"You're the wrong girl. I want the big girl.
Where is she?"* '

He paused for thought. He was not emotionally concentrated – he was piecing remembered and half-remembered
items together.

'What about the revolver, Bruce?'

'Thanks! Now I can do a bit more.' He looked down at
the weapon held firmly against her person. 'I don't think
either of us took the gun very seriously. She was holding it
wrongly, as you are, with her finger on the trigger-guard instead of the trigger. I didn't snatch it. I took it – like this.'

He pushed the muzzle to a safe angle and lightly smacked
her hand away from the stock.

Then he opened the chambers.

'Good Lord, Celia, this is loaded!'

'So was Bradburn's. That's why I held it by the trigger guard.'

But it need not have been loaded for the purposes of their test. Was she taking precautions against himself as a possible girl-killer? He refused to grope for an answer. . . . Dog chasing tail!

He shook out the cartridges.

'Now watch.'

He went to the bed, lifted the mattress and put the revolver under it – then threw the cartridges out of the window.

'Splendid again, Bruce! That's where the police found Bradburn's.'

'Splendid to you and many of 'em!' He laughed happily. 'If I had meant to kill that girl, I'd have used her own revolver. Besides, I wasn't angry then. I was thinking only that a girl like that oughtn't to be trusted with a revolver. By that time I was in an anxious mood, fussy and worried about something.'

His exhilaration vanished as he added :

'Of course, it doesn't prove anything to anybody but myself!'

'And me!' emended Celia.

'You never seemed to need any proof.' He added : 'Unfortunately, the police do.'

Presently, Celia asked :

'Do you really think there were two girls?'

'I – don't – know. Wait till it drops into place. I've only that last bit to remember, now.' He took out a cigarette case. 'Burmese doll is the next stop – and the terminus.'

'I don't smoke, thanks. You have one and relax. Make your mind a blank and let things drift in. I won't talk.'

He sat straddlewise on the single upright chair, his arms resting across the back. It was hard to think of nothing.

He was noticing the room itself. The bed was a single one, narrow, on a wooden frame; on it a mattress and dust cover. On the woodwork at the head, photographs of film stars had been nailed clumsily with tin-tacks – male and female stars impartially. The curtain across the corner, making a wide cupboard, was of faded cretonne. A chest of drawers with built-in mirror. On the other side of the gimcrack door an expensive trunk of seasoned leather, bearing a police seal.

Nothing in the appointments of the room that could tell him anything. Think about nothing. Practically impossible.

Then think about Celia, sitting on the edge of the bed. She was conscious of his gaze, accepted it contentedly.

Before the cigarette was half finished he observed that she was sitting upright, straining, listening. Then he, too, heard footsteps on the matting of the stairs – then in the corridor on the landing – knew from her astonishment that they were the footsteps of an intruder.

He motioned her to silence as the footsteps approached the door. Noiselessly he got up, stood clear of the chair, ready for action.

The door handle was turned, but the door did not open. It was locked and the key was still in Habershon's pocket.

Soundlessly, Celia's lips formed the word 'burglar'. He shook his head. Burglars did not waste time in servants' quarters at the top of the house. Nor would the police sneak into the house without notice. Habershon's pulse quickened. Someone had left something of vital importance in that room and had come to remove it.

From the other side of the door came a faint scratching : then through the keyhole appeared the end of a pipe-cleaner – a thin wire covered with cotton.

Habershon held the key in readiness to use it and rush out should the unknown walk away. That pipe-cleaner could never pick the lock, but the intruder might try some other means. Better to let him go on trying – better still if he succeeded in picking the lock; for then he could be taken by surprise.

There was more fiddling with the pipe-cleaner, then silence. Celia's lips outlined the word 'window'. With her hand she signed that the window of the next room was sufficiently close. Again he shook his head, knowing that the intruder was still by the door.

There was one more attempt with the pipe-cleaner, helped apparently with a knife. Then, with a muttered oath, the unknown stumped away – but in the direction of the staircase.

Habershon thrust the key into the keyhole. Half-way, the key was blocked by the twisted pipe-cleaner.

In a couple of seconds he had opened the window. It faced front – there was no car parked in the drive. The next sill was less than four feet distant and the gutter was within arm's reach so that he could steady himself.

Getting out of the window was the most difficult part. Every second was valuable if he was to reach the man before he could get clear of the house. He risked the noise of smashing the adjacent window with his feet, then swung across and half tumbled into the room.

In the corridor he invested another three seconds, listening – heard the footsteps on the parquet of the first-floor landing.

He pulled the pipe-cleaner out of the lock, inserted the key and released Celia, warning her to make no noise. Then he made for the staircase, whipping off his shoes in the hope of surprising the man before he could leave the house.

On the first-floor landing, intuition brought him to a sudden stop.

Using the settee as cover he peered under the outstretched arm of the Burmese doll. Diagonally through the banister rail he had a foreshortened view of the staircase, so that he saw clearly only the man's feet.

The feet were coming up the stairs.

Habershon ran back to the top floor, two stairs at a time. Celia, waiting on the landing, had guessed what had happened and beckoned him into the room next to that which had been Bradburn's.

Before joining her he locked Bradburn's door, removed the key and reinserted the pipe-cleaner. He was in the other room with Celia before the intruder had left the second floor. Evidently the latter was in no hurry, believing the house to be empty.

'Did you see him?' whispered Celia.

'Only his feet.' It would be impossible to open the door even the fraction of an inch without its being seen from the corridor. The footsteps, which were on the heavy side, were approaching – stopped at Bradburn's door. There came the sound of a tool in use – an effective tool – the door was heard to open in less than a minute.

'We'll give him time to get busy,' whispered Habershon. 'Then I'll horn in and see what he's up to.'

He was aware that his own pulses were thudding, and knew the reason. He was taking a big bet with himself that the intruder was either Clawson or Keller – the heaviness of the step favouring Keller. Whichever it turned out to be, the man's behaviour definitely established guilty knowledge pivoting on the murdered girl.

'I'm going now,' he whispered. 'Lock yourself in here in case I'm unlucky.'

19

WITH elaborate precautions for silence Habershon opened
the door and shut it behind him. The door of Bradburn's
room was ajar. Through the space he could see the leather
travelling trunk, the lid raised, some of its contents scattered
over the floor. He crept closer. The other's back was towards
the door – he was probing something which looked like a
brocaded pin-cushion. Even so, Habershon realized with pro-
found disappointment that the man was neither Keller nor
Clawson in fact, an altogether different human type.

As Habershon flung the door wide open the other dropped
what he was holding and whipped a knife from his belt. A
tough-looking customer, with wide nostrils, a cauliflower
ear and little piglike eyes which glared at him savagely.

The next second the piglike lids were raised in amaze-
ment. The knife clattered to the floor and the tough customer held his hands up, palms outwards.

'Don't hit me, sir. I bin in the ring same as you, and I
can't take another blow. Doctor said I couldn't.'

Habershon himself was astonished. This was the last type
of man to attend amateur boxing events, even of champion-
ship class. The general public and the fraternity alike
ignored amateurs.

'You needn't put your hands up – I haven't got a gun.'

'If you 'ad a gun I'd be all right. Fifteen years I bin in the
ring, from a nipper – and now me nerve's gone on account
o' me health. It'll be murder if you hit me.'

'Who are you? What are you doing here?'

'The Kilburn Kid, they called me – and that's good
enough for now.' Losing his first fear, he became aggressive.
'Come to that, what you doin' yerself in this 'ere room?
Don't happen to be lookin' for a diamond, I suppose?'

So the dead girl had been connected with the theft of the
diamond! He sized up the Kilburn Kid. The battered face

was leering at him. Cringing, blustering, smirking – a small-time bully.

'I see you know all my secrets. I'd like to know some of yours. Or would you rather talk to the police?'

'I can see you callin' the cops!' The Kilburn Kid made a noise resembling a laugh. 'I'll be candid with yer. I thought the gal had swopped me for a gent – meanin' you. When I see in the evenin' paper she'd been scuppered, it sort o' changed things round a bit. Somethink must 'a' gone wrong. So I reckoned I'd come up and 'ave a look round. Here I meets a gent – meanin' you – and I see he's come to 'ave a look round too. Two's company, eh? Come on – you turn out them drawers – I'll finish this junk. It's fifty-fifty on the diamond – or neither of us gets nothink.'

'All nice and simple, Kid. But if I scuppered the girl and took the diamond, why should I share with you?'

'If she'd given it to you, you wouldn't 've scuppered her. Not there and then you wouldn't, anyway. You scuppered her because you caught 'er passing it to me – though you didn't know it was me. And you didn't know she was double-crossing me as well as you.'

The one certainty that emerged was that the Kilburn Kid had been planning to steal the diamond with the dead girl, and that he believed she had obtained possession of it.

'Not much of a tale, Kid. If I saw her pass the diamond to you, why have I come here to look for it?'

'I dunno what she told you. Me – I was down below – standin' on the flower-bed under this very winder soon as I saw the light go up in this room. She was to drop it out the winder in a bag. As I was sayin', the light goes up, I takes me position – she opens the winder and the bag blamed well hits me on the napper.' From his hip pocket he took out and unfolded a small ration-bag of khaki twill, hemmed at the mouth, with metal apertures inset for a draw-string: he loosened the string and took out a match-box, opened it and displayed a large pebble, obviously picked out of a gravel path.

This bit of real evidence carried conviction. The Kid was too crude to be capable of inventing it.

'I got away – all accordin' to plan. Then I open this 'ere bag and see what she's swung on me. So I come back, meanin' to pay her out – not knowin' as you'd done it for me. There was no light in the kitchen, an' the door bein' on the latch, I went in. In the alley leadin' to the hall I hear voices. There's no sign o' the gal, but I see the young lady —'

'What young lady?' interrupted Habershon.

'The one that lives 'ere with 'er aunt – so the gal told me. She calls out to someone : "I can't come – it'll make me feel sick," she says. And then someone says somethink and the young lady says : "It's small enough to go in the safe," she says.'

Habershon was about to protest when through the open window came the sound of a car in the drive.

'I didn't send for the cops, Kid. But it looks as if they've come. Keep away from the window.'

'Cor blimey, it won't do me no good to be found with you ! Mine ain't a swinging job – yours is !'

'Don't talk. Help me get this trunk shut up.' He picked up some of the litter – the Kid scooped in the rest. 'Give it to me.' He grabbed from the other a double handful of dress oddments and knick-knacks, thrust them into the trunk and pushed it back into its former position.

'Wait here !'

He had intended to consult with Celia. But she, too, had seen the police car and was hurrying downstairs.

'Quick, Kid !' he called in a shouted whisper.

Together they had reached the first floor before Celia had crossed the hall. Habershon made for Mrs Rabethorpe's bedroom and when the Kid was beside him locked the door.

'It's only a routine call,' he whispered. 'Maybe they'll go in a minute.'

'It's bein' with you that's worryin' me. What've they got against me? Nex' door to nothink ! And now you've lost my evidence. You grabbed the bag I showed you, along of all that junk, and it must be in the trunk.'

'It wasn't evidence of anything.'

'I could 'a shown it to the cops if you 'adn't pinched it.'

'Shut up! Here! Catch hold of this.'

From his considerable hoard Habershon detached a rubber-ringed wad of ten currency notes. The Kid pocketed the cash nervously.

'They're coming upstairs,' whispered Habershon. Presently he heard Kyle's voice on the landing.

'That's not our difficulty, Miss Fenton. We have the girl's prison record but nothing else. We want to trace her associates and get some light on what did happen when Mr Habershon was in the house.'

The Kilburn Kid whispered close to Habershon's ear:

'Then the young lady must be at 'ome and let him in?' As Habershon nodded, the Kid grinned. 'Then it was you she was tellin' that the stiff was small enough to go in the safe.'

'You've got the young ladies mixed,' muttered Habershon.

As soon as Kyle saw that the police seals on the dead girl's trunk had been broken he would be active.

'Come on!' ordered Habershon. Down the stairs as quickly as was compatible with silence, and out by the kitchen, through the garden to the Chrysler.

'Don't slam the door. Hold it until we get clear.'

While he drove, Habershon was dissecting the other's story. 'The young lady' might have used those words, but not the one who lived in the house with her aunt. Apart from the absurdity of supposing for one second that she could be Celia, there were questions of time and place to be thrashed out with the Kid.

'We can't get a drink for an hour,' said the Kid. 'What about a nice 'ot cupper tea?' Ahead was a lorryman's pull-up calling itself The Kozy Korner Kafe.

As the Kid got out and Habershon switched off the engine, a patrolling policeman appeared at the driver's window.

'No parking here!' he said, ill-temperedly. 'Can't you see the notice?'

'Sorry!' The notice unequivocally directed patrons to park behind the café.

When Habershon returned, the Kid was not in evidence.

He was not in the café. By the time Habershon realized that he had been given the slip, the Kid was half a mile away on a London-bound bus – beyond the cross-roads, so that pursuit in the Chrysler would be futile.

Over a cup of unwanted tea he brooded over his loss. He could almost certainly have extracted essential information from the Kid – once the misunderstanding about the 'young lady' had been cleared up. On the afternoon's work the profit and loss account was depressing. If it did not actually increase his own fear that he might have committed murder, it certainly increased the evidence against him.

He drove back to Central London, put the Chrysler in the same garage. Remembering that he had told Prinny he would not be back until seven he loitered in the West End. At Hampstead Tube Station he rang Celia.

'Sorry I had to run away like that without even saying thank you !'

'I'm glad you did. But I had to tell the Inspector you had been here, because he saw that trunk had been tampered with. I implied that you had come immediately after lunch, and he didn't press me as to what time you left.'

'Splendid ! I'd no idea you were so cunning !' He laughed.

'It was easy. He had only come to look on the back of those pin-up postcards. He found nothing there, but he did find that dress almost at once. He was angry because his men hadn't reported it. I told him how we had found it in our reconstruction, and he was properly impressed.'

'Did he notice the size of the dress ?'

'He asked me about it and I told him how we had tested it. It's better to be frank with the police, don't you think ?'

'Oh, of course !'

That, reflected Habershon, might make Kyle a little less anxious to accept the gang theory.

'If I were you,' Celia was saying, 'I'd keep away from Prinny's flat. Kyle asked me for her address. Fortunately, I don't know it. She's no particular friend of mine, and when I've met her here she has generally been staying with Mrs Wellard. She rang me up about ten minutes ago – quizzing.

She really wanted to know if I had seen you and of course I told her nothing.'

'I'm being very careful with Prinny. I shall see her again because I think it possible she knows something we don't – though I can't give any reason for thinking so. The grim part is that I shall have to keep away from your house too – for as long as I'm dodging about.'

'Oh, that doesn't matter!' Celia assured him.

'Doesn't it? It does to me, and I hoped it did to you! I'm that kind of fool.'

'No, Bruce, you're the other kind! Hasn't it dawned on you that I'm desperately anxious for you to get out of this mess? Goodbye!'

It was the way she said it, thought Habershon, smiling with fatuous benevolence at a man who was waiting to use the kiosk. His sense of proportion had slipped into neutral. Celia was desperately anxious for him to get out of the mess. Then the mess was as good as got out of. The trouble with the police would doubtless adjust itself. Hampstead wouldn't be at all a bad place to live in – he would ask Celia next time whether she would like Hampstead.

A pity he had to spend another night under Prinny's roof. But Prinny wasn't so bad if you handled her the right way.

Up the stone steps of the one-time stable quarters to Prinny's flat. Nice of her to give him a latchkey! How nice would she be if she knew he was spying on her? She would turn back into the hell-cat, with the searing finger-nails. The gang would do their best to kill him if they suspected he was dangerous.

'Is that you, Bruce?' Prinny was calling through the door of her room in the opposite wall of the little hall. As he answered she appeared in a bathrobe and a turban.

'Thank heavens you're all right!' she exclaimed. 'Did the other man get away too?'

'Yes, but —'

'Don't look as if you'd seen a ghost. I rang Celia as I was waiting at the theatre. She'd got as far as you slipping out of the house, when *PBX* cut us off.'

'I'll give you what news there is when I've cleaned up,' he said dully.

He went to his room, taking the steep stairs like an old man. Celia had definitely stated that she had told Prinny nothing – definitely Prinny and definitely nothing.

That changed the whole set-up.

20

HABERSHON took a hot shower to soothe his nerves, followed by a cold one to brace him up to facing the facts. But the only fact he faced was that Celia was not taking him seriously as a man – was running him on a string. Which meant that his own estimate of the personality of Celia Fenton was hopelessly at fault – as no doubt were all his other judgements – for instance his judgement of Prinny. Clawson, Keller, even of Mrs Wellard.

He made no change of plan. Whatever happened he must go on trying to dig out all the facts he could, or he would be charged with a murder which he might or might not have committed. He was probably wasting time by staying on in the flat. The tang of personal danger had vanished.

'My dear, you look dog-tired!' exclaimed Prinny. 'You're not going to talk until you've had a square meal. But first you need a drink. So do I.'

She sat him down and brought the drinks. She was good, he noticed, at bringing drinks. No bustle, but no dallying – a clink of glass at the right moment. She passed it to him in a straightforward, pally way.

She was sitting opposite him in silence, yet contriving to indicate that she was not ignoring him. Presently she brought him another drink, then went to the kitchen. He found himself hoping she would not be long.

In time she returned with a contraption which carried two trays. While they ate she chattered about her misadventures that afternoon at the theatre. Nonsense, of course, but restful and slightly stimulating. Why didn't more women study the art of rippling nonsense!

His eyes lingered on her dress – one of those dark greens that seem to clash with red hair at first, but turn into a sort of harmony as you go on looking. Not an evening dress exactly, though it could hardly be worn in the afternoon.

Prinny had a genius for being the right kind of girl at the right time.

He realized that the meal had finished and that she was sitting the trays into the carrier.

'One of the mistakes you make about me,' he said, picking up the carrier, 'is thinking I think that plates wash themselves.'

She smiled – a domestic sort of smile which made him feel as if they were sharing the flat as lovers.

'You're rather rushing me, aren't you, Bruce?' Her voice was low and vibrant. 'I love being rushed.'

Retreat from that kiss in the morning was going to be difficult. Why worry? Why should he not enjoy Prinny's company without imposing limits? He had made a fool of himself over Celia and the sooner he forgot it the better.

The kitchenette, about twice the size of a telephone kiosk, was also the scullery. The difficulty of moving about put him on his mettle. He even enjoyed the washing up. Above the deep-down sullenness was a superficial gaiety, which might turn to dare-devilry, if he didn't watch it.

Prinny was bending over the percolator when he returned to the sitting-room. She straightened up to her full height. Other things being equal, he reflected, tall women have a special gracefulness of their own. There could be nothing else in nature so white as her throat; her cheeks held colour which might be their own, for there was no lipstick on her mouth. The deep-down sullenness kept his gaze calmly, critically appreciative though he experienced an undefined disturbance, like that provoked in him by certain kinds of music.

He took his coffee over to the long settee, almost as far away from her as possible, and plunged into a report. There was no reason why he should keep her in the dark. No reason why he should not speak as frankly as he would have spoken to Celia.

'The dead girl – Bradburn – was trying to steal the diamond. Whether she succeeded, I don't know. She was working with a confederate – a broken-down tough, whom she cheated. The tough was hanging about outside the house the night I was there, and may have very valuable information. But he gave me the slip when he had told me little more than I've just told you. He's an ex-pugilist calling himself the Kilburn Kid. My next job is to find him.'

'Oh, how maddening!' exclaimed Prinny. 'George ought to hear this at once.'

'Then let's tell him.'

'We can't get at George tonight. And tomorrow he has to go to court – or chambers or whatever it is – over Elsie Rabethorpe's property. He won't really be able to attend to this until tomorrow evening.'

'Anyway, there's nothing he can do, unless he can find the Kilburn Kid, which is unlikely. Keller seems to be one of the interested parties. Why not tell him?'

'Poor Frank is much too addled – the car smash shook him up horribly. He went on raving this morning after you left. Not much about Bradburn. He's obsessed with Velfrage.'

'So am I, in a sense. Everything that proves Velfrage wasn't in that house when I entered it proves nonsense.' He went on : 'I shall keep my bargain with Clawson to find the diamond if I can, but what I personally most want to find is Velfrage. When I know what happened to him I may be able to prove I didn't kill that girl. As it is, I can't. In fact, I've produced some more evidence that I did.'

'But, Bruce dear, this morning we agreed that you didn't. When I sent you to gape at that Burmese doll —'

'That wouldn't prove anything to a jury. What d'you make of this?' He told her of his discoveries during the afternoon.

'All this was very vivid and clear. When I entered that room I knew I had come to the end of my quest. When I threw Celia's apron away I knew that I must have changed tactics.' He paused, and added : 'Doesn't it suggest that I found the girl there and strangled her?'

'You may have.' Prinny agreed as if she were agreeing with a fractious child. 'But equally you may have found somebody or something else which made you forget all about the girl?'

130

'In that girl's bedroom this afternoon,' continued Habershon, 'we found a dress – a parlourmaid's dress – black, with apron – which I recognized as the one I had torn off the girl. And the dress had a huge tear in it.'

'I'm sold on your tearing the dress, dear boy.' Prinny persisted in the role of comforter. 'Let's get on to the murder part.'

'Remember I was chasing the owner of the dress, my face bleeding from her nails —'

'Yes, but why should you think that Bradburn —?'

'Because the dress was much too small for you, Prinny,' said Habershon. 'You could never have squeezed into it.'

It was no slip of the tongue. The sullenness had found expression in a cool defiance of circumstance. He would no longer tell any lies to placate anybody – least of all Prinny, who was making herself so agreeable.

21

SHE came a step nearer. He did not expect an outburst and none came. She looked astonished for a moment, then merely puzzled. She took his coffee cup and put it on the tray.

'Don't be angry with me, Bruce, but I'm afraid I've lost the thread.' She was beside him on the settee, thrusting a hand in his. 'I'll pick it up if you like to go on, but if you don't want to, we'll leave it. I'm sure you hate talking about all this !'

'I'd better go on, dear.' He spoke with detachment. 'I have the feeling that I ought to tell you. It would be a relief to get it off my chest.' The whiteness of her skin seemed to radiate through the short sleeves, turning them from dark green to pale green. He added : 'Mainly, because you have been so kind to me.'

He began by reminding her that Celia had helped him with his blackout in the hall of Woodville, with Kyle and Mrs Rabethorpe looking on.

'It began to work almost at once. I had a vivid memory of scrapping with two men and two women in that library. I opened the door – and faced two men and two women. Mrs Wellard clicked into place as the woman who had been carrying a bag with a peacock's eye design. I was equally certain that Keller and Clawson were the two men I had fought.'

'And what about me ?' she asked.

'You were far the worst !' He opened her hand, stroked her fingers, felt the tips of her nails. 'I was convinced that I had felt these on my face. You see, it's this gorgeous red mop of yours – though that poor little devil's hair was a doubtful ginger.'

'And you thought it was *my* dress you tore off ! No wonder you seemed a shy young man at our first meeting. You didn't know where to look, did you ! What did that Scotland Yard man say when you told him?'

His innate cautiousness warned him not to implicate Detective Inspector Kyle.

'He didn't say much. He was very friendly about it. He's had a lot of experience with drunks and hotheads "remembering" things that couldn't have happened. He wanted me to go home to bed and not try to rush things.'

'And he convinced you I'm not a brilliantly clever crookess?'

'He wasn't as absorbed in you as I was. Anyway, he didn't convince me, though he may have started me doubting. When Clawson turned up at my bungalow I still more or less believed it. I thought I'd play ball and see what these crooks – meaning you and your friends – were up to. Then – well, something I overheard you say to Clawson in here last night made it clear that there couldn't be a criminal conspiracy between you.'

'What did I say? Something nice?'

'Never mind! Listen! A bit of the theory survived this morning. Until the Burmese-doll incident. Obviously, if you were a crook you would encourage me to believe that I had killed that girl. And you'd have managed to work in Velfrage too. Instead, you put yourself to trouble solely to give me peace of mind. That registered right under my hide, Prinny. When I said you'd been so kind, I meant it – and I didn't mean the eats.'

'You're rather a dear, aren't you, Bruce! It's a charming way of saying you no longer see me as something pretty beastly.'

He frowned.

'I wish you hadn't said "see me",' he exclaimed. 'Visual impressions like this aren't affected by reason. I might prove to myself that you were miles away at the time – I could still close my eyes and "see" you got up as a parlourmaid —'

'Before or after the dress-tearing act?'

'You're laughing at me!'

'And you must laugh at yourself!' Her head slithered to his shoulder, drowning thought in a copper-red mist that held the perfume of unknown flowers. 'Poor boy, you've had to bear too much. I think I'm going to cry.'

There was a certain genuineness in Prinny. No doubt she had genuinely cried over the sorrows of other men and as genuinely rejoiced in their triumphs. She would repeat the whole process with other men after he had gone.

In the meantime —

'Just go right on thinking of me and nothing else,' she invited.

In the small hours of the morning she slipped away from him and, masking the telephone with a fur coat, rang Clawson. He answered with a snarl.

'What's the matter, George?'

'I went to the docks for nothing! Gallerton wasn't there. The passenger was another man of the same name. Maybe our man is crossing by air. If I can find out, you'll have to meet him and head him off until the judge has signed. Why did you ring?'

'Stop being sorry for yourself, George. I want to talk about my nice guest.'

'On the phone?'

'I know what I'm doing. Get this. He had a visual impression —'

'A what?'

'An impression that you and I and Frank and Margo were the crooks he ran into in Woodville that night – and that we were the people he beat up.'

'Huh! Has he told anybody besides you?'

'Try to listen, darling. He told the police – last night – and they laughed at him. He laughed at it himself tonight —'

'Because you had your arms round him?'

'It's nothing to do with that! He said he had found the dress he tore off the girl. In her bedroom. Under her bed. And it was much too small to fit me! What on earth does he mean by that, George? . . . Are you still there, George? That dress —'

'N'em mind now. Anything else, about – anything else?'

'Heaps! Have you ever heard of a tough called the Kilburn Kid?'

'No, but I can find out. Hold everything until I get clear tomorrow evening – if I do get clear.'

22

NEXT day, a little late for his appointment at one-thirty, Habershon entered the Casserole Café, to find that Miss Parker had already started her lunch. A waitress, in the manner of her kind, demanded attention.

'Oh, anything – bring me the same as this lady is having.'

Miss Parker promptly countermanded the order.

'My friend means that he would like roast beef, plain boiled potatoes and cabbage, but no horseradish.' To Habershon she said reprovingly : 'Have you forgotten that curry gives you indigestion?'

'I promise I'll remember it next time, Miss Parker,' grovelled Habershon as he sat down. 'Have you anything for me?'

'I need not trouble you with office routine, as no doubt you have enough on your mind. For the rest, I have that detective agency's report, but you'd better have your lunch before you read it.'

'Thank you, Miss Parker,' murmured Habershon. 'Does anything stick out?'

'Yes. That Miss Loftus whom you seemed to think so important.'

'She is important. What do they know about her?'

'She's a domestic servant,' announced Miss Parker. 'A housemaid.'

For a moment he was startled by a seeming coincidence.

'Oh no she isn't!'

'I am not prepared to argue about it. I merely quote the detective's report. He describes how she left the flat in Hampstead, made purchases at a fishmonger's, a grocer's, a dairy and a chemist's and then drove herself in her employer's car —'

'The fathead has been shadowing the wrong girl!'

'I think not.' He was startled again, because Miss Parker never used that phrase unless she knew she was right. 'The car was a two-seater Morris. The registered name was that of the other woman on your list – Mrs Wellard. Loftus drove to Mrs Wellard's house, The Chestnuts. In due course the detective knocked at the door, falsely describing himself as an insurance agent. Loftus, wearing a cap and apron, was cleaning the hall.'

'H'm! That doesn't mean she's a housemaid.'

But it did mean that Prinny had lied when she said she had spent the afternoon at the theatre. If she was next door to Woodville, she might well have seen him from a rear window when he was sneaking through the garden with the Kilburn Kid.

In that case, Celia's report of the telephone conversation was true. Celia, as she had said, had told Prinny nothing. He was so inordinately pleased that he was not even angry with Prinny. Poor Prinny! She had merely told a face-saving tarradiddle because she regarded it as undignified to clean another woman's hall.

'Are you listening to me?' demanded Miss Parker.

'I'm very sorry!' Hedging with Miss Parker never paid. 'Were you telling me something about George Clawson?'

'He was picked up on leaving his office. He went by train to Southampton to meet the *Caldragon* from New York, but returned alone on the midnight train. Keller, who is injured, is believed to have gone to bed at midday, and in a drunken condition. Of Mrs Wellard there is no report. Do you think,' added Miss Parker, 'that any purpose can possibly be served by having people followed about like this?'

'One never knows. Anyhow, it's one of the basic principles of detection.'

'But you are not a detective!' Habershon opened his mouth and shut it again because there was nothing that could be said. Miss Parker ploughed on : 'Is not a detective the product of specialist training plus practical experience?'

'I don't think you realize what I'm up against. It isn't a matter of soothing my own conscience. I am in danger of being charged —'

'That is why I think it would be so much safer to leave it to the police, who understand that sort of thing.'

It was hopeless. He had never yet convinced Miss Parker of anything, once she had made up her mind.

'You are quite right in supposing that I shall probably fail,' he confessed, feeling a trifle heroic. 'But it's now too late to turn back. It is absolutely essential that I should keep out of the way of the police for the present.'

'But you're *not* keeping out of their way. Mr Kyle tried to catch your eye as you came in. He's having lunch over there – with two of his colleagues.'

'Oh my hat! And you didn't even think it worth mentioning!'

'I have mentioned it! He seemed to be expecting you. He asked me to tell you, if you turned up, that he would like to see you when you've had your lunch. D'you think you could manage the milk pudding? You must take care of your health, or you'll make things still worse.'

By her carelessness – rather, by her sheer inability to understand the point of view of a fugitive – she had led him into a police trap. Useless to reproach her. Useless, even, to refuse the milk pudding. He was half-way through it when Kyle approached the table.

'Ah, Mr Habershon, I've been trying to get in touch with you. Could you come along to my office?'

'Right!' Habershon was ready to abandon the milk pudding.

'Not now! Sorry I can't give you a lift. Would three o'clock be convenient?'

'I'll be there,' promised Habershon, thinking it very civil of Kyle to accept his parole. Miss Parker would certainly have made a scene if Kyle had arrested him there and then.

'I'm so glad that's settled,' said Miss Parker, when Kyle had gone.

Habershon laughed bitterly.

'The next job is to find a good solicitor,' he said. 'Poor Velfrage used to do my personal work.'

'Isn't it premature – and perhaps a little unkind – to say *"poor"* Velfrage? We may still hope that it's only a case of temporary loss of identity. I feel in my bones that Mr Velfrage is alive.'

'If he's alive,' said Habershon, 'it means that he has turned crook.'

At a few minutes to three Habershon was being shown into Kyle's room at Scotland Yard.

'That's the distinguished caller's chair,' grinned Kyle. 'Sit down and relax. I congratulate you on not turning up at the inquest on the red-head. If you had, we couldn't have got a month's adjournment on formal evidence.'

'I was dodging you as well as the inquest,' sighed Habershon. 'The gang are shielding me from you people in return for my efforts to remember how I stole the diamond.'

'Good man!' enthused Kyle. 'That's pretty fast work!'

'Only, the gang isn't a gang!'

'D'you mean you were wrong when you said you recognized them?' Kyle was affronted.

'No. I don't go back on my recognition. I mean that things must have happened which I did not see, or did not understand. I mean that I do not, now, believe that they are a criminal gang committing murders and stealing the diamond.'

'Well, I'm jiggered!' Kyle's surprise was positively theatrical. 'What's behind all this, then?'

'A chain of small incidents – yes, I know all about the weakest link, but there isn't one.'

Beginning with Clawson's arrival at the bungalow, Habershon gave a full outline, including the conversation overheard between Prinny and Clawson and the events of the previous afternoon, ending with the burglarious intrusion of the Kilburn Kid.

'So you did see Bradburn and speak to her!' ejaculated Kyle.

'Yes. I can see that my statement is useless as evidence but at least it makes me sure I didn't kill her.'

Kyle turned away to ring Index and ask them to look up the Kilburn Kid.

'So you reckon all this proves they can't be a gang?'

'You saw that dress. And I daresay Miss Fenton satisfied you that it was yards too small for Prinny Loftus. In other words, I can't have torn it off Prinny. I recognize that you have no alternative to arresting me, and – thanks for doing it like this!'

Kyle frowned.

'If it'll put your mind at ease,' he said ponderously, 'I promise to arrest you the first real chance I get. You can have both murders, if you insist – and the theft of the diamond as a fall-back.'

Before Habershon could say anything, Kyle went on :

'You're a shipping agent, aren't you? Well now, I happen to own a sailing dinghy. I also own a small silver mug awarded for sailing that dinghy in a club competition. But that doesn't make me think I could drop my present job and set up as a shipping agent.'

Miss Parker's taunt. *'You're not a detective.'* But this man was not Miss Parker.

'I'm sorry you think I'm such an ass as to try to teach you your business,' he said stiffly. 'But I must point out that the principles of reasoning are universal. Now, I don't know anything about crime and criminals —'

'You're telling me!' grinned Kyle.

'But I do know the elementary principles of business – which you, apparently, do not. Please forgive me if that sounds offensive. But look at your actions from a business point of view. You are building a huge edifice of crime on the assumption that those four persons have conspired to steal the Rabethorpe diamond. What's that diamond worth by the time it has been sold to a fence? Not the hundred thousand pounds which the American, Sundius Gallerton, will pay for it in the open market, sold to him as the Rabethorpe diamond. What's it worth sold under cover – and after it's been made unrecognizable? Two thousand? A thousand?'

'I should think a thousand 'ud be a good price, after it's been cut up,' admitted Kyle.

'Right! Mrs Wellard owns a decent house and two cars, one of 'em a Rolls-Royce. The two men aren't on their beam ends. Prinny Loftus is comfortable and well dressed, with all the small expensive things she wants. What would the carve-up be after meeting expenses? Doubtfully a couple of hundred apiece – for a lot of careful planning and hard work and the risk of penal servitude – to say nothing of the gallows. The Kilburn Kid – yes, perhaps! But not that crowd, Mr Kyle. They can add up.'

Kyle had been listening with something approaching respect.

'I think you've got something there,' he said, thoughtfully. 'Keep going.'

'I can't. My account of what happened that night must be very incomplete. My positive statements are true. But other facts must have dove-tailed – facts which would provide a reasonable explanation, if we knew them. I now remember everything up to the moment when I threw that torn dress under the bed. The blackout coming then strongly suggests to me that I may have killed the girl.'

'I wish you'd stop making things suggest things,' grumbled Kyle. 'I'm going to give you some information now. It's confidential and it's against regulations. I'm telling you because I want you to keep up the gag that we're trying to arrest you – I want you to go on living with the gang —'

'The gang!' Habershon's voice indicated despair of making the other understand.

'You're going to pay for interrupting me. Listen. That torn dress that's worrying you wasn't under that bed when we searched the whole house – especially that girl's room and her things.' He paused. 'Go on. Ask me how I know my men weren't lying to me to cover up their missing it – I can see it in your eyes.'

'How d'you know they weren't lying?' asked Habershon obediently.

'Because I know they looked under that girl's bed. Because they found something under that bed and brought it to me, wagging their tails like the faithful doggie in the picture. And what's more – I'll show you what they found.'

Kyle opened a drawer and brought out a small dispatch-case.

'Velfrage's!' exclaimed Habershon.

Kyle nodded. After a long silence, he asked : 'Does that remind you of anything that happened in that girl's room?'

'N-no. That dispatch-case reminds me of nothing but itself – when Velfrage changed cars.'

Kyle replaced the dispatch-case.

'That dress was put under that bed *after* our search. We don't know why yet. Maybe it was put there for you to find, just as you did find it.' He continued, elaborating his own thought : 'That dress was put under that bed by, or at the instigation of, someone who had heard your tale about tearing a girl's dress off her back.'

'That limits it to Clawson and Co, and Mrs Rabethorpe,' cried Habershon.

'*And* Miss Fenton,' said Kyle.

Habershon scarcely heard the last. New theories sky-rocketed and collided.

'Your talk about the business side of the diamond,' Kyle was saying. 'There's a twist in it. You can forget the Kilburn Kid as a principal, though he may be a witness. The diamond was stolen from Velfrage, the theft taking less than three minutes. That means it was stolen by the people you scrapped with in the library. There was no time for some clever trick. They had to take it from him by force. Velfrage could have identified them afterwards. That means they must have planned his murder as well.'

'For a doubtful two hundred apiece?'

'Exactly! They would not have done all that for so little.'

'Well, if they didn't kill him, where is he?'

'I don't know – but I do know where he would be this afternoon if – if he could be. I want you to come along with me.'

Downstairs they entered a waiting car.

'The Law Courts,' Kyle told the driver.

'Of course! Mrs Rabethorpe's claim!' exclaimed Habershon. 'You don't imagine Velfrage will be there, do you?'

'We're not allowed to use imagination in our job,' chuckled Kyle. 'Wonders do happen. And if they don't happen this time, you or I may pick up a cross reference on why he's not there.'

23

ON the way to the Law Courts, Habershon showed Kyle the reports from the detective agency.

'Clawson went to Southampton in the hope of meeting the American, Gallerton,' mused Kyle aloud. 'The man who's burning to pay a hundred thousand smackers for the diamond. And Clawson hasn't got the diamond.'

'Makes nonsense,' agreed Habershon.

'When facts make nonsense it generally means you're holding 'em wrong side up,' remarked Kyle. 'Here we are. You needn't wait, driver.'

In the main hall Kyle consulted the Cause List.

' "*Rabethorpe v. Rabethorpe. Originating Summons. Before Mr Justice Holbeach in Chambers*",' he read, ' "*Court 194a*". When we get inside, keep your head down, Clawson will be there anyway, and he mustn't see you.'

In the corridor an official stopped them.

'Judge in chambers in that court. Public not admitted. Gallery door locked.'

Kyle showed his card.

'Scotland Yard. Okay, Inspector, I'll tell the judge's marshal.'

'But you might let us in, meantime. If the judge notices me he'll recognize me. I had a lot to do with him when he was Treasury counsel.'

In the empty gallery, Kyle looked down on a court-room containing fewer than a dozen persons. Counsel was addressing the judge, standing close to the Bench and speaking in low, conversational tones – but not about the Rabethorpe case. The fact that no witnesses are heard – and that principals are discouraged from attending – reduces formality to a minimum. On what was normally the witness's bench, George Clawson was chatting in a whisper with his counsel.

'No wonders this time!' whispered Kyle. 'Just Clawson!'

After a few minutes counsel finished. The judge signed a

document and made a joke. He was still enjoying his own joke when his clerk announced :

'Rabethorpe *v.* Rabethorpe is the next, my lord.'

Counsel left Clawson and approached the Bench. The judge glanced at the papers the clerk had placed before him.

'Elsie Amelia Rabethorpe,' the judge read aloud. 'Commonly called Mrs Rabethorpe. Why?'

'I am insufficiently instructed on that point, my lord,' said counsel, smirking a little, 'but I infer that my client's way of life has been such that to proclaim herself a spinster would be to invite disbelief.'

'Elegantly expressed, Mr Seaton.' The judge returned his attention to the papers in the case. 'I have not read your preamble.'

'I think I can save your lordship the trouble. In brief outline, the testator, William Rabethorpe, was divorced when his daughter, the claimant, was aged three, the mother obtaining custody. The mother removed herself and the child to Belgium, and father and daughter never met again. There seems to have been some malice on the mother's side, for she caused the child's surname to be changed to her own family name – that of Gallerton, my lord. The deed poll was never executed in Britain, so the child, never having married, remains Rabethorpe. When the mother died, which occurred when the child was twenty-two, the child, then a very headstrong and – er – broad-minded young woman, my lord – ignored the change of name, called herself "Miss" and subsequently "Mrs" Rabethorpe, though she seems to have believed that her father was dead, for she never wrote to him, or otherwise approached him.

'The solicitors in the case, as trustees, made every attempt to find this lost heiress of a fortune amounting to some quarter of a million pounds – to say nothing of the notorious Rabethorpe diamond, my lord. The trustees had no success until a couple of years ago, when the firm, in the person of Mr Velfrage, stumbled upon a clue and – as I feel sure your lordship will decide – established incontrovertible proof of identity.'

For some ten minutes, while counsel remained nearly

motionless, the judge studied the documents. At one point he picked up a pen.

'My hat!' whispered Habershon. 'I'd no idea it was so easy to claim a fortune.'

'It's only a rubber-stamp job if there's no opposition,' returned Kyle.

The judge was now turning the papers impatiently.

'Your identification has not been completed, Mr Seaton.'

'Oh, my lord!' Counsel contrived to combine a ritual deference with the suggestion that his lordship had made an absurd mistake.

'You submit a verbal statement that the deed poll was not executed in this country, but there is no affidavit to that effect. I shall not accept the negative certificate from Somerset House without an affidavit, executed in this case by – er – Mr Velfrage. Is Mr Velfrage present?'

'No, my lord, only his representative.'

'Then this will have to be adjourned. I repeat, I must have Mr Velfrage's affidavit. The signature of the firm will not be enough, as the other affidavits have all been executed by Mr Velfrage.'

Clawson was already at counsel's side, whispering energetically.

'My lord,' said counsel, 'I am instructed that the affidavit has in fact been executed. Mr Clawson, Mr Velfrage's representative, has handled it and can produce it. Its omission appears to be an act of unpardonable carelessness – for which, of course, my lord, I must accept responsibility and do profoundly apologize. In the circumstances, I do beg that your lordship will not adjourn, which would mean our going to the bottom of the list.'

The judge glanced at the clock. It was already past four.

'Very well, I will break instead of adjourning,' he said. Heading off counsel's effusive thanks, he continued: 'But I'm not going to penalize others for your carelessness. If that affidavit is not on my desk here when I come in tomorrow morning, I shall immediately call the next case. As you have remarked, you will then go to the bottom of the list.'

Inspector Kyle and Habershon crept out of the gallery,

leaving the Law Courts by the northern exit, to avoid a chance meeting with Clawson.

'You heard the name "Gallerton"?' asked Kyle.

'Yes, but the papers have already mentioned that he was a kinsman. Are we any the wiser for squatting in that gallery?'

'If Clawson produces by ten tomorrow morning a document signed by Velfrage, Mrs Rabethorpe steps into a quarter of a million pounds. No affidavit tomorrow – no fortune tomorrow!'

'But Clawson told his counsel —'

'Clawson didn't tell his counsel to say the document could be produced in a few minutes, his office being barely two hundred yards away.'

'You mean he wants time to forge the affidavit?'

'I'm not sure he's going to forge it, but I'm sure he's going to produce it tomorrow morning. There's a chance you might pick up something in that flat. And – look here, Habershon! – don't stick your neck out with that crowd.'

Habershon did not understand, so Kyle added :

'I can't get permission for you to carry a gun. And anyway you're quicker with that knockout. Don't argue about it – just keep your eyes well open, and don't turn your back on 'em if you can help it.'

Habershon pondered the advice on the way to the garage. It was difficult to take it seriously. Through Prinny he had dispelled any suspicions they might have had that he was spying on them.

He took out the Chrysler, drove to Hampstead, and garaged it locally. Movement would be easier now that he was no longer dodging the Yard, but only pretending to.

He let himself into the flat and called Prinny, without receiving an answer. It was a little after five. He went along the passage that looked like the corridor of a train to the sitting-room. On his way back to the hall he opened the cupboard door and had another look at the Burmese doll, an exact replica of the doll on the amber-upholstered bench in Mrs Rabethorpe's house.

Funny she should take all that elaborate trouble to ease

his mind – if she was a member of a gang. And then there was that conversation with Clawson he had heard through the floor-boards, which made nonsense of the gang theory.

'You're not a detective.' Certainly, he admitted, he came unstuck whenever he tried a spot of detection. He had been too ingenious in talking to Kyle about the business side of the diamond theft. He had proved the diamond could not have been stolen, when it had been stolen.

He turned back to the hall and knocked at Prinny's bedroom, then opened the door. No doubt about having the flat to himself. Up the ladder-like stairs to his bedroom.

He mustn't try to be a detective, but he must try to find out things, which meant nosepoking and ferreting and eaves-dropping. There was that locked door in the opposite wall of his room. And there was a short length of wire positively asking to be pulled out of the damaged fireguard on the electric stove.

The lock was a cheap affair. He found he could work the tongue in and out almost as easily as with a key. The room, as he had supposed, was a lumber-room, with re-markably little lumber in it. Prinny, he had noticed, was very tidy.

Half a dozen framed pictures leaning against the wall, all of railway engines. A dressmaker's headless dummy, clearly Prinny's luscious contour limned in bombazine! A couple of trunks and a large wicker travelling-basket. It was a touring actor's basket and it was filled with fancy theatrical cos-tumes. He turned them over rapidly, hardly hoping to find a black dress that would fit Prinny. A black dress torn to uselessness, of course!

Next, the trunks. The first was empty. The second con-tained beach and holiday garments, shorts, a stout pair of nailed boots. He rummaged and came upon a shallow wooden box covering a third of the floor of the trunk. In-side was a collection of studio photographs of Prinny. Prinny advertising a Mediterranean cruise, a hair tonic, a cigarette, an undergarment – and not a few of Prinny ad-vertising, he presumed, the human race itself.

There was, too, a series of group photographs – theatrical

groups in which he had to search for Prinny. They were amateur companies, he gathered from the inscriptions, supported by the more or less professional talents of Prinny. Some of her costumes he was able to connect with those in the wicker basket.

'*Thanton Amateur Dramatic Society in* Marjory Gets Married ... *Betsy: Miss Prinny Loftus (prof.)*'

Betsy was a parlourmaid character. And Prinny was wearing a fancy parlourmaid's costume with bib and apron.

He turned back to the basket, picked up the costumes one by one and shook them out, without result. Disappointed, he relocked the lumber-room and went downstairs.

He had barely reached the sitting-room when he heard Prinny returning. He went to the hall to meet her.

'Hullo, darling!' She said it as if she meant it. 'Don't come near me – I'm greasy and grimy. If you feel devoted, turn on that geyser for me – not too fast or the water runs cold.'

The bathroom was little bigger than the kitchen. Half the space was taken up by a full-size bath fitted with a shower enclosed in glass panels. In defiance of the safety regulations, what little space was left was occupied by electric gadgets – for drying one's hair, for thumping one's person with a rubber fist, for this, that and the other.

When he had finished with the geyser, the telephone rang.

'That's George!' Prinny called through the open door of her room. 'Take it for me, there's a dear!'

He lifted the receiver.

'Is that you, Prinny?'

'She's in her bath.'

'Then don't bother her. D'you mind telling her I'll be along about nine?'

Habershon relayed the message through the bathroom door and added : 'I'll clear out before he turns up.'

'There's no need. Stick around. I'll explain in a minute.'

When she emerged, in a white peignoir and turban, she thrust her arm in his.

'You aren't inclined to be dramatic about George, are you?' She sat him in an art wicker-chair by her dressing-

148

table, which creaked under his weight and had one groggy leg. 'My stuff about jealousy the other night was a light-hearted gag, at which you were both meant to laugh politely. I'm deeply indebted to George and I'd do anything for him except kiss him. Besides that, he has a rather fearsome female of his own. So forget him.'

'I thought p'r'aps you wanted to discuss things with him.'

'I want you to tell him what you told me last night. Not what you told me about *me* – he's too much of a prude for that! I mean about the Kilburn Kid and the rest of it. It might give him an idea about where to look for the diamond. He's no fool, though he is stodgy.'

He was faintly surprised that she had not herself told George. On Kyle's assumption that they were a gang, she would have told him at once.

'I'll do just what you say, of course.'

'That's the perfect answer!' She opened a wardrobe and studied the contents. 'You're a man who notices one's dress, unfortunately. That means a different dress every night. I can keep it up until – yes – next Thursday. Tonight I think we'll be on the prim side.'

She writhed into a simple affair in a colour which he deemed to be dark violet. Again there was a colour clash and again her rich physicality toned it to a vibrant harmony.

He met her eyes, to find that she in turn was appraising him.

'I'm the kind of woman you admire, but don't like!' she said, disconcerting him.

'You're not a kind of woman – you're a special invention of your own!' He met her gaze squarely. 'You've spotted that I don't trust you. But that's only because I don't trust myself. I may be a killer.'

'Specializing in red-heads, Bruce?' She took both his hands, raised them and pressed them to her throat. 'Here's another red-head!'

To Habershon it was a moment of revelation. On the staircase, that night, he had cried out that he would kill her

– he had tracked her from room to room like an angry lout. But he knew now that he would have curled up in horror from the act of strangling a woman.

Prinny slipped into his arms.

'Killer my foot!' she murmured, her lips against his.

24

THEY were finishing a tray-dinner in the sitting-room when the bell rang.

'If you'll let George in, I can put the things together.'

Habershon opened the door, not to George Clawson but to Mrs Wellard.

'H'm!' It was a dowager's grunt of disapproval. 'Good evening!' A shade of geniality. 'I understand that you're helping George find that diamond.'

'Haven't had much luck yet,' returned Habershon.

'A most unpleasant business altogether! Have you seen George? I'm wondering how he got on with the judge – Mrs Rabethorpe's claim – I expect you know all about that?'

Rather crude, thought Habershon. Prinny saved him from small-talking to Mrs Wellard by telling him to take the trays away. He spun the job out until George Clawson arrived.

'Hullo!' Clawson sounded disappointed, as if he had expected Prinny to get rid of Habershon for the evening. 'How've you been getting on, Habershon?'

'I've stumbled on something Prinny thinks you ought to hear. I'll tell you now, and then I'll vamoose for a couple of hours. Mrs Wellard doesn't like me.'

He told Clawson about the Kilburn Kid.

'It points that Bradburn was trying to get the diamond. And that's about all,' said Clawson irritably.

'I didn't guarantee results, Clawson,' snapped Habershon.

'Don't get huffy, old man! I was only inquiring whether you'd filled up any of the blanks.'

'I've proved to myself that I went to that girl's room. I found the dress I'd torn off her – under the bed.'

If Clawson had put it there, his face was giving nothing away.

'But you'd remembered that much the other night.'

'The size of the dress proved that the girl couldn't have been Prinny!'

'Prinny? How the devil does Prinny come into it?'

'She'll tell you. I'm going out.'

Habershon put on his overcoat. Clawson said nothing. But he waited in the hall until Habershon had gone, listened to his footsteps descending the stone staircase.

As Habershon passed through the archway, a taxi drew up. Out of it, with some difficulty, stepped Keller, his face still bandaged.

'Can I help you, Keller?'

'No—no, thanks!' He peered into the darkness. 'It's Habershon, isn't it? No thanks,' he repeated. 'I can manage.'

The taxi drove off. Keller hobbled through the archway.

A full conference of the gang – if it is a gang, mused Habershon. Now would be the time to settle that particular question.

He stepped back through the archway. A flood of light at the head of the stone staircase told him when Keller was admitted to the flat.

Up the stone stairs quickly and silently, pulling out his latchkey. The best moment to get upstairs would be while Keller was entering the sitting-room.

As he opened the door he could hear Prinny's voice in the corridor, chatting to Keller. He turned the Yale latch as he shut the front door behind him so that the tongue would not click.

When he heard the sitting-room door shut he crept up the ladder-like stairs to his room. Using only his torch, he removed his shoes and stepped on the bare boards at the listening point.

As before, every small noise in the sitting-room was audible.

'I know I look frightful, but I'm all right except for a little stiffness in the joints,' Keller was saying. 'You exaggerate everything, Margo – always.'

'When you two've done quarrelling, p'r'aps I can get a word in edgewise.' Clawson was still irritable. 'Here's how we stand. You needn't think any more about that affidavit.

It's all set. The signature is perfectly steady. Tomorrow the judge will give his assent before he starts his day's work. The whole thing is automatic. We don't want to chortle until it's over, but you can take it from me that it's all settled.'

'Except the problem of Velfrage himself.' This from Mrs Wellard.

'That's what's spoiling my beauty sleep,' Prinny chipped in. 'Just Velfrage!'

'As far as you girls are concerned, there is no problem of Velfrage,' said Clawson.

'That's ever so manly of you, George dear,' said Prinny, 'but we would like to *know*!'

'Calling me a girl isn't enough!' contributed Mrs Wellard.

'Questions! That's the devil of working with women! Why, it's against your own interest to poke and quiz! If there's something you don't know, you're not responsible for that something – and then you don't break down in cross-examination.'

'But, darling, we don't want a cross-examination to not break down in. Of course. I don't know how we stand legally —'

'I do!' rasped George. 'I'm begging you, for your own health as well as mine, to do what I tell you without asking why you're doing it. Now listen, Margo. Gallerton is staying at the Parnassus. He wants to meet Elsie. I don't want him to meet Elsie. She chatters – hands out unnecessary information with every breath. I can't stall a man like Gallerton – nobody could. You'll have to be Elsie.'

'How can I? He'll talk about family history.'

'Elsie doesn't know her family history. Gallerton won't probe – it's only a sentimentality on his part. At the end of half an hour of polite talk he can conclude you're not a very friendly sort of person. There's no snag. Gallerton never saw his aunt after she left Rabethorpe, nor the child. Be at the Parnassus at eleven tomorrow morning and I'll make the introductions.'

There was a short silence before Clawson added :

'Margo will have to leave about ten. Prinny, you'll have to be on duty in the morning instead of the afternoon. Don't be late, mind!'

'All right! Bruce can get his own breakfast. He's surprisingly handy with housework.'

'Bruce? Oh, Habershon! We've had enough of that young man. He made a damn funny remark about you tonight – that dress-tearing business – he said you'd explain.'

'I expect you riled him,' said Prinny. 'There's nothing to blow up about. It's only that he told that Yard man – Kyle – that I was the girl in the case and you were the toughs.'

'Good God!' cried Keller. 'Only that!'

'Anyone might mistake you for a tough with a gentility complex, George. I don't know about you, Frank.'

'What did he say about me?' demanded Mrs Wellard.

'Only that he snatched the bag from you while you were riding on his back, or something. We laughed over it. So did Scotland Yard, I gather.'

'Obviously, or they'd have tackled us,' said Clawson. 'Habershon has been a curse from the first. That memory stuff!'

'It's genuine!' Surprisingly, this came from Mrs Wellard. 'He wouldn't fool Celia. He's in love with her.'

'That, my dear Margo, is bilge!' said Prinny. 'But I agree that it did no harm, telling the police. And he himself doesn't believe it now.'

'There's always the danger of coincidence,' put in Keller. 'He might "remember" something which might happen to fit in and pickle us. I read a case —'

'I made a first-class bloomer in approaching him, and I admit it,' said Clawson.

'Don't be so magnanimous, George, or I shall cry.'

'If our Mr Habershon were to take it into his head to bump himself off, I should feel a lot better about it.'

'George, you're not going to try any *games* with my beautiful young man! God help you if you do, George! And besides, he's your one hope of collecting the diamond.'

'I don't want to collect the diamond. The police can do that.'

Habershon, in the room above, had the sensation of his attention fading out – was convinced that he had jumbled Clawson's words into meaninglessness.

'That damned diamond!' growled Clawson. 'I'm not superstitious. But when Velfrage put it in his pocket at the office, I had the feeling that we were sunk. I tried to persuade him that it was dangerous to carry it, but he snubbed me.'

'But in the legend it's only dangerous to the owner.'

'Then it's trying out a new line on us! What happens to us when we get in the way of that diamond? First, out of the sky tumbles Habershon. Then that servant girl, who tried to steal it. That pins a murder on to it and we have the police buzzing round. Anyhow, the girl is dead and out of it, but Habershon is alive – perhaps a darned sight more alive than any of you realize.'

There was a long silence, in which Habershon tried to snatch at the facts. Clawson wanted the police to find the diamond. Clawson had tried to persuade Velfrage not to carry it – in other words, Clawson had not intended to steal the diamond in Mrs Rabethorpe's house that night. His own theory that no man with a head for business would attempt to steal the diamond!

'Good Lord, look at the door!' cried Clawson.

'I wish you wouldn't explode like that!' Mrs Wellard was complaining. 'What's the matter with the door?'

'It's shut. Habershon could have come back without our knowing it. He'll be a bit sore if he's heard what I said about him.'

'He'll hear you saying that, too,' said Mrs Wellard.

'You all stay here – I'll go up and make sure.'

25

IT would be touch and go, thought Habershon, whether he could work the lock of the inner room in time. He lost three seconds finding it with his torch. Then he seemed to himself to fumble, but still there was no sound of George's footsteps.

The tongue slipped back. He entered the little room, listened, then relocked the door. Even so, there was quite a long wait before he heard a footstep in the bedroom and the click of the light switch.

There was nowhere in that small bedroom to hide, except behind the door when it was open. Therefore George might be expected to switch on the light, glance round the room, then go away, unless he wished to try the inner door.

He did not try the inner door and he did not go away.

The blighter is looking through my things, thought Habershon. Anyway, there was nothing for him to find. A minute passed, during which he heard George fumbling. Then the click of the light being switched off and George descending the steep staircase.

The next problem would be to get out of the flat in order that he might re-enter it in a natural manner. That must be done before the party broke up. Prinny would be sure to hear him when she was alone.

He listened until Clawson had returned to the sitting-room. He was about to move when Prinny's voice came through the boards.

'Celia has just rung up – from the Tube Station. She'll be here in a minute.'

'Whaffor?' demanded Keller.

'I can't imagine. She sounded a bit wintry. I didn't know she knew this address. I think I can hear her in the archway.'

A minute later Habershon was listening to a chilly exchange of greetings. Then a silence of which he could feel the awkwardness, broken by Prinny.

'Have a drink, Celia?'

'No, thanks!' A short pause. 'I thought you would be alone, Prinny, and I'm very glad you're not. I've come to talk about Bruce Habershon.'

Celia's voice coming from that nonsense-room, with its railway-train effects. The tone of it – the sanity and balance of it – seemed to be calling him out of a nightmare.

'You're interested in that young man, Elsie tells me,' Mrs Wellard was saying.

'Yes.' That word permitted no compromise. 'I'm doing all I can to help him reconstruct his memory. All I can!' she repeated. 'He needs a certain amount of prompting. So I've come to you – all four of you. I want some more material for the prompting.'

Habershon could hear a sound like a collective gasp – could visualize Celia ignoring it.

'I don't know what your plans are or what you are doing, and I don't care – provided they don't injure my aunt. I want to know what happened in that house before I arrived. And only in so far as it affects Bruce Habershon's memory.'

'You're being childish, Celia, and very impertinent,' rasped Mrs Wellard.

'Yesterday afternoon,' said Celia, 'Bruce and I found a torn black dress with a fancy apron under Bradburn's bed.' Prinny glanced at Clawson, who avoided her eye. Celia went on : 'Do you see the catch in that, Mrs Wellard – if I'm not being impertinent again?'

'Go on – we're listening !' urged Clawson.

'The catch is that Bradburn was the most dreadful little slattern. If she ever wore an apron, it was a kitchen apron – one of those brown things, made of hessian. This was a very fancy apron. The poor girl would have looked a clown in it. It had no belt – it was secured with pins. It came from Helin and Mawson's, the theatrical costumiers, and it's exactly like the one Prinny wore when she was propping up the Thanton amateurs in *Marjory Gets Married*.'

'That's a dreadful thing to say!' cried Keller. 'Innuendo.'

'Yes.' Again that utter lack of compromise. 'But it's not innuendo. It's accusation.'

'It is – and it's just funny!' Clawson's voice. 'D'you realize that you're accusing us, in effect, of murdering Bradburn?'

'And Mr Velfrage. Yes,' said Celia. 'I have, of course, taken precautions against being murdered myself in this flat.'

'Being a good little girl, why don't you have us all run in, instead of breaking the law by talking to us about it?'

'What I know may or may not be evidence —'

'Quite so! It may or may not be evidence. I'm not going to murder you, my dear, but I'm going to find out what you think you know. Lock the door, Prinny!'

'George dear, need we be so melodramatic —?'

'Lock that door!'

Sulkily Prinny crossed the room. As she locked the door the front door of the flat banged.

'That's Bruce Habershon come back. If I were you, George darling, I'd stop trying to be tough, or something ridiculous may happen.'

She unlocked the door and threw it open.

'Bruce darling, come and join the party!' she called.

26

COME and join the party! Habershon came in like a young man joining a party, intending to take the pace from the others.

'Good evening, Mr Habershon,' said Mrs Wellard, as if they had not met earlier.

Habershon returned the greeting, keeping a furtive eye on Clawson's hip pocket. This time Clawson would have to be knocked out before he could draw. Don't turn your back if you can help it, Kyle had warned him. It was a little difficult.

'I'm sorry I have to go just as you arrive,' said Celia. 'But it takes a long time by Underground.' She got up. 'I'll drop in tomorrow morning, Prinny.'

'You can't go all those miles round on the Underground.' Prinny put a proprietorial hand on Habershon's arm. 'Bruce dear, you can't come to the party after all. Take Celia home and use my car.'

'Rather! But I've got my own car up here – the police were not watching the other garage, so it seemed quite safe. May I, Celia?'

'Thanks, Bruce, but there's no reason —'

'If there's no reason against, it means yes,' he broke in. 'Good night, everybody!'

'Come in quietly, if you're back late,' said Prinny. 'And don't forget to bolt the front door, darling.'

Celia declined his help down the stone staircase, did not even, she said, need his torch. They walked in silence through the archway.

'Prinny evidently wants to turn in early,' said Celia. 'I can perfectly well go by Underground.'

That stuff of Prinny's about bolting the door, interpreted Habershon.

'Celia! Did you hear the front door bang just before I came into the sitting-room?' As she assented : 'I banged it from the inside. I was in the room over the sitting-room. It's a sort of sound-box. The gang have used it to feed me conversations and mislead me. They didn't know I was up there tonight. Clawson came up to make sure, but I succeeded in hiding. I heard all you said. I hurtled downstairs when I heard Clawson tell Prinny to lock the door. You will have noticed that Prinny was very anxious to convey to you that we have set up house together. So we have. But not quite in the bolt-the-door-darling sense.'

For a moment there was silence, then Celia laughed.

'I suppose I was a bit – hurt.'

'I'm so glad!' he said. And they both laughed again. He knew a twinge of unease as he remembered Prinny's kisses – remembered without regret. They reached the garage and he took out the Chrysler.

'Prinny will time the journey,' he remarked, as he made for the Great West Road. 'She makes it every afternoon – to do household chores for Mrs Wellard. And tells me she's been busy at the theatre.'

On the way he told her most of what he had heard before she arrived. Presently he asked :

'Didn't you realize you were risking your life, bearding them like that?'

'I left a note at home saying I was going to the flat, so they wouldn't have dared to kill me. They might have tried beating. But one never thinks of violence in connexion with men like that when one is talking to them.'

'That's one of their assets.' He went on : 'The funny thing that emerged tonight is that they're not particularly interested in that diamond, and certainly did not plan to steal it that night.'

'If they murdered Velfrage for some other reason, they may have taken the diamond as a blind,' she suggested.

'Never mind the reason. They take the diamond. The Wellard puts it in her bag. I grab the bag. Bradburn and the Kilburn Kid horn in somewhere. But Bradburn did not get the diamond. Can you see daylight?'

'No, Bruce, nor can you – so let's leave it !'

He slowed and turned into the drive of Woodville. Before

he had stopped, the front door was opened by Mrs Rabethorpe.

'Oh, thank you!' gushed Mrs Rabethorpe. 'So nice of you to come so promptly! But I do hope you won't arrest him – oh, it's you, Celia! – I thought it was the police. You might have stopped me, dear. Mr Habershon will think I'm behaving very strangely.'

'Not at all, Mrs Rabethorpe! Can I help?'

'Yes do, please, and we can tell the police we're sorry we've troubled them. The fact is, there's a most extraordinary man in the drawing-room.'

'What sort of "extraordinary", Mrs Rabethorpe?' asked Habershon, as he clambered out of the car.

'Well, he addressed me as "old lady"!' As if by afterthought, Mrs Rabethorpe added: 'He arrived by way of the drawing-room window, which he opened himself from the outside.'

'D'you mean he's a burglar, Auntie?'

'On the contrary, my dear, he insists that it is I who have robbed *him*. I found it all most confusing. So I thought it better to ply him with drink. He soon began to talk about himself – though in the third person, which I think is very difficult to sort out, especially as he calls himself a kid.'

'Oh-h! That explains everything!' exclaimed Habershon.

'I'm so glad – I knew you would understand, Mr Habershon.' With sublime confusion, she added: 'It's such a relief to have a man in the house!'

The Kid was lolling in a chair, his feet up on a settee, one hand holding uncertainly a tumbler of whisky.

'Cor, it's the gent! No ill-feeling now. Make yourself at 'ome. Help yerself. Ask the old lady to tell you all about the Kid. She unnerstan's. Agrees with ev'rythin' I told 'er.'

'You'd better get up, and I'll help you out,' said Habershon.

'You're too late, chum!' The Kilburn Kid grinned and chuckled. 'Lost yer chance. The cops 'ave come for yer.'

A local sergeant and a constable had come into the room.

'There's your man!' said the Kid. 'It was 'im put the girl in the safe. Ask 'im if he didn't.'

'D'you know this man, sir?' asked the sergeant.

'He calls himself the Kilburn Kid. I understand that he entered by the window and refused to leave when Mrs Rabethorpe asked him to, but he has stolen nothing. I also know that Detective Inspector Kyle wants to interview him.'

'Kilburn Kid – that's right,' said the sergeant. 'We've had a call from the Yard.'

The Kilburn Kid finished his whisky, dropped the glass on the carpet, then allowed himself to be escorted without protest to the police car.

It was midnight when Bruce Habershon reached Hampstead, though he had lost less than ten minutes over the Kilburn Kid. He hoped Prinny had gone to bed, but as he turned out of the archway he saw the light in the sitting-room.

He could not slink up to bed without speaking to her.

'That was kind of you, Bruce,' she said. 'I hated your going, but I simply had to make you believe I'm not jealous.'

'I was afraid you were not jealous.' He would have to keep up this nonsense with her until he had consulted Kyle. It was curiously difficult to make the senses understand that Prinny was a crook and a fake. In the physical grace of her – the warm, generous vitality of her – there was nothing spurious. He wished he need never see her again, to which was added the demoralizing suspicion that he would never wholly forget her kisses.

She was pouring him a whisky. He watched her hands with detached appreciation, the muscular economy with which she removed the cap from a new bottle and drew the stopper.

'I don't think I'll have a drink, thanks!'

'A nightcap!' she pressed. 'I can't drink mine all alone.' She continued to pour into the glass.

His brain, he thought, was still playing tricks. The subconscious was churning up half memories, ignored at the time – of George Clawson taking a long time to walk upstairs to the bedroom, of Prinny's hands – linking them all together and producing a flash of unreasoning, intuitive certainty.

She handed him the glass of whisky.

'Thanks, dear.'

Prinny picked up her own glass, of gin.

'Here's to us – and no heel-taps!' Her voice, gay and insistent, robbed the toast of solemnity, turned it to a frolic.

Habershon stared down at the glass in his hand. Suspicion was crystallizing into certainty.

'What's the matter, Bruce?'

He held the glass up, looked over the brim into her eyes. He would remember her eyes, always.

'Is this whisky poisoned, Prinny?'

Very slowly she set her glass down.

'You – asked – that – seriously! You mean it!' Her breath caught on a sob. Tears came into her eyes, dropped down her cheeks, streaking her make-up. 'I've had a good many lovers, Bruce. Not one of them could hurt me. I thought no man could. Just have a good laugh at that, Bruce!'

She was blubbering like a schoolgirl. Part of him was moved, part of him was whispering that she was a good actress off the stage. She could induce tears at will. He stood still, watching her, waiting for a false move.

She came towards him, put out her hand and took the glass from him. Of course! The next move would be to tip the whisky down the sink in the pantry and wash the glass. Destroy the evidence, as the trick had failed.

Without moving away, Prinny raised the glass to her lips and drank the contents – no heel-taps.

As she finished drinking, she drew breath and coughed, waved the empty glass. He stood it, perilously, on the back of the settee.

'And I do so *hate* the taste of whisky!' she whimpered.

The anti-climax broke the tension.

'Prinny, I don't know what the devil has happened to us! We've been tricked and trapped in some way. I was talking wild rot. I'm simply damnably sorry I said that!'

'I know. Don't worry, dear.' She put her arms round his neck. 'I was a fool to get hysterical about it. Oh, Bruce !'

It was a different kind of kiss, this time. It wiped out his self-contempt, forgave his blundering brutality.

'Now give me a cigarette, or I shall get maudlin again.'

The business of lighting the cigarette helped them both to normality. She moved away from him and sat by herself.

'I mustn't take any more alcohol, or I shall have a hang-over,' she said. 'But you help yourself.'

'You pinched my whisky – I'll pinch your gin,' he said, and they both laughed immoderately. They were still a little off balance. Prinny took refuge in small talk, jumping inconsequently from one topic to another. Presently she asked :

'When you arrived with Celia, did you see Elsie? She raves about you. Rather pathetic at her age.'

'I not only saw Mrs Rabethorpe – I also saw the Kilburn Kid. He was in the drawing-room of all places. He had apparently come to blackmail her. She couldn't make head or tail of it, so to be on the safe side she made him drivelling drunk —'

'The Kilburn Kid !' repeated Prinny, uncertainly. 'Wait a minute, Bruce ! Let's try it over without the music – God, whisky is a filthy drink ! D'you think it would really, honestly and truly hurt me to have a gin – just a baby one?'

'I wouldn't if I were you, dear. You're a tiny bit tight, as it is. Mind your cigarette !'

The tip was in contact with the upholstery. He took the stub from her. Her head dropped back and her eyelids closed.

He looked down at her, wondering. A girl who could put down a dozen or so gins in an evening without turning a hair ought not to get sleepy-drunk on a single whisky.

He raised his voice.

'Ladies oughtn't to go to sleep when gentlemen are talking to them.'

She opened her eyes, smiled at him, then shut them again.

'*Prinny!*'

He gripped her roughly by the arms and jerked her to her feet.

'Are you ill?' he demanded.

'Don't be cross with me! Whisky's not my drink. Gone to my head. I'm *fright*-f'l'y sleepy. Put me to bed, darling.'

He shook her violently, bellowing at her to wake up.

'Don't be horrid, Bruce! All I want – s'a good night's sleep.'

With his open hand, he smacked her hard across the buttocks – until she cried out with pain.

'You're not drunk, Prinny. You're poisoned! That whisky was doped! You've got to keep awake while I call a doctor. The whisky was doped!' Smack! *'Doped!'*

'Nonsense! It was a new bottle. George gave it me. Bruce, be kind to me! I'm so sleepy —'

'You've got to walk or you'll probably die.'

He slipped behind her, pushing her forward down the corridor, kicking her with his knee. She was still able to move her limbs. In the pantry he tried to administer mustard and water, but it spilt over her dress. While he telephoned, he held her with one hand, grinding the muscles of her arm. She was sagging on his arm before he had finished. He flicked her cheeks with his fingers and drew a moan from her. He marched her into the hall and flung the door open, then concentrated on staving off coma.

He shouted when he heard the ambulance outside. The doctor came running up the steps, followed by two students.

'She drank doped whisky about twenty minutes ago, doctor. She was drowsy in ten minutes.'

'Then we'll have to be quick! We'll raid the flat for what we want. You'd better keep out of sight.'

'I'll be calling the police,' said Habershon. He rang Scotland Yard and was switched to Kyle's private address.

27

BEFORE Kyle arrived, Prinny had been taken to hospital. Habershon led him to the sitting-room. The railway-train effects looked no longer freakish, only pathetic. A country girl had come to Town and had tried to be modishly bizarre – and that, indirectly, had been the end of her.

The glass that had held the whisky, still balanced incongruously on the back of the settee, recalled him.

'That's the glass! We both touched it. That's the bottle it came from – on that ornamental tray in the corner. I didn't touch that. She did.'

Kyle's questions broadened out until Habershon had reported everything from the moment when they had parted that afternoon outside the Law Courts.

'Come back to the dope business. You took this glass from her with the whisky in it. She took up her own glass of gin. You suddenly said "Is this whisky poisoned?"' Kyle sniffed the glass, without touching it. 'Did you smell anything?'

'No.'

'Then what made you think it was poisoned?'

'Devilish hard to say! I suppose – a vague feeling that everything was out of focus. Her pressing me to have a drink when I didn't want one. Clawson saying he wished I'd commit suicide. Clawson taking a long time to come up to my room and dawdling about when he got there. I know it doesn't sound reasonable – but there you are!'

'You've reinstated the gang theory then! You think the gang planned to bump you off?'

'Yes and no, in a way. Prinny couldn't have known, or she wouldn't have drunk it herself.'

'Let's fix the general layout. Clawson puts down a bottle of poisoned whisky, saying nothing about it. Anyone might have taken some, including Prinny.'

'But he knew she hates whisky. He knew I was coming

back later, and that I preferred whisky to gin. I gather he brings her bottles regularly – sort of business-hospitality allowance.'

'And after your remark Prinny drinks it, though she hates whisky?'

'She was rather overwrought by my suggestion, a bit hysterical, in fact.'

'Quite so!' Kyle nodded thoughtfully. 'A man tells a girl she has doped his drink. The girl knows she hasn't. To prove her denial, she drinks it herself. Very natural! You might almost say inevitable.'

Kyle looked round the room. Habershon found himself reversing the proposition stated by Kyle. If you want to poison a girl you put poison in your own drink, accuse her of doing so, then she drinks the poison of her own accord to prove you're talking rot.

Anyhow, Kyle wouldn't think that. There could be no motive.

'This whispering gallery stunt! Could you hear everything they said down there?'

'It's almost the same as being in the room – if you stand on the boards by the communicating door.'

'I'll go up, and you speak from various parts of the room. Ordinary speaking voice, of course.'

In the room overhead, Kyle turned on the light and looked quickly about him. He stood for a moment on the boards, and listened to Habershon's voice below.

'I am speaking from the chair Prinny generally uses. I will now go over to the settee. . . .'

Kyle continued his scrutiny of the room. He brought out a powerful torch for the corners, flashed it under the bed. Bare boards – and a shadow where there should have been no shadow. With his pocket forceps he picked up a small object – a cork, about one-eighth of an inch in diameter. He dropped the cork in an envelope, and went downstairs.

'I could almost hear you breathing!' he said when he returned to the sitting-room.

'You see how they used that the first time?' said Haber-

167

shon. 'They knew I could hear them, so they ran a dialogue for my benefit.'

'Could be!' agreed Kyle. 'When you were listening to-night, what particular remark of theirs made you certain they were a gang? You were doubtful about it this after-noon.'

'I don't know whether I could pick on one remark. Claw-son's talk about my being dangerous to them. Their reaction to Celia's accusation. The demand to know how much evi-dence she had. Locking the door. They'd have started beat-ing her if I hadn't cut in.'

'But in fact they didn't touch her! You'd be surprised how violently some innocent persons will sometimes behave if they think you're accusing them of murder.'

Habershon tried to guess the other's line of thought. The questions were not far removed from cross-questions.

'Didn't you tell me they had convinced you that they had not tried to steal the diamond?'

Obviously Kyle was trying to pick holes. Habershon felt resentment mounting.

'Then *you* have dropped the gang theory?' he blurted out.

'I never drop a theory because I never pick one up. I col-lect facts which can be used as evidence. Here tonight we have a fact or two pointing to Clawson. There's a long way to go before they add up to evidence.

'And it'll be a hard way by the look of it,' he went on. 'I want this flat kept exactly as it is. Do you mind clearing out to an hotel just as you are? You can come back about mid-day and collect your things.'

'I don't mind at all. I'll go back to my bungalow,' said Habershon.

He left Kyle packing the glass and the whisky bottle for analysis.

As soon as he reached the bungalow he telephoned the Hampstead hospital for news of Prinny. There was no report in the office, so he insisted on speaking to the matron.

'The fact that there is no report,' explained the matron,

'means that the medical officer in charge of the case has not expressed an opinion.'

As maddening an example of matronese as he had ever heard.

'I say, Matron, have a heart. Will she live?'

'Have a head, young man. I am sitting in an office. As soon as there is any report it will be filed at the porter's lodge.'

28

HABERSHON woke up every hour. At eight he decided to get up. From the hospital he learnt that Prinny was still on the danger list.

In his dressing gown he made a rambling tour of the bungalow. There was surprisingly little disarrangement, considering that Clawson had searched the whole place for the diamond.

He lingered in his sitting-room for a cigarette. The shabby old room, full of the associations of a normal and healthy existence, brought him a feeling of peace. There was no trace here of Clawson's activities. He wondered whether Celia would like that room.

He would have to get himself breakfast sooner or later, the later the better. He rang Miss Parker, asking her to hire a car and call on her way to the office.

He took his time over bathing and shaving, unusually reluctant to begin the day. Eventually he pottered into the kitchen and thence into the dining-room, where he became vaguely aware that there was something out of place.

The table had been shifted – he shifted it back, decided that it was not the table after all that was wrong. It was the floor. The drugget had been rolled back and badly rerolled. By one wall there was a line of bare boards.

The nails had been drawn from the boards.

Now why should Clawson leave the sitting-room practically untouched yet assume that the diamond must have been hidden in the dining-room? Why, indeed, take up the floor-boards in one room and not in another?

Why worry? All it meant was that Clawson had had the devil of a lot of exercise for nothing. He wandered back to the kitchen.

There came a subdued knock on the back door and he hurried to admit Miss Parker, who was carrying a shopping basket.

'Sit down somewhere, or you'll get in my way,' she commanded.

'It's very good of you, Miss Parker, but I don't really feel much like breakfast.'

Miss Parker grunted and the conversation lapsed until he had consumed a cereal and a roll and butter.

'We can pay off that detective agency,' he announced.

'I'm glad to hear it. Inspector Kyle said you were only wasting your money. I have their latest reports, as they call them.' She put them on the edge of the table. 'Are you coming back to the office?'

'Not today. I'm still in the thick of it. Only I'm taking your advice —'

'That means, I'm afraid, that you're more worried than ever.'

'I wouldn't put it as strongly as that.' He shrank from telling her about Prinny. But he had to tell her something. 'I've met a girl I want to marry. I don't know whether she wants to marry me. If she does, I know you will approve. I mean, I can't imagine her ever doing anything of which you would disapprove.' He added : 'I haven't asked her, of course.'

'I don't see any "of course" about it !' pronounced Miss Parker. 'If she hasn't as much faith in you as I have, you'd better put her out of your mind.'

'She may have faith in me. But I haven't any in myself. I say, Miss Parker, you know that gag *"in vino veritas"* – meaning you don't know what you're like till you've had a blackout. It's possible to think you're an averagely decent sort and yet – be chock full of criminal instincts without knowing it.'

'I don't know. I've heard that sort of thing said, but I've never believed it. In your case, it proves that you oughtn't to have come back to London until you'd had a proper holiday.'

When she had gone, he glanced at the detective agency's report, which told him nothing of any value.

'Miss Loftus left flat one fifteen. Purchases at fishmongers' and chemist. Arrived The Chestnuts 2.15; left 6.20 p.m.'

Afternoon duty, Clawson had called it. And he had said that she must do morning duty instead this morning, arriving at ten – when Mrs Wellard would be leaving to meet Gallerton at the Parnassus and pose as Mrs Rabethorpe.

'Prinny does the chores for Wellard. Wellard will leave the house at ten. Prinny – had she been able – would have entered the house at ten. Why?

'Now I'm trying to be a detective again after I've sworn off. Leave that sort of thing to Kyle. We don't want theories, we want facts.

'That's a fathead slogan! How the devil can you link two facts together without a theory? You'd get child's babble. "First a man disappeared and then a man tore a dress and a woman was in a safe and a diamond was stolen."

'My theory is that there's something funny in that house besides poor Prinny's housework.'

At ten he was in the Chrysler at the end of the road, saw Mrs Wellard drive off in a hired car, the Rolls being still out of action.

He drove on to The Chestnuts.

Prinny was not there – a fact possibly unknown to Clawson – the house was presumably empty. He drove up to the door, as if making a legitimate call.

He rang and knocked, three times each, stretching it over a period of five minutes. The front door looked difficult. He walked round the house to the rear. The back door was locked and looked difficult too.

He set to work on the scullery window with a penknife. But the catch had a safety lock, and he broke his blade trying to shift it. Then he kicked the window-pane and smashed it, pulled back the safety catch and entered the scullery.

Neither scullery nor kitchen gave any sign of nefarious practice. He passed along a short corridor to the hall, which was like the hall of Woodville next door, except for the furniture. The house was probably built on an identical plan. There were the same doors in the same place.

He would start with the room corresponding with the library in Woodville.

With his hand on the door knob he hesitated. Up to that

moment he had been sustained by a sense of boyish adventure. Now came sudden reluctance. He had to force himself to open the door.

The room was as inoffensive-looking as the kitchen. It was more definitely a library than Mrs Rabethorpe's room. The walls were lined with bookshelves, which were crowded. The furniture was good, not new but modern, probably late Edwardian.

Try every room in the house, he told himself, and crossed the hall to the dining-room.

Nothing there. Very well – every room in the house! Just as he had gone into every room in the other house when he was trying to remember what had happened.

But this time there was a difference. In that other search he had feared only failure. Now it was as if he feared success. There came a shivery feeling that he would find something it were better for him not to find.

Morning-room empty. Drawing-room empty. Up the wide staircase, so like the other, that he noticed the absence of a settee with a Burmese doll on the landing.

The first room, presumably Mrs Wellard's. A museum of Edwardian New Art curtains. He looked under the bed and in the wardrobe. There was no need to look behind the curtains.

Across the landing to the room opposite Mrs Wellard's. As he opened the door he started back, for the blinds were drawn and the room was in near darkness. There was a smell of antiseptics.

He turned on the light.

There was a man lying in bed. On the edge of certainty, Habershon ran forward, switched on the bed light.

'Mr Velfrage!'

There was no doubt that Velfrage was alive. The breathing was audible, being little short of a snore.

Habershon pulled up the blinds.

'Mr. Velfrage. Wake up.'

One hand was outside the bedclothes. Habershon noticed that Velfrage was wearing a day-shirt. He squeezed the hand and shook it.

Velfrage moaned and opened his eyes, then yawned extensively.

'Ah!' he exclaimed. 'I feel much better this morning. I've had a splendid night. The morphia was effective, but of course the pain is coming back now. One must expect as much for a while yet. Can I have my letters, please?'

'Mr Velfrage, do you know me?'

The hand on the coverlet twitched.

'I think I do.' The voice was restrained and nervous. 'The light from the window is in my eyes. D'you mind coming to the other side of the bed?'

Habershon had got over his first surprise. Velfrage, he supposed, had been doped with some memory-destroying drug.

'Good heavens! It's Bruce Habershon!' exclaimed Velfrage. Then, with a mixture of timidity and indignation – as if the solicitor in him were trying to reassure the patient – he added : 'What are you doing here, Habershon?'

It was the very question Habershon himself had intended to ask. Turned on himself he could find no immediate answer.

'Does Mrs Wellard know you are here?' demanded Velfrage.

The quickest way to understanding, Habershon decided, would be to make use of the time factor. Three weeks and two days had passed since Velfrage got out of the Chrysler and disappeared.

'Mr Velfrage, we are at cross-purposes. We can clear it up if you will answer one question. How long do you think you have been in that bed?'

'Twenty-three days,' answered Velfrage. 'And how can that fact clarify what you are pleased to call a cross-purpose?' He added testily : 'I am not conscious of a cross-purpose.'

'Twenty-three days ago you entered Woodville to see Mrs Rabethorpe and show her the Rabethorpe diamond. You were struck down in the house —'

'Struck down! I was bludgeoned and fired at, if you call that being struck down. I would have been killed and robbed

174

of the diamond had not Mrs Wellard and her friends arrived by chance and rescued me. I am very deeply indebted to Mrs Wellard, not only for saving my life, but, further, for allowing me to be treated in her house. The doctor said that to move me might prove fatal.'

A simple tale – and Velfrage had swallowed it whole.

'But Mrs Wellard has not allowed you any contact with the outside world!' Habershon pointed out. 'Try to follow this, Mr Velfrage. You have been robbed of the diamond. The doctor is a crook, and so is Mrs Wellard. Scotland Yard has been looking for you – is looking for you at this moment – believing you to have been murdered or kidnapped. You have been kidnapped, but you don't seem to know it.'

Velfrage closed his eyes. His face twitched. Then he rallied.

'*Tch!* What possible object can you have in talking to me like this? Scotland Yard indeed! Didn't it occur to Scotland Yard to inquire at my office – when my managing clerk, Clawson, would have informed them that he sees me every day, that I deal with the more important correspondence! At this very moment Clawson is presenting a document to a judge in chambers – but I cannot continue this absurd conversation. What is your object in coming here?'

Habershon tried a new tack.

'You're speaking to me damned rudely, Mr Velfrage. Do you think I robbed you of the diamond?'

'No one has robbed me of the diamond. It is in Clawson's possession – Mr Gallerton has come over from New York to complete the purchase.' Even in bed, Mr Velfrage clung to the jargon of his profession. 'In answer to your question, my information is that you were concerned in the attempt to rob me, which was, fortunately, unsuccessful. I hope I have been misinformed, but I confess that your present conduct renders the hope a slender one.'

In short, Habershon had to admit that he had failed to put over a single item of the truth. Clawson had made a pretty good job of it. Kidnapping without unpleasantness on either side.

'Good enough, Mr Velfrage. I shall bring an Inspector

from the Yard to see you. You can tell him how kind Mrs Wellard has been – and the doctor – and Clawson. I will leave you now —'

'Quite so ! You have heard Clawson's voice downstairs, as I have.'

Habershon was startled. He had heard nothing.

'I understood you to say that you would leave me,' said Mr Velfrage.

Habershon stepped on to the landing, leaving the door ajar. He tiptoed until he could see through the banisters.

Clawson was coming up the stairs.

29

HABERSHON crouched low by the newel. Within arm's reach of Clawson he could beat a gun, but not otherwise. Moreover, if Velfrage had heard Clawson's voice, Clawson must have been speaking to someone.

'I want your gun, Clawson. Better keep still.'

'*Habershon!*' It was a long drawn breath. 'Where's Prinny? I haven't got a gun.'

Habershon satisfied himself that there was no concealed weapon of any kind.

'I don't know what all this is about,' sneered Clawson. 'I thought it was your car and then I thought it couldn't be. Where's Prinny?'

'Prinny was poisoned last night. I'm going. I think Velfrage wants to see you, Clawson.'

Habershon walked round the other to the stairhead.

'Velfrage can wait. Just a minute, Habershon. You can't be serious about Prinny?'

Habershon made no answer. Clawson followed him downstairs. Habershon wheeled round.

'If you come within my reach I shall hit you. Can't you see you're washed up, Clawson?'

'Yes, yes, I daresay! But don't get excited, old man. You ought to be careful, in your condition. I wish you'd tell me what all this mystery is about Prinny.'

'You can ask Inspector Kyle. I'm going to ring him now.'

'A pity!' said Clawson. 'You're your own worst enemy, Habershon.'

At the foot of the stairs Habershon reminded himself that there was someone else in the house. Probably Keller – who was probably armed. Keeping his eyes about him, he got into the Chrysler. He had to back out of the drive, as Clawson's Buick blocked the straight run.

It would be quicker to drive to a kiosk than to turn in next door. Mrs Rabethorpe was well meaning, but an infernal nuisance. Within seven minutes of leaving The Chestnuts he was connected with the Yard.

'Inspector Kyle? Habershon here. Listen hard. This morning I had a hunch there was something queer about Mrs Wellard's house —'

'Detective work again?'

'Yes, sir! Detective work! I burgled the house and in the house *I found Velfrage*! Can you come along?'

He heard an exclamation from Kyle.

'Next door to Mrs Rabethorpe's? No mistake about it being Velfrage?'

'Mistake be damned! I talked to him for a matter of minutes.'

'D'you mean he's *alive*?'

'He's alive and doesn't know we're looking for him. He doesn't know he's disappeared.'

'Then he must be loopy!'

'He isn't. He's absolutely clear-headed. He thinks I attacked him, that he's been ill – he's in bed, by the way. And he thinks he's running his business. Clawson comes to see him every day to deal with letters.'

There was a long pause, and then:

'I'll come right away.'

That would mean about forty minutes, with traffic luck, reflected Habershon as he hung up. It hardly mattered. Clawson would already have had time to get away in the Buick. He rang Celia and told her about Velfrage and then about Prinny. Then he drove back to The Chestnuts, noted that, as he had supposed, the Buick was no longer there.

He parked a dozen yards from the gate and settled down to wait. A local policeman arrived on a bicycle and looked him over.

'Your name, please, sir?'

'Habershon. I'm waiting for Detective Inspector Kyle.'

'That's correct,' said the constable and put himself on point duty by the gate.

Habershon kept looking at his watch. Twenty minutes since he had spoken to Kyle. Call it half-time. When he looked again, only ten minutes had passed. It was now twelve thirty-three.

A car approached from the London end of the road. It slowed to turn into the drive. The constable stopped it.

A rear window was opened and Mrs Wellard put her head out.

'What's the matter, constable?'

'Sorry, ma'am. Orders are that no one is to go in until – until further orders.'

'That doesn't apply to me. It is my house. Kindly let the driver pass.'

'No car may enter until further orders.' The constable was digging his toes in, but Mrs Wellard changed ground.

'Very well!' She got out of the car and paid off the driver.

'I don't think you will take it upon yourself to restrain me by force from entering my own house.'

The constable did not think so, either. Mrs Wellard walked sedately down the drive and let herself into her house.

At ten minutes to one the Yard car arrived with Kyle.

Habershon hurried down the drive on foot, caught up with Kyle as he was pressing the bell-push.

'In the room over this one on the left – over the library. If you look up, you'll see it – the one with the blinds drawn. It's the first door on your left on the first-floor landing.'

Kyle nodded. Mrs Wellard opened the door.

'Good morning, Mrs Wellard. How many persons are there in the house beside yourself?'

'At the moment there is no one but myself – and a sick friend upstairs.'

'I would like to see the sick friend, please.'

'He's asleep and I won't have him disturbed.'

Kyle stepped over the threshold.

'You intend to search my house? Kindly show me your warrant.'

'I have none and need none. I have reason to believe that a felony is in course of being committed, and —'

'Thank heavens, here's George Clawson!' exclaimed Mrs

Wellard as the Buick drew up and parked behind the police car.

'Hullo, Margo!' shouted Clawson. 'It's all right! I've just told Elsie she's a rich woman. Good morning, Mr Kyle. I know why you're here.'

'He wants to search the house and he has no warrant.'

'He doesn't need one. He'll arrest you if you obstruct him. Habershon told him you're concealing Velfrage.'

'Con-*cealing*! It's a perfectly monstrous suggestion.'

'That's no good, Margo! If you don't want to take Inspector Kyle over the house, I will.'

As a dowager bowing to the inevitable, Mrs Wellard led the way. At the foot of the staircase she turned.

'I see no reason why Mr Habershon should accompany us.'

At a nod from Kyle, Habershon waited in the hall.

Kyle followed Mrs Wellard, Clawson followed Kyle. They disappeared round the bend of the staircase and Habershon heard the door of the sick-room being opened, then shut.

A full minute passed, a minute and a half. Once Habershon thought he heard Kyle's voice. A moment later Kyle himself appeared, walking briskly down the stairs, alone.

He called through the open front door to a junior waiting by the police car.

'On the first-floor landing, you'll find a bedroom door on the left. Miss that. Search the rest of the house and report anything unusual to me in this room.'

He indicated the library, opened the door and invited Habershon to join him.

'Were the blinds up or down while you were in that room?'

'Down when I entered. But I pulled them up.'

'Are you absolutely certain that it was Velfrage?'

'Yes!' Habershon felt his head spinning. 'What on earth — ?'

'And that he talked to you for some minutes in a clear-headed way?'

'I had difficulty in waking him. He said he was shaking

off a sleeping draught. Then he was perfectly clear-headed – and accurate about dates. I told you what he said. Hold on and I'll fill in the details.'

Habershon reported the conversation in full.

'Quite all right! I believe you!' said Kyle. 'Only, the man in that bed upstairs is Keller!'

As Habershon gasped, Kyle went on :

'Keller is dicky after that car smash. He was taken worse when they were coming away from the Hampstead flat last night, and Mrs Wellard took him in.'

'Why tell me their tale? I saw Velfrage.'

'Keller,' continued Kyle, 'was asleep when we went in. He woke himself up, and his first words were : "Sorry I dropped off to sleep, *Habershon*. What were you saying?" Then he recognized me and explained that he had taken a sleeping draught. And I noticed he was wearing a day-shirt, as you described.'

Habershon had listened without concealing his impatience.

'I can see what's happened!' he exclaimed. 'There would have been time to get Velfrage out of the way. I didn't mention it before but there was someone else in this house when I surprised Clawson. Clawson had been speaking to him.'

'Ah!' said Kyle. 'You certainly didn't mention it before. I wish you had.'

The junior knocked and entered.

'All the other rooms in the house unoccupied, sir. I didn't notice anything unusual in any of them.'

'Well, that's that!' sighed Kyle when the junior had gone. 'We'll have a look round outside as a matter o' form, and then I'll get back and see if I can shake anything out of the Kilburn Kid. I think you'd better get out of here. You're not exactly popular with the household.'

'*Mr Kyle!*' Habershon laid a detaining hand on the other's arm. 'Will you tell me – please – whether you believe I saw and spoke to Velfrage, exactly as I described?' Kyle scrutinized him closely, then made up his mind.

'I believe you're on the level, Habershon, or I wouldn't answer you in the way I'm going to answer you. I don't know whether you saw Velfrage. That doesn't mean I'm sure you didn't. I don't know. I'm going to find out, if I can. Right now, I'll tell you there's one darned thing sticks out against you.'

'Please do. I'm more likely to be able to help if you sort of half trust me.'

'Take it slowly, then. According to you, Velfrage has been up here since he disappeared, semi-invalid but sane and coherent. Okay? Clawson comes to see him every day, talks business, lets him sign letters – but of course destroys them – and makes Velfrage think that everybody else thinks that Velfrage is convalescent in the ordinary way, and keeping a whip hand on this business? Okay?'

'Exactly! There's nothing wild in that, from Velfrage's point of view. He lives alone in a flat. His only relative is a married sister whom he rarely sees.'

'Right! But what will happen to Clawson when Velfrage eventually gets out of that bed, goes to the office, learns that the diamond was stolen, and that Clawson has been pulling his leg?'

'I haven't worked it out from Clawson's angle.'

'Clawson works things out from Clawson's angle.' Kyle let his words sink in, then : 'Obviously, Clawson would have to make sure that Velfrage never did get out of that bed. He'd have to bump Velfrage off.'

'Obviously! But —'

'Then why not do it at once instead of footling about in that room and running a troublesome deception?'

'I don't know why he waited all this time. But he simply must have meant to kill Velfrage. I believe he killed him after I left there this morning. By God, he may have buried him under the floor-boards of my bungalow! He'd have had time!'

'Steady! You don't want to jump at things like that.'

'It isn't jumping. I noticed this morning that the floor-boards have been lifted and not nailed down. I gave him leave to search there for the diamond. I bet he prepared a grave – I bet he's been keeping a grave all ready for an emergency like this.'

Habershon was aware that he was panting.

'I know I'm getting excited, and I don't care. Let's have my floor-boards up – before you go back to the Yard. If you tread on the gas you can get there within ten minutes.'

In the Chrysler, Habershon trod on the gas and the police car held on. The bungalow was one of a row, well spaced, with box hedges ensuring a measure of privacy. Double gates gave a twenty-foot run across the strip of front garden to the garage.

'Those aren't your wheel tracks,' said Kyle, indicating fresh tracks to Habershon's garage. 'Your tyres are on the old side.'

'Agreed!' Habershon spoke tonelessly. 'And why should anyone but Clawson drive into my garage?'

He let them into the bungalow.

'Suppose you were to take a spot o' fresh air in the garden while we look round?' suggested Kyle.

For some ten minutes Habershon paced the narrow path before Kyle appeared.

'You guessed right!' he said. 'Under the boards in your dining-room. Only just covered, too. The spade had been left all handy for us.'

'And is it Velfrage?'

'Take it from me! The formal identification can wait. Keep on walking. I'll come back presently.'

Another half an hour on the garden path, no longer thinking of anything. In that half-hour the doctor had come and gone.

Kyle turned up, stuffing a pipe. He began to light it as he spoke.

'I've been – a policeman – for twenty-two years. Inspector for five years. I never believed in the clever criminal until now. Never met him. A bit o' foxlike cunning, of course, in getting away – faking an alibi and the like. That's all.'

'It doesn't seem to me frightfully clever to plant Velfrage on me like that.'

'Depends how you look at it.' The pipe was drawing badly. 'The very obviousness gives it a sort of – perverted – cleverness.' He looked sideways at Habershon. 'Two murders – Bradburn, Velfrage — A third attempted – yourself. Only it was Prinny Loftus who swallowed the poison. Almost points to a maniac murderer.'

'Surely there's too much method for mania!'

'If there's any method at all? It was you who pointed out that Clawson and Co couldn't get enough for the diamond to make it worth pinching. Meaning there was no method, if he was on that line.

'Besides, murder mania isn't the neat, tidy horror some people think it is,' continued Kyle. 'I've handled a few cases. The maniac takes a sort of personal pride in the crime. He doesn't tell a lot of covering lies about it like the ordinary crook. He even turns sulky when someone else gets the credit for it – that's how he looks at it! Result – it's nearly always the maniac killer himself who provides the chief evidence against himself.' Kyle paused and added : 'Very much as you've provided most of the evidence against yourself in this case.'

'Cheerful for me!' muttered Habershon.

Ambulance men were removing the body from the bungalow. Kyle went on :

'Velfrage was suffering from a bullet wound in the leg —'

'That lay figure – as I thought it was!' cried Habershon.

'Quite so! And who told me you fired at it? You!' chuckled Kyle. 'Only, death was caused by suffocation – anything up to three hours ago. So you *would* have had time!

'And another thing! Who handed me that glass and whisky bottle on a plate? You did. In the room you occupied I found a cork and, later on, the powdered-up glass phial which had contained galvanium – the quick-fire narcotic which the girl swallowed. You couldn't buy it anywhere in Britain, so it was imported – which means we shan't be able to trace purchase.'

'But —'

'Let me finish my little piece. There's the servant girl, Bradburn. You're sure it wasn't her dress you tore. But you're not sure you didn't strangle her. We don't go in for theories, as you know, but – *there's* a theory for you! Three

184

murders planted on one man! By a lawyer clever enough to see that he was on velvet the moment you bleated about not being able to remember whether you were a murderer or not. The maniac killer – with the self-accusation all laid on, all okayed by the case-books! If Clawson had the sense to bump me off right away you'd be convicted.'

'As he hasn't – you're going to pull me out of it?'

'I don't know,' answered Kyle.

'Anyhow, I'm not a maniac killer!'

'I don't know.' Again Kyle repeated: 'I don't know – just as you don't know that this ramble of mine isn't a trap. I'm taking a bet that you are not a maniac killer. You must take a bet that I mean what I say. And if you find any more evidence against yourself, throw it at my head at once. So far the only witness in your favour is Miss Fenton. She can prove you didn't put that black dress under the bed yourself. And she brought out the point about it probably being bought by Loftus or Clawson at the theatrical costumier's. That's all we've got. And it's only subsidiary stuff. Here and now I want a promise —'

'Better be careful about promises,' said Habershon.

'This one's easy. No more discussion with Miss Fenton – about what you remember and the rest of it – until I give the word, which may be tomorrow.'

Habershon promised. Promptly his thoughts flew off in another direction.

'You've cocked my tail for me, Inspector, and I'm more grateful than I can say. But – it's all based on Clawson committing two murders and trying to commit a third – me, though Prinny actually swallowed the stuff.'

'Well?'

'What the purple hell did he do it all for? We know he didn't plan to steal the diamond, even if the gang actually took it from Velfrage. But nobbling Velfrage had method – which disposes of the maniac theory – it must have been planned. Why? Where's the pay-off?'

'Hm! That's a knobby one, isn't it? We're working on it, of course.'

'Working on the assumption that Clawson and his gang

are irresponsible fatheads endangering themselves for nothing?'

'Ah! I see what's troubling you,' chuckled Kyle. 'You don't want someone else to get the credit for the crime!... Hi! What's the matter, Habershon? I was only trying to make a tomfool joke!'

Habershon had the illusion that his lawn had floated upwards and hit him softly on the head.

For a moment Kyle was unable to help. He stood stock still, holding his breath, staring down at the white, drawn face of the man upon whose sanity he was staking his own reputation.

30

HABERSHON sat up and blinked, barely aware of his surroundings. Kyle helped him to his feet and steadied him.

'I'm all right now, thanks. I wonder what happened. I've never fainted before.'

'You've had all you can take, the last few days.'

'I know what it was! Something you said made me suddenly think I must be a maniac killer.' He laughed, very loudly. 'If poor old Velfrage proves anything, he proves there's nothing wrong with my mind.'

'Who's asking for proof? I'm not.' But Kyle had to listen to the proof, all the same.

'Just a minute! You said I would have had time to bring him here this morning. And kill him. Bring him from where? From Mrs Wellard's house? And if he was not in that house – where did I keep him hidden?'

'Quite so!' soothed Kyle. 'There's nothing in it.'

'He's only been dead three hours, if as much as that, the doctor said.' Habershon's words came quickly and high pitched. 'Where could I have hidden him yesterday – the day before – while I was in Cornwall – while I was in hospital?'

'You're pushing an open door, old man.'

'And what about that doped whisky? If I had doped it myself and tricked Prinny into drinking it, I wouldn't have told you all about it.'

'You're preaching to the converted. And another thing – Miss Loftus is out of danger. I heard it when I was ringing headquarters on your phone. She's made a statement to our man that dovetails with your statement. So suppose you stop proving your innocence to me, will you?'

'Sorry!' Habershon added: 'I think I'm trying to prove it to myself rather than you.'

Kyle's unease had been growing steadily since Habershon had fainted. As he drove away he tried to put his finger on the spot. Fainting in itself meant nothing – the man was living on his nerves. But that excited insistence on the fact that he was sane might well be a danger signal.

The poisoned whisky incident was full of loopholes. Every main incident was full of loopholes. The 'gang theory', as Habershon called it, was supported solely by Habershon's evidence. No single fact had emerged independently of Habershon except the fact of the dress thrust under the bed – which could have more than one explanation.

There was the dynamic fact that Velfrage had been alive a few hours ago. Admittedly, it was impossible that Habershon could have kidnapped Velfrage and hidden him for twenty-two days.

But it was not impossible that Velfrage might have hidden himself.

There were a good many combinations to tick off. Velfrage as master criminal. Clawson as master criminal, with Velfrage as associate or victim. Whatever the original plan was, it had gone wrong. It had been upset by Habershon's entering Woodville. That entry tangled the lines and spoilt the grouping.

The plan may have contained no murders. The murders may have been acts of homicidal mania by Habershon. Habershon stealing the bag with the peacock's eye by mistake and in ignorance that it contained the diamond – as, in fact, had happened.

On the way he stopped at The Chestnuts. Clawson was having lunch with Mrs Wellard. The two men went into the morning-room. Kyle told him where Velfrage's body had been found – sprang it on him and watched his reaction.

'On the whole I'm not so surprised!' he exclaimed. 'Of course, it was obvious that Velfrage had been murdered when he disappeared. Men like Velfrage don't disappear.'

'Velfrage was alive a few hours ago,' stated Kyle.

Clawson scowled, then forced a weak smile.

'If he was alive a few hours ago, where has he been locked up for the last three weeks? I'm not challenging your information, Inspector – I just can't add it up.'

'Habershon says he was here.'

'Yes – poor devil! But that doesn't help much. You know, Habershon loathes me, but I rather admire him. I'm terribly sorry for him. It'll be Broadmoor, of course. That chap believes every word he utters, including the impossibilities.'

'We have to sort out the impossibilities, Mr Clawson. Can you help?'

'Afraid I can't. Unless you mean the bit about Velfrage being locked up here. Even then – well, how does one prove a negative?'

Correct – and detached. Exactly as an innocent man or a level-headed crook would behave.

'You could begin by giving me Keller's address.'

'He has a house in Brighton, but after the car smash I took him to a small nursing home in Kew.' Clawson gave both addresses and went on : 'I know, by the way, from Miss Loftus, that Habershon said we'd killed Velfrage and stolen the diamond. You don't take it seriously, or you'd have followed it up. Any questions, now you're here?'

That might be as innocent as it sounded. It might be an anxious feeler. In either case, Kyle was not ready for action.

His next call was at the nursing home at Kew, where he satisfied himself that Keller had been expected to return the previous night. Shortly before midnight a Mrs Wellard had rung up and explained that Keller was spending the night in her house.

Habershon, on his way to the hospital in the hope of seeing Prinny, was methodically calming himself – which is not a good sign in a young man. He began with elaborate fairness to both sides. Let it be granted that I am a homicidal maniac and don't know it. How then would I behave in the following circumstances?

Almost in the first round the theory collapsed. He had done things that no maniac had ever been known to do. Ever been known by Habershon. The theory simply would not stand up.

On the other hand, there was a cast-iron case that Clawson was leader of a gang which had stolen the diamond, killed the girl, tried to kill Habershon, killed Velfrage. True that the whole series of crimes was apparently without motive. In the last ditch, it would be more sensible to assume that Clawson was the homicidal maniac. Anybody could be a homicidal maniac.

There was, therefore, Habershon assured himself, no earthly need to worry about his own sanity. He repeated the assurance, using different words at each repetition. No one could fail to be convinced by the positively staggering volume of evidence amounting to overwhelming proof of sanity.

At the hospital he learnt that Miss Loftus, against medical advice, had returned home. He hurried to the flat. While he was inserting his latchkey the door was opened by a hospital nurse, who motioned him to silence.

'You are Mr Habershon? Come in, but please be quiet. Miss Loftus is resting.'

A handbell tinkled vigorously through the bedroom door and a few seconds later Habershon was being shown in.

Habershon saw burnished copper red against a green pillow slip. Her face, without make-up, took an extra pallor from the slip, as did her arms lying outside green sheets.

'Bruce! Don't kiss me, darling – I'm all hospitally. Sit and hold my hand and keep saying you're so glad I'm alive. Do I look like a ghost?'

'Yes, dear – one of the new de luxe models! I'm as glad you're alive as you think I am, but I wish you hadn't left hospital against advice.'

'I fled *because* of the advice. They advised me not to think about myself and to try to take an interest in wholesome things. So I escaped while I still had the strength. Margo got that nurse for a few hours.'

The hell-cat who had clawed his face. There was, of course, just the bare possibility that he might be wrong about that bit. Her hand was smooth and affectionate.

'They cleaned all the dope out of me. I'm only weak and lazy now. Margo will be along this evening when the nurse goes.'

'If it's only weakness, I can fuss round you.'

'That's the awful part, darling. I shall have to kick you out for a few days.'

'I don't mind what you do, but I do hope you won't have Mrs Wellard here.'

There was a gentle pressure of his hand, but no promise followed.

'Prinny! Don't have Wellard. She's closely linked with Clawson. You know he planted that bottle of doped whisky, intending to get me!'

'Darling, if I thought George had tried to kill you, I'd go straight to the police.'

'How can you be in doubt! That bottle —'

'But he produced a bottle of whisky a few minutes after he arrived. And he and Frank and Margo punished it quite a lot. It's still in the flat. The police found it behind the settee. It wasn't the bottle from which I poured the doped stuff.'

As he looked puzzled, she explained:

'The police showed me the poison bottle as soon as I was conscious. There'd only been one drink taken from it. And it wasn't George's brand and it hadn't been bought at his retailer's. I don't know where it came from.'

'Someone put that bottle where you'd pick it up without thinking, and pour me a drink. If it wasn't Clawson —'

'Darling, don't let's do plots and plans. I'm not strong enough yet, really!'

His eye travelled from her wrist along her arm, to the green-white pallor of her throat. Ghost-like perhaps, if one could imagine a ghost being humanly attractive. Hell-cat too, perhaps – and perhaps no more hell-cat than ghost.

'Do you think I planted that bottle, Prinny, and tricked you into drinking it?'

Her eyes were closed. She answered without opening them.

'I don't know, Bruce, and I don't care. I never thought I would love a man like that, and I'm ashamed of it. But I do love you like that.'

He faced the stark fact that she did believe he had tried to kill her.

'And you think I return your love by discovering that it would be rather fun to murder you?' He laughed because he thought it genuinely funny. 'We won't pursue that, dear. The truth is that you're in danger from those three, and I'm going to make you see it. Listen with both ears! This morning I burgled Wellard's house and I found Velfrage there.' He remembered the private detective's report that Prinny did the housework. 'Is that news to you, Prinny?'

'Yes – no. I mean, tell me all about it, darling. Drag it out into the light of day and let's look at it together.'

'I found Velfrage!' he repeated. 'He was in bed, convalescing. He told me he had been there three weeks – ever since he was attacked and robbed of the diamond.'

He paused, watching her, uncertain whether she had taken it in.

'Yes, dear – I'm listening. I only close my eyes because of the light.'

'I telephoned Inspector Kyle. When he arrived, Keller was in the bed previously occupied by Velfrage. At my suggestion Kyle searched my bungalow. He found Velfrage's body under my floor-boards. The doctor said that Velfrage had been alive three hours previously. So he was murdered and planted on me. The plot failed, as you see, or Kyle would have arrested me. Do you understand now that Clawson and Wellard are dangerous to you?'

He was still holding her hand. Her other hand crossed over and held him above the wrist.

'Bruce! Do you remember I told you the other night that I had spent the afternoon at the theatre? It was a harmless lie, because the truth was too dull. I was doing Margo's housework. I do it by arrangement whenever I haven't an appointment with the theatre people – which means nearly always. So of course I know.'

Her confession gave added weight to her words – a weight that was crushing what was left of his belief in himself.

'Are you telling me you don't believe I saw and spoke to Velfrage in that house?'

'No, Bruce, I believe that you saw him.' She pulled him closer to her. Still uncertain of her viewpoint, he acquiesced.

She drew his head to her breast, and crooned over him.

'Don't worry, darling. I don't. It's no good. Spoils our moments together.'

He waited, but that was all she had to say. Her murmurings were not of Velfrage.

'Prinny – do you believe I'm a homicidal maniac who totally forgets his crime?'

'I think you're mad, beloved. I didn't want to say so, but you've called my bluff. I think you'll kill me one day, and I'm not trying to protect myself. I'm not even afraid of dying – that way – which shows I'm mad too! And I don't care! . . . Do I really smell of hospitals?'

He parted her arms and stood up.

'You may be wrong,' he said. 'You may be right. If I decide you are right, I shall kill myself.'

He drove to the Heath, got out and walked for half an hour. Prinny believed him to be a homicidal maniac and she was not even afraid of him. Dear, amoral Prinny! . . . Burnished copper red cascading over green!

As a result of his amateur detectiving, he had nearly killed Prinny. He made for a telephone kiosk and rang Miss Parker.

'Did you think up a solicitor for me in case I should want one?'

She answered, as he knew she would, with a name and address. Miss Parker never forgot and never failed him. He drove to the solicitors, waited in their office while a will was drawn up, bequeathing his business to Miss Parker – with a charge of fifty per cent of the net profits in favour of Prinny Loftus.

Phew! Miss Parker would not in the least object to the fifty per cent charge. But by all the genteel gods of middle-class spinsterhood she would object to Prinny Loftus!

He found himself laughing, not because he was amused, but because he suddenly felt free.

31

AFTER checking on Keller and having a bar lunch, Inspector Kyle went back to the Yard. He was about to make a second attempt to interrogate the Kilburn Kid when a query came from another department.

'A Mr Gallerton, an American gentleman staying at the Parnassus, is on the phone with a query touching Mrs Rabethorpe. Will you take it?'

Kyle was eminently willing to take it.

Mr Gallerton was a man who prided himself on his ability to come straight to the point and stick to it.

'This morning a lady was introduced to me as Mrs Rabethorpe, daughter of William Rabethorpe. In the course of a short general conversation she said she regretted she had no means of accepting my offer to buy her diamond, as it had disappeared.

'This afternoon a different lady called, giving herself the same identity and adding that the said identity had been this morning accepted by a judge "in his private sitting-room" – meaning, presumably, a judge in chambers. She thanked me for my offer and gave me the impression that she accepted it. But she couldn't deliver the diamond because she said it had been temporarily stolen – whatever that may mean. She was quite sure, she said, it would be returned. I don't know which of these women was the fake. Neither tried to touch me for money, so I'm doing nothing officially, but I thought you might like to know.'

'We're very grateful, Mr Gallerton. It's important information. Could you spare me a few minutes?'

'If you can come right along.'

Kyle could. In the hall of the Parnassus he was received by a white-headed man in the later fifties. Gallerton had the bearing of a successful business man who no longer needs to assert himself, and can afford to be as genial as he likes to anybody.

'Before we talk about the diamond, Mr Gallerton, d'you mind telling me whether you know Mr Velfrage personally?'

'I certainly do. He has been to the States twice in the last ten years to see me, and when I come over here we always forgather. I have interests in Britain and he acts for me. From time to time we exchange gossipy letters. He wrote about his finding Rabethorpe's daughter – which has nothing to do with our business. He expressed the hope that I could help him clinch the identification with information about the family.

'As a matter of fact I don't know anything worth knowing.' He took another look at Kyle, decided that he was the right sort. 'Frankly, my recollections on that topic are none too pleasant. I only saw Elsie Rabethorpe once – when she was eleven and I was fifteen. It only sticks in my memory because she was the means of getting me into disgrace with my aunt, her mother, and with my own parents. Our family was staying in London and I was sent over to spend a week with my aunt in Brussels. She was a moody woman and I was very bored. Elsie was an ugly little thing, but chock full of mischief. It sounds an ungallant thing to say now, but that kid pestered me into taking her on the quiet to a travelling circus. Owing to a mishap we were caught and her mother sent me back to London.'

There followed the anecdote of how and why the children had been caught, to which Kyle gave such close attention that he was startled when Gallerton asked in the same breath:

'Now *you* tell me something. What has happened to Velfrage?'

Kyle told him and induced him to make an appointment for the following day. The main inducement was the promise – given in strictest secrecy – that the Rabethorpe diamond would be produced for his inspection.

In spite of the anecdote, the whole interview had lasted less than ten minutes. It was the anecdote that sent Kyle hurrying to Mr Justice Holbeach – the judge who had authenticated the claim to the Rabethorpe estate.

By the time he returned to the Yard it was close upon five. He had very nearly forgotten the Kilburn Kid, and promptly had him brought in.

The Kid was unshaved and generally bedraggled. He looked older than his thirty-five years, and almost pitiably afraid.

'You can sit down, Kid. Charged with making a burglarious entry and molesting Mrs Rabethorpe, eh!'

'Pardnin' me for contradictin', I never did no molestin'. I never did no harm to the lady, sir, and I never stole nothink. I was drunk, sir.'

'And now you're here what do you know about conspiring with the girl Bradburn to steal the Rabethorpe diamond?'

The Kid swallowed hard.

'I never —'

'Shut up! I might get Mrs Rabethorpe to drop the charge. I might forget you were after that diamond —'

'Thank you, sir.'

'If you didn't kill that girl – and I don't think you did – you've nothing to be afraid of – until you tell me a lie. Tell me a single lie and I'll make things as damned hot for you as I can. Are you ready?'

'Yessir.'

'If you don't know the answer to this question, say you don't know. If you answer at all, it's got to be right. How many times have you looked on at an amateur champion boxing contest?'

'*Amachoors?* Me!' The Kid's obsequiousness left him, and he laughed coarsely. 'I never been near any amachoor boxing in me life, and with Gawd's 'elp I never will.'

'Then how did you know Habershon was a boxer? When he caught you in that girl's room the other afternoon you said something which showed you knew he was a boxer. How did you know?'

'Pardnin' me, sir, you said *amachoor* boxer.'

'Habershon is an amateur boxer.'

'No, sir. Pardnin' me for contradictin' – not an amachoor, sir. Why, he's got a right-hand punch that I'd *call* a right-hand punch!'

'He has. He didn't punch you. Where did you see that punch?' As the other hesitated : 'Don't make a mistake, Kid.'

'Lookin' through the corner of the blind the night of the shemozzle.'

'What else did you see in that room?'

'Nothink, sir. Only a piece of an old woman – it was only a sort o' slit, like, I was lookin' through.'

'Did you see the man whom Habershon hit?'

'Did I see him! I saw 'im when the gent made contact. I saw the other bloke's head go up first, then round a bit, then sort o' curl round sideways. And I could 'ear the contac' through the winder-glass. Sort o' *flang,* only splashy. Nearly stopped my 'eart in my state of 'ealth.'

'You saw the other man's face. Would you know it if you were to see it again?'

'Betcher life I would, sir !' The Kid chuckled ghoulishly. 'That is, if 'e's still got a face.'

'Then come along.'

Kyle took him in a police car to Chancery Lane, hid him where he could hold a clear view of Velfrage's office exit.

'If you see him come out of that building, don't say anything. Pull my sleeve.'

It was ten minutes to six. There were other offices in the building. In the next few minutes a dozen or so men and twice as many girls trickled out, singly and in couples.

As six was striking George Clawson came out, alone. Kyle said nothing but saw to it that his sleeve was easily accessible.

The Kid looked well at Clawson, but gave no signal. When a few others had come out of the building Kyle asked : 'Have you seen the man Habershon hit?'

'Not yet, sir.'

Kyle sighed. Another promising theory gone wrong.

'All right, Kid. You can scram.'

32

On the following morning Habershon rang Detective Inspector Kyle by appointment.

'What are you doing at six o'clock sharp tonight?' asked Kyle, a chortle in his voice. 'If you haven't anything else you might turn up at Woodville. Mrs Rabethorpe will be sure to give us cocktails.'

'Six o'clock tonight,' repeated Habershon, understanding only that Kyle was pleased with himself.

At a quarter to six exactly Habershon was being admitted by Celia Fenton.

'They're all here, including Prinny,' she said in an undertone. 'She's reclining prettily on the settee and being an invalid. She says she had to come because you might need her. Am I being catty?'

'You wouldn't know how. The trouble is that when Prinny says that kind of thing she believes it.'

In the study, Mrs Rabethorpe was dispensing cocktails.

'Mr Habershon! I'm so glad you could come. It feels just like a seance, though of course it's all so sad.'

Confused as usual, but impressive in a brocaded gown of royal purple, Mrs Rabethorpe had the air of giving a party 'to meet Detective Inspector Kyle'. Mrs Wellard ignored Habershon. Keller waved his glass from a corner of the room. Clawson nodded.

Prinny held out her hand. She was reclining on the settee as one who has planned to recline on a settee.

'Bruce darling! Aren't I magnificent. Don't say that I oughtn't to have come.'

'You oughtn't to have come. You'll steal the act.'

A couple of minutes later Kyle arrived, instantly adapting himself to the atmosphere created by Mrs Rabethorpe, which happened to suit his purpose. Middle-class respectability had been used as an effective cloak for a double murder – a device which could be used with equal effectiveness by Scotland Yard.

He accepted a whisky and soda, and congratulated Mrs Rabethorpe on establishing her claim to the family fortune.

'But it has all happened too late!' wailed Mrs Rabethorpe. 'What is the use of money when one is old?'

'You'll know – in thirty years time,' smirked Kyle, and turned to inquire tenderly after Prinny's health. He informed Mrs Wellard that the weather was unexpectedly mild. In a sudden silence, Clawson guffawed.

'I call upon the secretary to read the minutes of the last meeting.' Prinny clapped her hands. Keller was believed to have muttered 'Hear, hear.'

'That's a good idea,' said Kyle. Glass in hand, he stood astride the Indian hearthrug which had been used to cover that which Habershon had believed to be a lay figure.

'At approximately five-thirty on the afternoon of the fifteenth of last month,' he began, 'Mr Velfrage, carrying the Rabethorpe diamond, rang the bell of this house. The door was answered by the dead girl, Bradburn. Bradburn obtained possession of Mr Velfrage's dispatch-case – how, we do not know – and took it to her room.'

'Oh – h!' It was a small collective murmur of surprise.

'Approximately three minutes later, Mr Habershon, who was a little light-headed owing to influenza and a liberal dosage of quinine, got out of his car and rang the doorbell, being anxious about Velfrage.

'The door was answered not by Bradburn but by a woman purporting to be a housemaid. As you are all aware, Mr Habershon has stated to me that the woman was Miss Loftus. But he has himself robbed that statement of value as evidence by warning me that he feels he must have made a mistake. After furthering his acquaintance with Miss Loftus, he came to believe that she would never lend herself to any kind of trickery that would hurt someone else.'

'That was dear of you, Bruce,' said Prinny, looking at Celia.

Clawson stood up, and raised his voice to drown interruption.

'I can tell you what's coming next,' he said. 'Mr Kyle is about to give us a theory based on poor Habershon's delusions. I'm sorry, Habershon, but I have to speak plainly for the sake of the others. Remember this, everybody. When a detective wants to talk, it means that his case is incomplete. He hopes to complete it by picking up something from the comments of the suspects.'

Kyle beamed on Clawson, made him a little bow.

'Mr Clawson is quite right. The case is a long way from complete.' He spoke like a provincial councillor conceding an opponent's point. 'As you ladies and gentlemen don't belong to the criminal classes, I thought you might like to talk things over in an unofficial way.'

'There's no unofficial way of talking to a policeman,' put in Keller.

'If you all prefer it, we'll stick to Regulations.'

'Oh, do let's go on!' begged Mrs Rabethorpe. 'It's about those awful murders, of course! It's so lucky Mr Habershon is here to clear the air.'

The impetuous personality of Mrs Rabethorpe invariably triumphed over her own misconceptions of nearly everything. She had the genius of creating in others a subconscious desire to do as she asked.

'Mr Habershon states that he forced his way into this room,' resumed Kyle, 'where he saw Mrs Wellard sitting in – that – chair, holding by its chain the bag with the peacock's eye design. Mr Clawson threatened him with a revolver. Mr Keller was standing by the safe, which was open. In front of it was an object in an upright chair, covered with this rug on which I am standing, which Habershon took to be an artist's lay figure.

'Mr Clawson threatened him with a revolver and was knocked out. A brawl followed in which the – er – ladies took part. Mr Keller also produced a revolver, which was taken from him. Habershon tried to shoot Keller but hit the supposed lay figure, knocking it over. The brawl ended with Habershon pursuing Miss Loftus, intending – as he himself insists – to kill her. At the top of the stairs he caught her by the dress, but she escaped, leaving the torn dress in his hand. He continued his pursuit through the upper rooms, coming in time to Bradburn's room, where he found Bradburn. He had a brief conversation with her, which makes clear that Bradburn was aware that something of a criminal nature was being perpetrated in the house. At this point, or soon afterwards, he seems to have fainted, leaving an unaccounted period of approximately twenty minutes before the meeting with Miss Fenton in the hall.

'After leaving the house in his car, Habershon was stopped at the gate by Mrs Wellard who demanded the return of her bag. Mr Keller attempted to enforce the demand with a revolver, but was shaken off. Before he reached home Habershon had an accident and was taken to hospital.

'I will add that a number of the items in Habershon's account have been substantiated. In Velfrage's body, in the thigh, there was a bullet wound from a heavy calibre revolver. As to the brawl, we have an almost expert witness. A down-at-heel ex-pugilist, called the Kilburn Kid, was prowling round the house for his own purposes. He looked through the window at the edge of the blind and saw the knock-out. The bag —'

'How could he have seen my bag if —'

'Don't interrupt, Margo,' cut in Clawson. 'Do you tell me, Inspector, that this feller recognized me as the crook Habershon laid out?'

'No,' admitted Kyle. 'He was absorbed in the technique of the blow. That is one of the weak spots. I can't prove that you were the crook Habershon knocked out.'

Silence fell. Kyle glanced at his wrist-watch. Prinny's eyes were closed. Celia was standing by the door, looking doubtfully from one face to another.

'I think it's perfectly wonderful of Mr Habershon!' exclaimed Mrs Rabethorpe. 'Prinny and the others are psychic symbols, of course! And later on you'll tell us who the real criminals are, won't you, Mr Kyle?'

'Quite right, Mrs Rabethorpe,' agreed Kyle.

'Let's look this thing squarely in the face!' Clawson addressed the room at large. 'Inspector Kyle doesn't know whether we are a gang of cooks—or whether poor old Habershon is seeing double again, as in the case of his seeing Velfrage in Margo's house. We admit we can't prove we weren't here at that time. But Mr Kyle knows jolly well that crooks can always fix an alibi. Take the thing in the round, from a common-sense angle. The whole bag o' tricks amounts to an attempt to steal the diamond. On that assumption, why did we kill the Bradburn girl? Why didn't we kill Velfrage? Come to that, why didn't Velfrage communicate with Mr Gallerton —'

'Perhaps he did,' interrupted Kyle. 'We can ask him. He'll be here in – let me see – about ten minutes.'

Clawson opened his mouth, as one taking a deep breath. Mrs Rabethorpe was indignant.

'Why didn't you tell me?' she reproached Kyle. 'The fishmonger would have let me have a little ice for the cocktails.'

Mrs Wellard got up.

'I can contribute nothing to this discussion,' she said. 'I'm going home, Elsie.'

'Mrs Wellard,' said Kyle, 'I particularly request that you remain.'

'I'm sorry, Inspector, but I cannot comply with your request.'

Celia Fenton moved from the door but did not open it. Mrs Wellard had to open it herself, the dowager stance suffering a little.

In the hall stood a man of the uniformed branch, and near him a policewoman, also in uniform.

'Excuse me, madam. No one is to leave the room without the Inspector's permission.'

'This is intolerable!' blustered Mrs Wellard.

'Margo, please don't make a scene,' begged Clawson. 'This is a serious investigation. Come and sit down and don't interrupt.' With a gesture, he stopped an outburst from Mrs Rabethorpe. When quiet had been restored he returned his attention to Kyle.

'As crooks out to steal a diamond – which could be sold for only very little – we show up as rather imbecile, don't you think? We allow Velfrage to escape and tell his tale to the police. But he does not tell his tale to the police. He was alive until yesterday morning. Why didn't he come to you?'

With a glance Kyle warned Habershon to silence.

'I don't know,' said Kyle. 'Why didn't he?'

'Either because he was forcibly prevented – or because he did not want to, for his own reasons,' said Clawson. 'Now, if Miss Fenton will let me, I want to ask her a question.' As Celia assented : 'Did you say, in Mr Kyle's hearing, that you rang Velfrage during the afternoon, told him that your aunt could not keep the appointment here that evening, and that you had some small conversation with him?'

'Yes,' said Celia indifferently. 'That is what happened.'

'Thank you, Celia.' Clawson turned back to Kyle. 'There are seven persons besides myself employed by the firm. They will tell you that Velfrage was last seen in that office when he left for lunch – it was the last time I myself saw him. Miss Fenton, therefore, could not have spoken to him on the telephone in the afternoon.'

'And so what, Clawson?' demanded Habershon.

'I am suggesting, Inspector, that the persons with whom Habershon scrapped in this room were not trying to steal the diamond but trying to protect it.'

'Trying to protect it from me?' asked Habershon.

'Well, old man, you've said yourself you aren't certain you didn't scupper the girl. How can you be certain that you didn't pinch the diamond and hide it where you can't find it yourself?'

'Mr Habershon did not hide the diamond.' The words came from Detective Inspector Kyle and caused an instant hush. Kyle added : 'He handed it to the police. It was under the lining of Mrs Wellard's bag.'

There was a general gasp of astonishment, Habershon himself as astonished as any.

From his pocket-case, Kyle took out the little box which might have been mistaken for a pill-box.

'Here it is !'

'Oh, do let me see !' shrieked Mrs Rabethorpe. 'Don't touch it, any of you – unless you have a small piece of iron in your hand. A curse doesn't work through iron. I think Mr Kyle is safe – the police are sure to be exempt!'

Kyle was holding the Rabethorpe diamond in his palm, so that all who wished might peer at it. Clawson stood apart.

'Can you identify the Rabethorpe diamond, Mr Clawson?' asked Kyle.

'No,' answered Clawson. 'I've never seen it before.'

Behind them the door was opened.

'Mr Gallerton is here, sir,' boomed the constable.

Kyle returned the diamond to his pocket-case.

33

GALLERTON came in, with a faintly conspiratorial air. He
stole a glance at Kyle, as if for instructions. Mrs Rabethorpe
pounced upon him.

'Mr Gallerton! Isn't it wonderful! The diamond has
turned up literally as you entered the house!'

'You warned me that it was only "temporarily" stolen,
Mrs Rabethorpe,' smiled Gallerton.

'It appears that the police had it all the time. Only they
couldn't tell us because of the trouble over poor Mr Velfrage. Margo dear, meet Mr Gallerton – my friend, Mrs
Wellard.'

Mr Gallerton bowed stiffly.

'I have already the privilege of this lady's acquaintance,
but at our last meeting, which was yesterday morning, her
name was "Mrs Rabethorpe".'

'I'm afraid that's my fault, sir,' said Clawson. 'I didn't
make it sufficiently clear that Mrs Wellard was being introduced as a friend of Mrs Rabethorpe – not as Mrs Rabethorpe herself.'

'Indeed!' Mr Gallerton made it clear that the explanation was not acceptable.

So did Mrs Rabethorpe.

'But how deceitful of you, Margo! When I was telling
you how handsome he was, you pretended you did not
know him.'

Celia created a diversion by providing Mr Gallerton with
a drink. Mrs Rabethorpe introduced him to everyone in
turn.

'Now that you know everybody, you'll naturally want to
see the diamond. Where *did* we put it? Oh, it's in your
pocket, Mr Kyle!'

Mrs Rabethorpe had taken charge of operations, and
Kyle knew that there was no means of deposing her, short

of putting her out of her own room, which would have defeated his plan.

He handed the diamond to Gallerton, who promptly produced a pocket lens. For a minute or more he examined it, while even Mrs Rabethorpe was silent.

'This is it!' he exclaimed. 'I have coveted that diamond for thirty years. That's why I've offered an outsize price for it.'

As if it hurt him to do so, he handed the diamond back to Kyle.

'At the same time, I feel sure you will appreciate, Mrs Rabethorpe, that I'm not paying out so large a sum without indisputable proof of title.'

'There'll be no trouble there, sir,' said Clawson. 'Mrs – more accurately Miss – Rabethorpe's claim to the estate, which includes the diamond, has been authenticated by a High Court judge in chambers. It is indisputable on any ground whatever —'

'Except the ground of fraud,' interrupted Kyle.

'I resent that remark!' snapped Clawson.

'Oh dear!' wailed Mrs Rabethorpe. 'Who is being a fraud now?'

'No one, I sincerely hope,' said Gallerton. 'I take it, Mrs Rabethorpe, that you know yourself to be William Rabethorpe's daughter?'

'Well of course I do, now that the judge has settled it!'

'But you were not sure *before* the judge settled it?'

'I suppose I was. Poor Mr Velfrage knew I was fond of money, and I'm sure he wouldn't have been so unkind as to raise false hopes.' She went on: 'You see, I had never heard of my father or the diamond until Mr Velfrage tracked me out in Brussels a few years ago, so how can I know that I am his daughter?'

Mr Gallerton, perceiving the danger of being dragged up a blind alley, tried a new approach.

'If you are William Rabethorpe's daughter, you are also my first cousin, Mrs Rabethorpe, and I —'

'Oh, how nice! Won't you call me "Elsie"?'

'Thank you, Elsie. I was going on to say that I can enable you to satisfy yourself – and everybody else – that you are the lawful heiress —'

'Not a birthmark, for heaven's sake!' groaned Prinny.

'Certainly not a birthmark!' Mr Gallerton had taken a dislike to Prinny. 'Mrs er – Elsie, do you remember a callow youth of fifteen coming to stay with you for a few days – when you were eleven?'

'No. Was it you? You mustn't mind my forgetting. Eleven? No, I would not have noticed a boy particularly – not until I was perhaps fifteen.'

'Possibly I can refresh your memory. Your mother had refused your request to take us to the circus. One afternoon – no doubt, at my suggestion – we gave her the slip and went to the circus. You and I alone.'

'Yes – so we did!' said Mrs Rabethorpe, without marked enthusiasm.

'Do you remember a special incident – an incident that would be certain to remain in the memory for life?'

'It's really rather difficult,' said Mrs Rabethorpe. 'You see, I went lots of times to that circus. Always giving my mother the slip. Always with a boy. Sometimes there were, as you say, special incidents, but I never made a fuss and certainly never bothered to remember.'

Mr Gallerton came perilously near to blushing.

'I'm not beaten yet!' He spoke to Kyle. 'Elsie, do you remember going on a sort of scenic railway in little box cars for two —?'

'Yes, but they all took me on those.'

'— when our car jibbed and the car behind ran into us?'

'Oh, you were *that* boy, were you?' shrieked Mrs Rabethorpe. 'I couldn't possibly have guessed. I didn't like that boy at all.'

'But you remember?'

'I remember that I was hit and you weren't. And when I began to bleed rather revoltingly, *you* cried and *I* laughed, and you said when I grew up I'd never be a lady.'

'William Rabethorpe's daughter!' said Gallerton to Kyle. 'I guess I'll take that diamond.'

'There's no proof there, Mr Gallerton,' objected Kyle.

'You supplied the essential details. Mrs Rabethorpe, in effect, merely said "yes".'

'I was coming to that.' Gallerton was not too pleased at being directed. 'You may like to know, Elsie, what actually happened. The bumper of the rear car was smashed, and a sharp length of rusty iron pierced your – er – pierced *you* – in your – er – in a part of your back.'

'How very delicately put, Cousin Sundius!' simpered Mrs Rabethorpe.

'They put seven stitches in, leaving you with a permanent scar and a discoloration of the skin owing to the tattooing effect of the rust.'

'Don't answer that question, Elsie!' shouted Clawson.

'It isn't a question – it's an insult!' shrilled Mrs Rabethorpe. 'I have no scar and no discoloration – *anywhere*! It is a monstrous thing to say of me, now that I am no longer young. I would have you know, Cousin Sundius, that when I was twenty-four I sat in the nude for Vortiot, and at thirty-five, Cousin Sundius, I sat in the nude for Maerlinger. Maerlinger's picture was bought by England and you can see it in the Tate Gallery, where you will look in vain for a scar or a discoloration.'

'The artist would know better than to paint it in,' said Gallerton. 'Anyhow, your mother sent my mother the doctors' report. I have it to this day. It definitely says a scar of an inch and a half —'

'Then it was another accident and another child of eleven, and I think, in the circumstances, you may wish to apologize.'

'Mrs Rabethorpe!' cried Kyle. 'Do you realize that you are saying you are not William Rabethorpe's daughter?'

'That is absurd! How can an accident at the age of eleven affect one's parentage?'

Kyle found that one too difficult. Gallerton carried on.

'You admit that you did have an accident when you were eleven?' he pressed.

Mrs Rabethorpe was angry to the point of hysteria.

'I admit nothing of the kind. But I see that I am not believed. That is enough! All my life I have laboured to keep my skin unblemished, only to be told in my own house that it is scarred and discoloured. Very well! I am going to take all my clothes off.'

Mr Gallerton reached the door first, Kyle hard on his heels to cancel the order about leaving the room. Habershon and Clawson followed, with Keller panting in the rear.

Kyle spoke to the policewoman, who promptly entered the library, closing the door behind her.

The men gathered round the foot of the staircase.

'I wish that lady were my kinswoman,' said Gallerton. 'She's eccentric, but by heaven, she's absolutely honest!' He glanced contemptuously at Clawson. 'Her claim to the fortune may be a fake, Inspector, but she doesn't know it.'

'Quite so!' agreed Kyle. 'We shan't touch her.'

'You'll have difficulty in touching anybody,' said Clawson.

The door of the library opened and the scraggy Mrs Wellard came out. No longer a dowager, she looked about her in a bewildered manner, then approached the group by the stairs. She was walking oddly, with a gait that suggested the sleepwalker.

She stopped opposite Clawson.

'George!' she exclaimed in a voice little above a whisper. 'You bungling fool!'

'I did my best. I told her to keep her mouth shut. The case could never have been reopened if she hadn't denied the scar in the presence of witnesses.'

'*You – bungling fool!*' Mrs Wellard was trembling, as if shivering violently with cold. 'She has the scar and the discoloration! She is William Rabethorpe's daughter – you bungling fool!'

With a sound like the growl of a cat, Mrs Wellard flung herself at Clawson, scratching, biting, trying to gouge his eyes.

Kyle and Habershon dragged her away, as the policewoman appeared.

'Take this woman into one of the rooms, please,' he ordered. 'If you can get her calm, bring her to the library.'

'Very good, sir. I found a scar about an inch and a half long, and considerable discoloration. Mrs Rabethorpe denied there was any scar, but she refused to look in the mirror I held for her. She said I was to tell the American gentleman that her skin is flawless, so I said I would – but it isn't true.'

'It's the most magnificent lie in history!' enthused Gallerton. 'I'll be able to buy that diamond. I reckon you don't want me any more, Inspector.'

'Very grateful to you for your help, sir.'

'You're welcome. And I'll regard it as a favour if your authorities will let me take that diamond back with me the day after tomorrow.'

'I'll do my best,' promised Kyle. 'It will depend on the nature of the charge. Good night, sir.'

Clawson waited until Gallerton was out of earshot.

'What charge, Inspector? And against whom?'

'You thought that claim was a fake, Clawson. You were as staggered as I was to hear that she really is Rabethorpe's daughter.'

Clawson looked at the detective with cold defiance.

'What charge?' he repeated. 'And against whom?'

'The charge? Murder, of course!' answered Kyle briskly. 'Against whom? I don't know yet, Clawson. The case is still incomplete.' He added: 'Let's go back to the library, as Miss Fenton has just signalled the all-clear. We shall want you too, Keller.'

34

HABERSHON stood by the staircase, one hand on the newel. In that brief exchange between Clawson and Kyle lay the blue-print of the crime. Clawson had believed he was backing a fake heiress. It turned out that he had been backing a genuine heiress. That was the formula which would make reasonable the apparently imbecile behaviour of the gang.

Yet Clawson seemed certain that he had nothing to fear. And Clawson probably knew much more about the rules of evidence than did Kyle.

Celia was helping Mrs Rabethorpe up the stairs. Habershon went on to the library, where Clawson was pouring Prinny a drink. Keller was staring out of the window at the lights of the police cars. Kyle, his back to the others, was tapping a cigarette.

'We'll wait a few minutes for the others,' said Kyle, as if by way of apology.

If Clawson was an unusual criminal, thought Habershon, Kyle was an unusual official. Habershon felt something approaching aversion creeping over his admiration, pulling against the gratitude he felt to the detective. But for Kyle's breadth of vision he himself would have been arrested before doing anything to disentangle himself. He had been encouraged and sustained by the detective's forbearance, his genial, friendly manner. But in the last few minutes an impersonal ruthlessness had revealed itself. The geniality remained, but Habershon saw it now as a mannerism – a screen for the mechanism of Scotland Yard.

Celia came in and stood near the door. Habershon crossed the room and joined her, bringing her a chair.

'Mrs Wellard will be here in a minute,' she announced.

When Mrs Wellard came, she glared at the company and sat in the chair in which Habershon had first seen her.

'I'm going to give you a chance to sort yourselves out,'

said Kyle, without preliminary. 'If you don't take it, we'll go back to Regulations.'

'It's a fair cop, guv'nor, and we'll go quiet,' mocked Clawson.

Kyle grinned good-humouredly.

'Meaning I haven't copped you yet,' grinned Kyle. He went to the door.

'The Kilburn Kid!' he ordered. 'You know a lot of law, Clawson. D'you know any chemistry?'

'No. Is that where I made my "fatal slip"?'

'It's where you made one of 'em. That affidavit of Velfrage's you produced in court yesterday morning! We have a whole team of science boys to swear the ink hadn't been on the paper for twenty-four hours. The signature itself was genuine. Means you contacted Velfrage after the court rose on Tuesday afternoon.'

'Charge denied. No statement,' said Clawson.

The Kilburn Kid stood near the door, twirling his hat.

'Come in, Kid. Look round at everybody and tell me how many you have seen before.'

'There's the gent!' The Kid jerked his thumb at Habershon and continued his survey. 'And there's the young lady that lives with the old lady.'

'Don't describe her. Point your finger at her.'

The Kid pointed at Prinny, lolling on the settee.

'Is that the lady you saw in the hall when you were in the corridor leading from the kitchen? What was she doing?'

'Nothink, sir. Only standin' still. She called to a bloke I couldn't see: "It's small enough to go in the safe," she says.'

'All right, Kid. Turn up at the Yard tomorrow and draw your expenses. You can hop it.'

' "It's small enough to go in the safe," ' repeated Kyle when the door had been shut. 'The Kilburn Kid was referring to the corpse of Bradburn. This statement – unless modified by statements of yours – is evidence against Mrs Wellard and Miss Loftus and a man unknown.'

Prinny closed her eyes as if to remind all concerned that she was an invalid. Mrs Wellard was moving her lips soundlessly. Keller was hunched up in an armchair. Clawson was sitting at the writing-table, his eyes on Kyle, while he doodled on the telephone book.

'When we are dealing with a bunch of crooks, we question them separately,' Kyle was explaining. 'We tell Crook A what Crook B has said to the detriment of A. That makes A so angry that he supplies a fact to the detriment of B. Then we reverse the process.

'That method would not work with persons like yourselves. I am keeping you together until you yourselves insist on separation. I am revealing the weakness of the police case – in order that you may understand its strength.

'Let me tell you a little more about the strength – a footnote to what I told you about yourselves before Mr Gallerton arrived and greatly increased our strength.

'Bradburn, as I told you, went up to her room with Velfrage's dispatch case no doubt believing that the diamond was inside. When Velfrage came into this room, one of you knocked him senseless. What you did about the diamond and why you did it, I admit frankly I don't know. I can say this, though – when I handed the bag to Mrs Wellard the other night I saw her feel inside the lining. Evidently she believed the diamond might be there. Further, on the night of the crime, she stopped Habershon's car in the drive, demanding the bag. She thought Habershon had it. She didn't think Bradburn had it. That alone disposes of her statement that Bradburn had stolen the bag.

'Leave the diamond out for a minute. You sat the unconscious Velfrage in a chair, and put a rug over him – a pretty desperate device, but you had no time for anything else before Habershon burst in on you.

'After the brawl you carried Velfrage to Mrs Wellard's house next door. Now, Habershon had unknowingly wounded him – a large wound. But the local police found no blood on this carpet. One of you mopped it up – Clawson, I think. Keller, who took his medical degree but was struck off, was probably attending Velfrage.

'The lapse of time between Habershon entering the house and the Kilburn Kid hearing Miss Loftus say "It's small enough to go in the safe", is only about twelve minutes. You had barely started washing the carpet when Bradburn caught you at it. That was the end of Bradburn.

'I don't know why you didn't kill Velfrage at once. I was in the gallery when you were before the judge in chambers. I don't see how you could have guessed that the judge would suddenly want that affidavit signed by Velfrage. Anyhow, Velfrage made it clear to Habershon how you fooled the old man so that he never knew he had been kidnapped.

'When you buried him under Habershon's floor-boards, you were counting on a lapse of time before we turned up. Quite reasonable, too! We might not have found the body for weeks if Habershon had not demanded that we should search at once. The fact is, Clawson, I admit I was taken in by your trick of putting Keller in that bed. I did believe, for a short time, that Habershon was lying. Which meant I was ready to work on your theory that he was a maniac killer.

'I wasn't sure that Habershon hadn't tried to poison Miss Loftus – until the analyst reported that the dope could not have been in the whisky for more than twenty-four hours. And I knew Habershon couldn't have laid hands on it in that time. Another slip-up on chemistry, Clawson!'

Prinny sat bolt upright, pointing a finger at Clawson.

'Shut up, Prinny!' cried Clawson before she had spoken. 'Mr Kyle hasn't finished.'

'I have finished,' said Kyle. 'It's up to you all now to sort yourselves out, as I suggested.'

'So you believe,' said Clawson, 'that you have evidence on which you could charge me with murdering Bradburn, murdering Velfrage, and attempting to murder Miss Loftus – or would it be Habershon?'

'I don't believe anything of the kind!' Kyle was offended. 'I couldn't prove that you murdered either of 'em, Clawson. Same applies to Keller – and, of course, to the two ladies. I couldn't pin even one of the murders on any one of you.'

'Then what the hell are we talking about?' cried Keller.

'Mr Kyle!' Prinny gazed at him sadly. 'Don't play cat-and-mouse with us, there's a dear!'

'You must blame Clawson,' Kyle told her. 'As a lawyer,

he knows that – though I have no evidence on which to charge any one of you with murder – I have a cast-iron case against the four of you of jointly murdering Bradburn and Velfrage. And the judge would tell the jury they needn't bother their heads about which of you did what.'

35

FOR a moment Habershon felt weak about the knees. In the same genial manner in which Kyle had chatted with him in Cornwall – with the same infernal friendliness with which he secured co-operation in London – he had brought these four into the shadow of the gallows.

In the silence, Celia took Habershon by the arm and pushed him into the chair which she had occupied. She kept a hand on his shoulder to still his protest.

'George dear!' Prinny raised herself so that she could see him above the back of the settee. 'You haven't forgotten your promise, have you?'

'I have not! I can keep it, if you three have the sense to keep your mouths shut tight. Don't make a single comment, and you'll be safe. And you'll damned well give me a pat on the back. You, Margo, tried to scratch my eyes out. And you, Prinny, threatened to betray me to the police if Habershon were arrested for killing Velfrage. Don't say I'm a malicious man, that's all!'

He turned to Kyle.

'I confess that I murdered Bradburn and Velfrage by strangling them. The others assisted me indirectly without appreciating what they were doing. If you'll write that down, I'll sign it.'

'Ah! Does you great credit, Clawson!' Kyle made no move towards taking it down. 'Only, our people are rather suspicious of heroes.'

'Hero be damned!' snapped Clawson. 'I can't save myself by dragging my friends into the dock with me. Incidentally, I let them down by letting you spot that I thought Elsie was *not* Rabethorpe's daughter. I knew about that accident at the circus, and Velfrage didn't. But he did know that Gallerton had made that trip to Belgium as a boy. He intended to get Gallerton talking – and I intended that he should not meet Gallerton.

'Elsie told me she had no scar on her body and I believed her – damn her pathological vanity! I reckoned that if I could put her in possession of the fortune and then explain that it was all a mistake, I could put pressure on her to carve up the quarter of a million.

'I knew Velfrage's movements and planned to use this house. As you will want me to account for the small details – I fixed a business dinner so that Elsie should not turn up here. I impersonated Velfrage when Celia rang up.'

For the first time he spoke with bitterness.

'The whole thing would have been plain sailing if it hadn't been for that damned diamond! I was not such a lunatic as to want to steal the diamond – no fence would touch it. It was to my interest to leave it in the Rabethorpe estate – to protect it, in fact. And of course I didn't know that Bradburn would be in the house when we arrived – still less that she was after the diamond. The first thing that went wrong was that Bradburn got to the door to admit Velfrage before Prinny, though I didn't know that until afterwards, because Bradburn didn't announce him. He just walked in.

'I batted him on the head. I was standing behind the door – the others were over in the corner there, so he never knew what struck him. Frank Keller, as previously planned, opened the safe with Velfrage's key – we were looking for correspondence and documents. I took the diamond from Velfrage – for safety – and asked Margo to take care of it. She put it in the lining of her bag.

'Prinny Loftus, who had been in the drawing-room getting herself up as a parlourmaid to admit Velfrage, discovered that Bradburn was in the house, saw her going upstairs carrying something which you have since told us was Velfrage's dispatch-case. Prinny was coming in here to tell us about it when Habershon rang the bell.

'We lifted Velfrage into a chair and covered him with a rug – there was no key in this door – before Habershon broke in. He has told you what happened then – he saw more of it than I did. When I came round from the wallop he had given me, I found Frank and Margo wringing their hands. Margo told me that "that madman", meaning Habershon, had chased Prinny upstairs and probably killed her.

'My first thought was to get Velfrage away. I took the rug off him, found he was bleeding from the leg. Frank patched him up, and we carried him into the Rolls.

'I went into the kitchen here, got a bucket of water and mopped up the blood. When I was half through the job, Bradburn took me by surprise. She had crept in – she grabbed the gun which I'm told Habershon had flung across the room, and held me up. I don't know why she wasn't carrying her own gun. I heard you found one in her room.

' "Might do meself a bit o' good if I was to call the cops," she said, grinning at me. Little beast! I bluffed her that the gun was mine and that I knew it wasn't loaded. She dropped it and bolted. I chased her into the drawing-room – caught her as she was trying to get out of the window. I've told you how I killed her.

'I was wondering what to do next when Prinny burst in, blue with cold, in her underclothes. She told me she had dodged "the madman" by standing on the window-sill of the bathroom. She said he was lying on the first-floor landing, unconscious, and we'd better get out. While she was talking, she was putting on her proper clothes. Then she saw Bradburn. I told her the madman had killed Bradburn.'

'And I believed him, at the time!' cut in Prinny. 'I did think you had killed her, Bruce, but that you didn't know what you had done.' She went on : 'It was nice of you to admit that, George, but you've given away such a lot that you might as well do the rest in comfort.'

'I've promised you that none of you will be charged!' snapped Clawson : 'My confession is not evidence against you. But if I tell a single lie Kyle will break it and upset the confession and start work on all of you.'

'Then let me say my little piece myself,' insisted Prinny. 'I waited in the hall —'

'Shut up, you little fool!' bellowed Clawson. 'If I say it, it isn't evidence against you.'

He turned to Kyle.

'At her suggestion I put the body in the safe, and Prinny and I went over to Margo's house. We got Velfrage into bed. Then Margo suddenly spotted that she had lost her bag. She and Frank went back for it. They stopped Habershon's car at the gate, but he denied that he had the bag, and scraped them off. They saw lights go on and off in the house. They didn't know it was Celia and thought it might be the police.

'Frank doctored Velfrage – very efficiently, too. Habershon has told you what Velfrage was made to believe. But to go back a bit – when Habershon walked into this room a second time the other night we had time to get our breath, because we had heard a bit of what was going on in the hall. That lapse of memory gave us a break. We palled on to him, mainly to watch him, but partly in the hope of finding the diamond, which would mean another hundred thousand pounds to be divided up. But he was the sort of man whom no one would believe to be a criminal. So I hit on the idea of suggesting homicidal mania.'

'You *brute*!' cried Prinny. 'You made me believe it.'

'Fighting for one's life is a brutal process,' said Clawson, indifferently. 'But although he suspected himself, he was so infernally sane that he became too dangerous, and I tried to get rid of him with the whisky, planting in his room evidence that he had doped it himself. When I met him coming out of Velfrage's room yesterday, I thought I could pull off a double with that whisky. So I could have, Kyle, if you hadn't tripped me up on that ink. And, of course, Gallerton's scar story destroyed the useful camouflage of apparent motivelessness on my part.'

'Why didn't you kill Velfrage at once?' asked Kyle.

'Because although I didn't foresee that particular affidavit the judge demanded, I did foresee the possibility of some query arising which I couldn't have answered. The documents in the case were very complicated. I had to keep him alive – without his seeing Gallerton – until the claim was decided. And then, at the last moment, Habershon broke into Margo's house and spoilt it all. I did not give up, even then.'

He paused. Something of an artist's pride in his work showed in his face as he went on :

'You will say I had luck, in that Frank really did spend the night in Margo's house. But it's not luck. I knew that fact and used it. In a few minutes after Habershon had walked off to telephone you, I analysed the circumstances and turned them to advantage. I seized the chance to rivet your suspicion that Habershon might be a maniac killer. I would stage a brilliant repetition. He would again report fact which would seem to be fantasy. And you would disbelieve, as you had apparently disbelieved his story that I was the original man with the gun, and that Prinny was the red-headed housemaid.

'I saw that I must kill Velfrage at once and put the corpse in the bungalow, where I had already dug a grave for that purpose. But I had counted on a lapse of time before you found the body – so that the doctor could not be precise as to how long Velfrage had been dead. Habershon spoilt that too, by prodding you into making an immediate search of his own place. His honesty is so infernally energetic I wish I could manage to hate him instead of admiring him as a bright man wasted.

'If Margo keeps her mouth shut, you will not be able to disprove that she behaved as Velfrage told Habershon she behaved – as a kind hostess who did not know there was any concealment of his whereabouts. Any questions, Mr Kyle?'

Before Kyle could answer, Celia cut in.

'I have a question. A black dress, torn —'

'— was found by you and Habershon under Bradburn's bed,' interrupted Clawson. 'I bought it from a theatrical outfitter's to pile up the evidence against Habershon.' He glanced at Kyle.

'You certainly seem to have covered most of the ground, Clawson.'

'Then I'll write out my confession now, and the others can buzz off home.'

'We needn't do that here,' said Kyle, moving to the door.

'If there's going to be a formal confession, Mr Kyle, it's going to be written here,' said Clawson. 'Prison would cramp my style.'

'All right!' agreed Kyle. 'Perhaps the others will kindly wait in another room.'

While the room was emptying, Clawson went to the little writing-table and opened the drawers, assembling paper and carbons.

'Just a minute, Clawson!' Kyle felt him for a weapon. 'We don't want a last-minute melodrama.'

All the same, there was a last-minute melodrama. Kyle had neglected to examine the drawer in the writing-table.

In the hall the policewoman and her male colleague were hovering. Celia opened the door of the drawing-room. When Prinny had followed Mrs Wellard, who was being supported by Keller, Celia shut the door on them.

'We'd better leave them alone to congratulate themselves on their escape,' she said to Habershon, and led him to the little morning-room.

She was cool, almost detached, whereas Habershon felt his head whirling with thoughts which collided and produced emotional confusion, centred on Celia.

'Your nightmare, as you called it, is all over,' said Celia. 'Slip into reverse and forget all you can.'

'Thanks to you! You helped me to remember enough to feed Kyle when he most needed it. I shall not try to forget that bit, Celia.'

'I'm glad if it really helped!' He did not notice her expression, because he was not looking at her. She went on: 'It was generous of you to whitewash Prinny. Most men would be spiteful about those scratches.'

'It wasn't whitewash, exactly,' he protested. 'She thought I was mad, or fighting drunk, and would kill everybody within reach. One can't blame her for that!'

'Can one blame her for dressing up as a parlourmaid?'

That, he reflected, was the sort of thing Miss Parker might have said.

'It's futile to judge Prinny by our standards,' he asserted. 'I bet Clawson told her some innocent tale of an estate held up in Chancery because Velfrage was so fussy – I bet he made her see the whole thing as a lark in a good cause. Then grisly things happened, and she had to do what she was told.'

'She must be very gullible, Bruce.'

'She *is* – most extraordinarily gullible! She gulls herself. With a fake sophistication which makes her easy prey for men like Clawson.'

'Fake sophistication!' repeated Celia. 'That never occurred to me. Perhaps you're right, Bruce. I'm sorry I was catty about her. I suppose it's impossible not to be jealous of Prinny.'

'She might say the same of you, Celia – if she had the sense, which she hasn't. She can be true to a person but not to an idea. She should envy your balance, which makes you demand an orderly life and a methodical routine. Most of all, your outlook – what my friend Miss Parker calls "moral and social background" – which poor Prinny so conspicuously lacks. I'm afraid I'm ranting, rather, but you set me off.'

In short, he admired her for her ability to stand on her own feet. And of course he was grateful for the help she had given him. That was all! Celia faced the facts without flinching. The bit about moral and social background was true.

'I'm forgetting Aunt Elsie!' she exclaimed. 'I wonder whether she understands that she really is a rich woman at last. Probably we shall go to Brussels to sneer at all her old enemies. Come and see us before we go, Bruce.'

'Be sure I will!' Gratitude to her welled up in him – a vast gratitude, the nature of which he failed to understand, though it was crystal clear to Celia. He loved her for letting him off love.

In the drawing-room Habershon was surprised to find Prinny lolling on the sofa alone.

'Kyle said Margo could go home, and Frank took her,' she explained. 'George will probably be hours with his confession.'

Habershon grunted and sat down.

'So now you know all about Clawson!' he ejaculated, unable to keep a sneer from his voice.

'Don't rub it in, dear. I've learnt my lesson.'

'You haven't! You couldn't learn any lesson, or you wouldn't have got yourself into this mess. And all the other messes.'

Prinny was not taking him very seriously, though his roughness puzzled her.

'You aren't being very helpful in a crisis, darling. I did think you were going to say something strong and silent about a brave little woman – meaning me, of course. Why are you so angry all of a sudden?'

'Because you're such a muddled little idiot, Prinny. A lawyer protects your financial interests – and you think he's most wonderfully kind and brotherly to do his job. You come up to Town with some grandiose idea of carving out a career for yourself – and what happens? You rub the bloom off by landing yourself in for imitation love affairs because you think it's modern and broad-minded.

'And another thing!' he went on. 'You're a thundering bad actress. You didn't look a bit like a real parlourmaid. With every possible gift in the matter of appearance, you can't even get a job in the chorus. You never will. With no occupation, you'll lurch from one horror to another until you've jiggered up your whole life. You can't go on like that. You must see that. You'll have to do something about it.'

'I do see it, dear. I always have. The question is – what?'

'For one thing, you can marry me.'

Prinny swung her legs off the sofa and sat up.

'Am I raving, Bruce – or did you really ask me to marry you?' As he glared at her she went on : 'But *why,* dear? Do you think I would make you a suitable wife?'

'No! You'll be an endless anxiety. Every night when I come home from the office I shall wonder what sort of muddle you've got yourself into. But at least I shall *know*! Whereas if you're not there – if you're alone in that nice but beastly little flat – I shall perpetually suspect that some Clawson or other is imposing on your exasperating innocence.'

She looked up at him with eyes solemn as an anxious child's.

'Thanks awf'ly, Bruce darling, but – no. You'd hate it after a month or two. And a month after that, so would I. But I'm ever so glad you asked me.'

'*Prinny!*' He was shouting at her. 'You simply can't muddle my life away as well as your own by turning me down. I – I don't know why I want you so much – and want so much of you. I want you to bring me a meal on a tray sometimes, and sit opposite me, looking pally and efficient and scandalously lovely. But it isn't that sort of thing at all, really. You'll be fat in a few years – and then you'll know I wasn't lying – this evening in this horrible house – when I told you I loved you.'

'I didn't know you loved me.' Her voice was unsteady. 'You didn't happen to mention it, Bruce dear – really you didn't! Look out! I believe I'm going to howl.'

In the library, Clawson had finished writing his confession. He initialled each sheet and signed the last, then reversed the sheet so that Kyle, who was sitting opposite, could witness the signature.

As Kyle was signing, Clawson took the revolver from the drawer and shot himself through the heart.

The report of the revolver was heard in the drawing-room.

'Whatever that was, it's nothing to do with us,' said Habershon hastily, as Prinny tried to rise from the settee. 'Stay put, darling.'

'I can't – let me get up. I must know for certain.'

He helped her to rise. Before they reached the door it was opened by Mrs Rabethorpe.

'Oh dear! That was George, of course!' she exclaimed. 'Poor George! I suppose he had to kill himself.' The large eyes seemed to peer into time and space. 'I do *hope* things won't be made too difficult for him!'

Her eyes dropped. Absent-mindedly, Bruce and Prinny were holding hands.

The smile that spread over the wrinkled face would have explained why so very many men had found this very plain woman so very attractive.